# INTRO 8

## EDITORIAL BOARD

# INTRO 8
## THE LIAR'S CRAFT

*Edited by*

GEORGE GARRETT

Assistant Editor—
Stephen Kendrick

ANCHOR BOOKS

ANCHOR PRESS/DOUBLEDAY

GARDEN CITY, NEW YORK

1977

The Anchor Books edition is the first publication of *Intro 8*.
Anchor Books edition: 1977

Library of Congress Cataloging in Publication Data

Main entry under title:
The Liar's craft.

(Intro; 8)
1. College stories, American.   2. College verse,
American.   I. Garrett, George.   II. Kendrick, Stephen.
III. Series: Intro (New York, 1968–   ); 8.
PS508.C6I63   no. 8      810'.8s     [813'.5'408]
ISBN 0-385-12375-2
Library of Congress Catalog Card Number 76–27705

# CONTENTS

## III POETRY

# INTRODUCTION

Each time, with each new edition of *Intro,* there seems to be less need for an editorial prologue. This one will be brief.

The system (for the time being) remains the same. Submissions of manuscripts by beginning writers of all ages, but mostly young writers, come to us from professional writers and writer-teachers at a hundred or so colleges, universities, community colleges, etc. These professionals act as scouts, preliminary editors, and, finally, as sponsors. The manuscripts are then read and judged by others and passed along to the editor, who must make the final choices and decisions.

The job is never very easy and was especially difficult this time. For one thing, in spite of strict preliminary selectivity and screening, there were still roughly twice as many submissions for *Intro 8* as we have ever before received. That's the good news, maybe: that the series and the idea have caught on, that beginning writers want to appear in *Intro.* And why not? Besides the pleasure and achievement of appearing in print and in the context of an anthology composed of other young writers, there is always the chance of being "discovered" by someone or other in a position to act upon discovery. Many writers who first appeared in *Intro* have had books of poems, collections of stories, and novels published. Sometimes this happens rather quickly. For example, at this writing, poets Carolyn Forché, H. A. Maxson, and Stephen W. Pett and short story writer Lee Zacharias, all contributors to *Intro 6,* already have their first books in print. A good many of the poets from the whole *Intro* series are represented in Daniel Halpern's *The American Poetry Anthology.* All to the good.

And yet . . . and yet what is going to happen to all these gifted people, a large number growing constantly larger, at a time when the possibilities for publication of poetry and serious fiction, especially short fiction, are dismally limited and continually shrinking? I am thinking not merely of the published contributors, but also of the many more whose work was sponsored and submitted and not chosen for one reason or another, or for editorial considerations which often have very little to do, in the abstract at least, with quality. The point is that, for better or worse and with a few special exceptions, the work of a great many beginning writers these days mainly demonstrates a high degree of skill, a high shine of technical competence. But, it must be admitted and understood, there is still, perhaps inevitably, a kind of uniformity at this level. Which is no reason to question the validity of the idea of *Intro*. These writers need a place (and *we* need such a place) to show and tell; and, at the moment, aside from the literary magazines, this is it. What is depressing is the realization that, after all the submitting, reading, and judging have been done, a simple lottery system might have been just as fair, quite as accurate. For each story and poem that appears here, there are half a dozen which could just as well have been published. It is always the same, only more so, every year.

And that is offered in explanation of one small change in the *Intro* format this year. Instead of the usual "symposium" on a subject thought to be of interest to beginning writers, I have preempted the space to unburden myself of what is really a harangue, though I call it a "monologue." I do so hoping to pass along—despite the knowledge, from years of teaching, of how little that matters can be passed on without hard experience to support it—some basic and probably obvious thoughts about the place of the serious writer in our time. Hoping, then (as much like a foolish parent as a pedagogue), to spare the beginning writer certain pains which arise from comforting and false illusions, illusions which persist year after year in the face of contrary facts and common sense. To check myself on my own excesses and illusions, I asked Stephen Kendrick, an excellent young writer and editor, to read over the "monologue" and then, using a tape recorder so I had no place to hide, to question me on the contents. It may be an odd expendable gesture: but if it can serve to start some writers and readers thinking (if only to disagree), then it will not have been a waste.

The real work, the fiction and poetry in this volume, speaks for itself. Of course things seem to change a little every year, and patterns of interest and concern shift subtly in direction. The prose fiction is (again) more various, thus in some ways more interesting, than the poetry. Much of the fiction submitted this time was less overtly experimental than in previous years. Clearly the models of excellence for young writers of fiction are not quite the same as those noticed and named, established by the critics. Clearly, also, the models for the poets are more limited, more so than they ought to be, one feels. There are good poems here, indeed some very good ones by any standards; but there is something here that is also noticeable in the literary magazines and recent anthologies—a curious sameness about much of the work. I believe this can only come from a severely limited idea about what a poem can, may, should be. Most of these poets do what they do very well. Yet there are so many other ways and means—explored, but still largely unexploited, by a great variety of twentieth-century poets—of which the present generation seems mostly ignorant. Like everything else, poetry has its trends and fashions. It is no discredit to these very good poets to say that one wishes they may grow more adventurous, expansive, perhaps more eccentric.

We have been faulted in the past, and perhaps justly so, by some reviewers and others for failing to publish contributors' notes. Even though it seems to me preferable to save the space for poetry and fiction, we have decided to try to remedy that situation in this volume. The trouble has been that the majority of the writers do not submit any biographical information and a significant number do not wish to do so. Then there are the others who have a tendency to conceive of the note as a creative genre— "Mary Gumbo is a desultory student but a wonderful kazoo player. A prominent figure in various ongoing liberation movements, she earns her living as a topless go-go dancer in a pool hall and spends her vacations backpacking in Bedford-Stuyvesant." Our compromise—there must be a middle way—is a brief note with uniform information. Read the work; then, if you really like something, why not write the author a postcard or a letter? Something like that could make a lot of difference.

*George Garrett*

# I FICTION

*She refuses to accept responsibility for the isolated prepositions,
the of's, to's, unders, and aboves: arrowheads with no shafts, no
targets, setting up unresolved tensions, snapping and snarling on
the page. Or for the dismal nouns, the catalogue of subjects and
objects motionless and dumb as skeletons in a closet, or for the
verbs (the Prussians of the language) advancing in columns to
rattle the bones.*

from "The Liar's Craft,"
by SARA McAULAY

*James L. Bond*

## BREAKFAST WITH THE
## PIONEER CLUB

Walter Kimbel crept back into his six-by-six office, drew shut the purple curtain which substituted for a door, and squeezed himself in behind his desk. He sat down. Several newspaper clippings, a dozen blank typing pages with bent corners, a worn eraser—these along with an assortment of writing instruments littered the desk top. Walt selected three of the longest pencils, studied their sharpened points, then broke all three in quick succession.

"Attend their little gathering," Fat Al the editor had told him. "These old-timer things are really important you know. People like to read about these old folks. It lets them know who's still around." Fat Al had swung sideways on his swivel chair and blown cigar smoke at the nude calendar girl hanging on the wall. "Might prove to be good experience for you," Fat Al had added.

Walt wished he'd told Fat Al to go fish. That slob of an editor along with his dime-and-penny newspaper could sink into the damn river for all he cared. Some newspaper. Why, they didn't even own a printing press; photocopied everything then sent it off to Spokane to be printed by a real newspaper. He'd give a couple of fingers, Walt decided, for the chance to work at a big newspaper again; where they printed real news, not this local backwoods gossip about cousin Dick from Panguitch who spent the weekend with his Aunt Jane. Yeah, he'd give both thumbs to be writing real news about real interest material like rapes, murders, interviews with senators, and big bank jobs. That's what real reporting was all about. People want to read a newspaper that shows action, people meeting other people, people doing things. It wasn't as though he was some young punk reporter; he had qualifications, he had an eye trained to find facts, he had experience. Heck, in two months he'd be thirty. Walt swore he'd cut a hand off before he'd attend an old folks' breakfast. On Saturday morning he arrived at the grade school cafeteria ten minutes late.

Walt met with the amused stare of a hundred senior citizens as the steel-and-glass door slammed shut behind him. He shifted his gaze to the floor and followed his feet to the nearest unoccupied place setting. He sat down just as a platter of hash browns passed by. On Walt's left sat a bent, skinny man of eighty; he wore no tie, a narrow sparse band of gray hair encircled his skull from temple to temple. On Walt's right was a heavy-set woman dressed like a Christmas tree in mourning. She wore a black cotton dress with a series of big green and purple blotches descending diagonally from left to right. The dark plastic frames of her glasses were studded with dozens of rhinestones, around her neck hung a triple-strand china-bead necklace, and miniature replicas of the Capitol building dangled from her ears. Walt chuckled.

Glancing in his direction, the woman smiled, exhibiting a pair of polished, bead-white dentures.

Walt looked elsewhere.

Jack Sadler, seated directly across from Walt, stared at the slight crouching figure hiding behind thick glasses. Jack found it amazing that the young man's blunt knob of a nose could support such a clumsy set of eyepieces. Jack was further amazed by the total lack of expression on the young man's face, the complete absence of lines, creases, or a wrinkle. Jack tried to think what the young man's face reminded him of, but he couldn't remember. Jack grinned at the young man. Walt appeared not to notice, his gaze fixed on the activity beyond Jack's left ear.

"You knew Jake Stong didn't you?" the woman asked Jack.

"Jake and I were good friends," Jack said, his protruding larynx bobbing up and down as he spoke. "He was a considerable bit older than me, but we got along well. That's just how Jake was."

With his trained eye, Walt was searching the room for food. Three rows of collapsible tables placed end to end stretched the length of the cafeteria. Two high school girls carrying pitchers of orange and tomato juice intermittently appeared and disappeared through the swinging door of the far wall. At the tables, baskets of muffins, platters piled high with sausage, bowls filled with scrambled eggs, and plates of hashed-brown potatoes were handed from one partaker to the next. Walt glanced down at his empty plate.

"He was a wonder with animals that Jake was," Jack said.

"My father said the same thing of him, said there was no better man with animals than Jake Stong."

Walt watched a sausage platter at the adjacent table as it was passed, placed, lifted, and passed on. Walt's stomach growled. People were beginning to eat. The old man on his left gummed a sausage. Reaching inside his raincoat, Walt removed a note pad and pen. He placed the note pad next to his fork and opened it. On the pad he printed:

FALSE TEETH. A LOT OF FALSE TEETH.

Walt laid down his pen; he glanced at his empty plate.

"Animals loved Jake," Jack was saying. "Old Doc Kelly for a long time had a boxer, a big animal, big and mean. Why that dog would bite you for just being on the same street as him. He'd bite anything that moved, even Doc. But whenever Jake came around that dog would take to wagging his tail and bouncing around like a three-month-old puppy."

A plate of hash browns was handed to Jack; he took the plate and thrust it across the table to Walt. "Here you go, son . . ."

Walt grimaced.

". . . dig your spoon into this."

Meeting with the plate at eye level, he took it from Jack's hands. "Thank you," Walt mumbled. After dumping a sizable portion onto his plate, Walt returned the hash browns to Jack.

"Yeh, Doc's dog was tame as a puppy when Jake was around but soon as Jake was out of sight that dog would sink his fangs into the first flesh that walked by. Why that dog was so mean, he'd bite himself if nothing else was handy."

The woman laughed, her beads rattled against each other. The toothless man on Walt's left handed him a bowl of scrambled eggs. Jack and the woman spent several minutes in silence as they ate.

"What's your name, son?" Jack asked.

Walt gulped down a mouthful of egg. "Walt. Walter Kimbel. I'm a reporter, a reporter for the *Newport Miner*."

"Oh."

The woman flashed a quick smile at him, then continued eating.

Walt picked up his pen; on his note pad he wrote, forming slow, careful letters:

WHEELCHAIRS. LOTS OF WHEELCHAIRS.

Jack Sadler laid down his fork. "Yeh, Jake Stong had a way with animals, mules in particular. Why I remember this one mule that he had: Alabaster, Jake called him. Now there was a mule, he would do anything for Jake. Why if Jake had wanted him to—that mule would have swam through fire, or towed away hell and the devil himself." Jack frowned. "Maybe his name was Asbestos. Anyway that mule had real intelligence, why you could look into his eyes and see that right off. He was almost human he was so smart; he didn't even smell like a mule. And work, why that mule loved to work. Most mules are like Wobblies, they might work all morning without a complaint, but come afternoon they'd set down on their ass and not budge an inch."

The woman giggled; she dabbed her mouth with a napkin.

"I never saw that mule sit down, why I never even saw him sleep. Every morning he'd be just trotting about the barn there waiting to go to work. Jake and him, they'd skid three times as many logs as would any team of oxen or horses, and there was more than one good team of them around. Why I've seen Asbestos skid whole trees, limbs and all, big yellow pines four feet at the butt, and he'd walk 'em out of the woods as if they were only a feather. Why you could actually see that mule smile, cocky as could be he was, and Jake there walking alongside never had to use a whip. I never even saw Jake carry one."

"What did you say his name was?" Walt held his pen poised above the pad.

"Jake."

"No the mule's?"

"Alabaster, Jake called him Alabaster."

"How do you spell that?"

"I don't know."

"Oh." Walt placed his pen back on the pad.

"There was this one time," Jack continued, "that we fell this giant cedar, biggest tree I ever saw; we dropped it down into about two and a half feet of mud. We sawed it into sixteen-foot logs, then Bob Crawle and his oxen team began dragging them off. They had one heck of a time in that mud and finally they came to the last one but they couldn't budge it. It was a big butt log, big as a house."

"A big house or a small house?"

The woman turned about in her chair and glared at Walt. She reached up with a hand and began to tug on her beads.

"Small house, I guess."

"Thanks." On his pad Walt wrote:

SMALL HOUSE.

"Anyway along came Jake and Alabaster, well Jake he walks up to Bob Crawle and says, 'You get your oxen out of the way and my mule he will move that log.' Bob Crawle he laughs and says back, 'Your mule can't move that log in this bad mud.' And Jake says to him, 'You move your oxen, and if my mule can't move that log you can have him.' Then Bob Crawle says back, 'If you want to give a good beast like that away, then you go right ahead, my good oxen says you can't.'

"So Bob he moved his oxen out of the way, and Jake hitched up Alabaster to that butt log. Jake gave Alabaster a slap and that mule began to pull—straining against the brace, but that log didn't budge. And that mule began to dig with his hooves sinking deeper in the mud, and we were all thinking: that mule he is going to dig his own grave. But that log it did start to move—no more than an inch at a time at first, then pretty soon it moved a foot, and there was a white lather rolling off that mule he was working so hard, but pretty soon that mule he found solid ground and he drug that butt log off like it was no more than a matchstick. Bob Crawle and his oxen team followed along behind."

Jack Sadler sat back; he lifted his glass of orange juice and took a long drink.

"Did Jake keep Bob Crawle's oxen?"

"No, he wouldn't take 'em, said he had the only animal he needed. No, that was the way Jake was; he'd of looked upon taking Bob's oxen as stealing. Jake was one honest man. That must have been why he got along with animals so well; they could sense that of him."

Walt looked over to the old man next to him; the old man had cleaned his plate and now his chin was beginning to sag toward his chest.

"Not long after that, maybe a year, a wagonload of logs dumped over and Jake, he came up underneath. It smashed his legs terribly bad and he ended up having to sell Alabaster, sold him to a cousin of Ralph Chase. Funny thing about that mule, they worked him one day and he worked good the whole day too. They led him back to the barn, and Alabaster he walked into that corral, layed right down, and died."

"Where's he buried?" Walt asked.

Jack Sadler frowned. He peered at Walt trying to see what sat behind those thick glasses. Jack saw nothing. Leaning forward Jack said, "I don't know but I imagine behind the barn."

"Good." Walt sat up quite straight and grinned first at the woman and then at the napping, toothless old man.

Throughout the cafeteria the hum of conversation increased in volume as more people finished eating. The high school girls were sitting off to one side. An elderly gentleman wearing a plaid sports coat stepped up to the podium and announced that the program would begin in fifteen minutes. The announcement jerked the toothless old man awake.

"Now Jake he'd bought this hog," Jack Sadler was saying. "He was a good-looking beast, long, and his belly hung real close to the ground. He was clean too. I never knew a hog to be so clean. Jake kept him in a pen about ten feet from the house, Jake not being able to get around so well on his crippled legs. It was a good hog, would eat most anything Jake dumped in for him except root vegetables. Hog wouldn't eat root vegetables, carrots or the like; he wouldn't even eat their tops. But Hog he liked lettuce and cabbage and broccoli. Vic Kilburn, who's an old bachelor too, lived just down the road a ways from Jake. This one day Kilburn caught Jake's hog eating lettuce in his garden. Well Kilburn kicked Hog home, and Jake and him found where the hog had crawled out from underneath the pen. They mended that hole and everything was fine. The next day Kilburn caught Jake's hog out in the middle of his garden munching on the lettuce. Well Jake and Kilburn buried boards all the way around that pen along the bottom so that Hog couldn't crawl out. Next day that hog was in Kilburn's garden working over the cabbage. Jake figured that Hog must of climbed over the top so they built the pen two feet higher all the way around. That was one rough job; they worked for maybe ten hours doing that. Now things were fine for about a week then Kilburn came over one morning and told Jake that Hog had eaten his beet tops off. Well, they both went and studied that pen, but they couldn't find no hole where no hog could of crawled out. Kilburn was pretty mad and he told Jake that if he caught that hog over in his garden he'd shoot him. Well, that upset Jake since he liked his hog so awful much. Jake studied that pen and studied that pen, but he couldn't see where Hog could crawl out."

"So where was he getting out at?"

The woman rattled her beads.

"I'm getting to that. The next day Hog never budged out of his pen. Hog squatted down there in a puddle and all you could see of him was those eyes peering up and out of that gray mess. He stayed like that for a week, wouldn't even come eat. Jake was getting real worried about his hog; he'd leave the gate wide open all day but Hog wouldn't budge. Jake would get in the pen there and talk with that hog for hours but Hog would not budge one inch. Jake finally went over to see if Kilburn wouldn't drop by and apologize to his hog. Well Kilburn, he wasn't too awful excited about Jake's idea, seeing as his beets were now all gone and most of his carrots. Kilburn he just turned right around and walked right back into his cabin only to come back out not a half a minute later packing his rifle. He stepped on past Jake and started off down the road. Jake hobbled along after him."

"So the pig was crawling out at night and eating the man's garden wasn't he?" Walt interjected.

The woman turned on Walt and hissed, "Let him finish."

"No it wasn't like that, the hog never left his pen."

"So what got to the man's garden?"

"I was getting to that. Deer, two does were creeping in at night; Kilburn never even took notice of the tracks all over in his garden, never noticed they were deer tracks."

"What happened to the pig?"

The woman leaned over and hissed in Walt's ear, "Now you just be quiet and let him finish." She rattled her beads within a hands-breadth of Walt's face.

"The hog died. Kilburn with his rifle got to the pen there, but Hog was already dead."

Leaning away from the woman, Walt said, "So I suppose that Jake died then, after the pig."

"No." Jack no longer was looking at the woman or Walt, but was speaking to the window in back of and above Walt's head. "Jake couldn't explain it, nothing like that had ever happened to him before. He'd never had an animal just lie right down and starve to death like that. He worried about it, and talked some about it, and worried some more. No, Jake didn't die. He grew old."

The woman stared at Walt. She stared at the puny little man clutching a pen, wearing an oversize raincoat. She thought about her son, a skilled carpenter with big shoulders, and polite too. She rose to her feet. "You're not very kind, you know that? You're not very kind at all." She waddled away, over to where a small cluster of people had gathered at the end of the table.

Jack picked up his spoon and placed it beside his fork. He slowly stood up, a hand on the table to steady himself.

Walt turned to his left, and in so doing peered into the red pit of the toothless old man's mouth.

"So?" Walt said to him. "So what? What was the big deal anyway?"

The toothless old man's mouth snapped shut.

Picking up his pen, Walt wrote on his note pad:

GREW OLD.

Walt drew a thick blue line through the words. Beneath them he wrote:

HE GREW OLD.

Walt chewed on the end of his pen for a moment, then drew three quick lines through the three words. Walt snapped the notebook shut; he slipped it and the pen inside his raincoat preparing to leave. He'd tell Fat Al to go fish, he decided. He'd tell Fat Al to stick an elbow in his ear and go swim. Some news. There wasn't enough news here to fill a want ad. Yeah, Walt swore; he'd give his right arm for the chance to work at a real newspaper again. Walt stepped outside, the steel-and-glass cafeteria door slamming shut behind him.

Vaughn D. Brown

# GODDAMNED HUNTERS

## I.

*Goddamn You, Jesse Sloat*

In the blue-gray, late evening of that fall day, Ralph Baxter, twenty, sat on the cold plank backsteps skinning squirrels and drinking whiskey from the bottle. That morning Ralph had seen one of his friends get his head blown in with a shotgun. Another friend, a good friend, had done the killing.

Hard to absorb, hard to accept, he wasn't ready yet to dissect what had happened for reasons. Perhaps it was only an act of God. That was the easiest thing Ralph could tell himself, though he didn't particularly believe in God. Now he drank whiskey to numb the hurt. He drank whiskey to simplify. He drank to cancel out doubts as he told himself easier things to believe.

His sister's big, yellow-striped cat came out from under the porch and crouched at his feet, watching. Ralph cut off the head and feet of a skinned squirrel, laid it aside. He took another swig of whiskey, then spat it out from sheer disgust.

For there, across the garden, by the trashcan in the alley, sat Jesse Sloat's car: an old black Chevy station wagon with a little blue light on top. Jesse Sloat was watching him.

Then he got out of the car, the fat man with the gun at his side, balding, big-eared Jesse Sloat. He got out and started across the dead garden toward Ralph. He was going to want to ask questions.

Ralph coughed and spat on the ground again. He found Jesse Sloat immensely disgusting, as essentially repulsive as a shit-faced hermaphrodite. For a time the dogcatcher of Quantril, Arkansas, he had also served two terms as night marshal and worked in the civil defense, directing traffic at county fairs. Now he was the constable of Taboria, a tiny hamlet six miles out from Quantril up on Crowley's Ridge. It was where two gravel roads crossed by a church and an old shack of a country store, the roof of which was supported mainly by rusty signs nailed to the walls. There, late on certain Saturday nights, cars from Tennessee and Missouri could be seen, parked for the gambling games. For Jesse Sloat was a would-be cop even to his share of graft.

Ralph pretended to ignore Jesse. He cut a neat incision with his knife around the middle of a squirrel. He pushed his fingers in under fur, skin, and fat, then pulled the pelt up over the squirrel's ears, shook and worried it off the front legs. It was like removing a sweater, twisting it off of a drunk or a dead man.

"Just like undressing little people," Ralph remarked softly.

"What?" said Jesse.

"I said skinning them, it's like undressing little people."

Jesse didn't seem to know what to say to that. He just stood watching.

The cat reared up on its hind legs and sniffed at the squirrel. Then it dropped down again, too well-mannered to attempt theft until sure of success.

Jesse hitched up his gunbelt and said, finally, "Ralph Baxter . . ."

"I don't want to talk right now," Ralph replied, half belligerently. "The sheriff, the cops, the coroner, they've all already asked. You talk to them."

Jesse looked at Ralph and the bottle and pursed his lips in a disapproving way. He said, "I've already talked to them. But there's still a few things that need clearing up."

When Ralph didn't answer, Jesse went on, "I mean everyone knows that the three of you used to be buddies. But there was talk too."

"Yes?"

"Talk was that there was bad feelin' between Lloyd Jones and Jerry Walker over that Stacey girl. Some said that she broke her engagement with Lloyd because of Jerry. I know for a fact that she was out with Jerry, 'cause I seen them weekend before last parked out in Linsom's tree nursery. So it seems sort of strange to me that those two boys would be huntin' together with you."

"Well," Ralph told him, "me and Jerry had agreed to go huntin' a month ago, when he visited me down at the college. First I heard of Lloyd comin' was last night when Jerry called me. He said he'd asked Lloyd himself."

"Odd. Mighty odd. Did he say why?"

"Not exactly."

"You ain't got no idea?"

"They had patched things up," Ralph said. "Jerry swears . . . swore that he hadn't seen her while she and Lloyd were still engaged. Just dated her a couple of times later on whim."

Jesse Sloat grunted, his eyebrows cynically arched.

"Believe it or don't," Ralph told him. "I'm just telling it like they told me. True or not, Lloyd seemed convinced. And they weren't mad at each other when I saw them."

"Seems to me that you and Gwyn Stacey used to go together, didn't you?"

"A long time ago. Junior year of high school." Ralph picked up the fifth and last squirrel.

"She's a real pretty little girl. I guess you might have had it bad for her one time?"

"If I did, so what?"

"Maybe," Jesse said, "maybe you had it bad enough for her to have begrudged Jerry. Maybe as much as Lloyd begrudged him."

Ralph tightened up for just a second. Then he made himself relax. What Jesse was insinuating was par for the course. Idiot. Too many TV detective shows for Jesse. Ralph said, "It was an accident. Just a goddamned accident that *got my friend killed.*"

Then the back door opened and Ralph's father came out on the porch, kicking empty Mason jars and tools out of his path.

"Goddamn you, Jesse Sloat," he said hoarsely. "What are you doin' here?"

"Just askin' Ralph a few questions, Mr. Baxter."

"You get the hell away," Ralph's father wheezed. Fat and emphysemic from too many years of too many drinks and cigarettes, still he was fired up and nearly jumping with rage now as he said, "You leave or I'll have you in. For trespass."

"Now Mr. Baxter," Jesse said soothingly, "I'm a duly elected county official. I've got official business here."

"The hell you do. This ain't Taboria. You go."

"Now looky here," Jesse said.

The old man bent down. Ralph had to jump then to keep from being stepped on as his father rushed past, waving a socket wrench handle.

Jesse Sloat backed up repeating, "Looky here. Now you looky here. . . ." Then he turned and ran for the car, a fat man's rolling, lard-assed run, barely fast enough to outdistance Ralph's father.

"Goddamn you, Jesse Sloat!" Ralph's father called out one more time as Jesse drove away. Then he coughed and gagged as though he were about to vomit, crouched over with his hands on his knees. When he came back to the porch he was still gasping, mouth open and chest heaving.

Finally he sat down and said, "He was fuckin' with you. Wasn't he?"

Ralph just nodded.

"You should have called me. Or run him off yourself. Meddlesome. He's meddlesome as an old woman."

"He thinks Lloyd shot Jerry on purpose."

His father was silent for a second or two. Then he took a deep breath and said, "People will talk. Huntin' accidents. Accidents with guns. Not a season goes by without some son-in-law shoots his wife's old man. Or a businessman accidentally gets his partner. 'Accidentally' shoots him three or four times sometimes."

"But I saw it. Lloyd didn't mean to."

"If you say so, I believe you. But wait and see. People will pick at Lloyd. Some will. Just the way they'll look at him. Be enough to give any man the spooks."

"Jesus," Ralph said softly, mostly pitying Lloyd.

They just sat there thoughtfully a few moments. It was almost dark. Then the old man helped himself to a swig of the bourbon and said, "It's cold out here. You go on in. I'll finish cleanin' these squirrels."

"No. You go in and I'll be through in a minute."

"Well, all right. But you just be careful not to freeze. And don't worry about Sloat, son. Don't let him make you feel bad. You got grief enough."

When Ralph was finished with the last squirrel, he gathered up the heads and feet, took them out to the garden, and threw them down for the cat. He put the skinned meat into plastic bags to refrigerate.

He took another stiff drink. Perhaps he could sleep. Perhaps now he could sleep, with one more drink from the bottle, untroubled by insinuations or implications of what could not be changed.

That morning, waiting for Jerry to pick him up, Ralph had been more pleased than concerned at the prospect of seeing both his friends together. Whatever it was that had been going on with them and Gwyn was foggy and confused to him, pieced together from gossip that the other few people from Quantril brought back to the college from their visits. Besides, he had doubted that it made much difference in the long run.

Cradling his shotgun in his arms, he paced around the front yard, moving to ward off the cold. He enjoyed being out, to feel the crisp morning beginning: hickory nuts plopping down into the frosted leaves and grass, a pickup truck rattling past the house, a tang of woodsmoke and wild onion in the air, the silence when the truck was gone.

Both his friends, his friends—strange to say that after only two years of being not very far away from Quantril, Ralph had to number Jerry and Lloyd most highly among his friends. They always made a point of looking him up whenever he came home. Not the guys with whom he'd played legion baseball nor his other old classmates did as much. Those people were all out cutting their own paths now: studying to be accountants or looking after the wife and car payments.

But Jerry and Lloyd had always been around when it counted, Jerry with an empty bread wrapper and a tube of Testors with which to while away dull summer afternoons, buzzing in the cool dirt under the cotton gin warehouse. And Lloyd, Lloyd wasn't quite as good crazy as Jerry. More serious, he had read some and felt, like Ralph, that most of the things respectable people in Quantril worried about were not worth the effort. Better to think, drink, talk about something else: Aldious Huxley, John Ingersol,

Vikings, and fighting with knives. They used to do that. Practice with pocketknives. Cut the shit out of each other's hands and arms sometimes.

They were the people with whom Ralph hauled hay and pitched melons to earn the money for fifths of Kentucky Beau to drink and be sick on around a campfire in the woods, with whom he went plinking tin cans and spotlighting for rabbits; or just cruised the country roads for the sheer animal joy of cutting cat-asses in the gravel, leaping Thrill Hill, drinking beer; stopping when it was time under the moon and stars to piss on the whole weird god-damned world. Not the yearbook most likelies—Ralph had known and been one of them too—but Jerry and Lloyd were still in Quantril, still his friends. Why was it that risks and hell-raising brought people closer than any work-a-day worthwhile thing ever could?

He looked down and frowned as the cat yowled and poked its head against his leg. Blood was oozing out of half-healed gashes all over the cat's yellow head and neck.

"What happened to you?" He set his gun down and picked up the cat. It cried again, protesting at being lifted.

Examining the wounds, he decided that it must have been fighting with another cat. Or perhaps with a squirrel. Those were deep bites like a squirrel makes. Tough cat, to take on a squirrel.

In the bathroom Ralph held the cat with one hand while he rummaged through the medicine cabinet, looking for the blue dye lotion. After some struggling he managed to catch the cat in one hand by all four of its legs. He laid it on its side in the bathtub and poured the medicine on.

The cat went wild at the first touch of the stinging lotion. It arched and flexed, wriggled and shook. Ralph poured on more. Then the cat got hold of his hand and bit until he had to let it go, clawing out of the room.

Ralph cleaned the spilled dye out of the tub, washed his hands, and put iodine on the bitten hand, wincing, himself, at the sting.

Jerry's old brown Valiant pulled into the driveway just as Ralph came out of the house. He sat there, big blond Jerry, a cigarillo clenched between his teeth, one eye squinted, grinning at Ralph.

"Long time no see, college boy," said Jerry.

"Long time indeed." He got in the car and set his gun beside Jerry's, butt on the floorboard, barrel leaned against the seat.

The heater was on but it was still kicking out cold air as they pulled away. The windshield was fogging up, so the two of them wiped at it with their hands and coatsleeves.

"What happened to you, Ralph?"

"Hmm?"

"Your hand. Looks like you caught it in a fence."

"Oh. I was doctorin' the cat. He didn't want to be worked on."

They drove past the court square: the new courthouse all glass and white concrete, the empty park benches and tables where the spit and whittle club met when it was warm; the storefronts with poised and graceful mannequins displayed, roto-tillers, jewelry, and hardware. The doughnut shop was open for the few early Saturday risers. They bumped across the railroad tracks and passed the bean siloes that they used to sneak up into nights, years ago, to catch pigeons in tow sacks.

"Hey, Jerry," Ralph said. "I don't mean . . . well, I'm curious. Why is Lloyd comin' with us? You know, fill me in." For Jerry had been very nonchalant when he called the night before, just mentioning that Lloyd was coming after arranging details of the hunt.

"Oh, well, we're gettin' along," Jerry said.

"Yeah?"

"See, late last Friday I ran into him at the A & W. He and Flash Eliot had just come back from the line and they had some beer. Lloyd invited me to help drink it. So I went and got in with them."

"Weren't you scared of gettin' your ass kicked?"

"Naw. I know I can take Lloyd. And old Flash was wearin' his false front teeth. You know. He always carries them in his pocket if he thinks there's gonna be a fight. Scared he'll swallow them or something. But anyway we went out drinkin' and we got talkin' friendly. That's when I mentioned us goin' huntin' and he said he'd like to go and I said it would be fine if he did."

"So he ain't mad at you and Gwyn anymore?"

Jerry downshifted and made the car whine through a turn. He rolled down the window and tossed his cigarillo out.

"Look," he told Ralph, "I explained myself to Lloyd. I mean, I never so much as looked hard at Gwyn all the time they were goin' together. After they broke up, well, I kept meetin' Gwyn and it wasn't my planning and it wasn't accident. You know how she can do. So yeah. I thought I'd see what I could get."

"And now?"

"I ain't really sold on her. Doubt if I'll see her again."

"Yeah," Ralph agreed. "I always did get more status than pleasure from knowing her. But what did happen with Gwyn and Lloyd?"

"I'm not sure. One thing, Gwyn ain't gonna marry no one who's still workin' in his daddy's store, like Lloyd. And too, Gwyn's sort of . . ."

"Fickle?"

"Could be."

They pulled up in front of Lloyd's house and Jerry leaned hard on the horn.

"It's not really any of my business," Ralph said. "I was just surprised."

"Well," Jerry said, "Lloyd seemed friendly enough last time I saw him. And if he's willin' to be friends, I am too."

He honked again.

"I'll go get him," Ralph said.

Lloyd's mother answered the door when Ralph knocked. She was in her bathrobe, rubbing her eyes and trying mightily to suppress a yawn.

"Lloyd not up yet, Miz Jones?"

"I think he is. Don't know why he couldn't come to the door." She sounded more than slightly annoyed. "Come on in and get him if you want to."

Ralph found Lloyd in the kitchen pouring coffee into a metal thermos. He'd had his dark hair cut short and he'd grown sideburns and a short beard since Ralph had seen him last. His hands shook a little as he poured, and Ralph noticed that there were rings under his eyes, as though he'd been missing sleep.

"Hey there. Good to see you, man." Lloyd looked up.

"Good to see you too, Lloyd."

"I'll be ready to go in just a bit. How are things goin' down in Jonesboro? You gettin' into any good meanness?"

"Every now and again. Weekends. I'm pretty busy the rest of the time."

"Guess you're glad to be back here for a while. Relax some."

"Yeah. And I'm glad to hear that you and Jerry are gettin' along." Ralph looked at him questioningly.

"Well, you know how it is," said Lloyd as Ralph followed him down the hall. "I guess it isn't Jerry's fault if Gwyn grooves on his big dick more than mine."

In his room Lloyd unhurriedly put on a camouflage hunting jacket, opened his desk drawer, and scooped a handful of shotgun shells up. He got his shotgun down from the gunrack, an old .12-gauge Winchester pump gun. He pumped the chamber open, checked to make sure it was empty.

When they came out the front door, Ralph's footprints were still visible in the frost on the lawn.

"Hey, Lloyd."

"Hey, Jerry."

"How's it hangin'?"

"Why it's danglin' in the cold, cold breeze."

They piled into the front seat, guns and all, and took off driving fast out of town.

"What took you all so long?" Jerry asked.

"I had to get this coffee," Lloyd said, holding up the thermos.

"Well. How about a cup now?"

Lloyd slowly and carefully poured a cup as the car rocked along. He handed it to Ralph who was sitting in the middle. Ralph took a sip before passing it to Jerry, realizing by the sweet kick that it had been heavily laced with peppermint schnapps.

Jerry took and drank. "Whoo!" he whooped. "This ain't coffee. It's panther poison."

"Yeah," Ralph agreed. "Give me another snort."

"Let's finish this cup. But save the rest for later," Lloyd said.

Jerry slowed down when they reached Chalk Ford, a little town on the Saint Francis River, which was the state line between Missouri and Arkansas. At the edge of town, almost at the bridge, he turned and they rocked and bumped up the levee and along the road on top of it.

It wasn't much of a road, just two uneven ruts with dead weeds between them, axle high, and even higher weeds on both sides. It was a sort of no man's strip between the river and the brown-leaved woods on their left; the stubbled rice, bean, and wheat fields on their right.

They turned down a fishing trail to their left and stopped, got out with a slamming of doors near a pile of trash someone had dumped there.

"What time is it?" asked Lloyd.

"Little after seven-thirty," said Ralph.

The clicking metallic sounds of shells being loaded was the only sound for a few seconds. Then Lloyd remarked, "It's a little late to be starting. We should have got here earlier."

"We would have if you hadn't taken so long getting ready," Jerry said, staring at the woods.

Lloyd was about to say something else, but Ralph cut him off.

"You're just lookin' for excuses," he told both of them. "You know neither one of you is goin' to get as many squirrel as I am."

"Five'll get you ten I bring in more than you," Jerry said with mock belligerency. "Five'll get you ten."

"I'll bet you five even. How about you, Lloyd? You in?"

Lloyd just shook his head impassively. That was just as well by Ralph. For Lloyd was far and away the best hunter of the three of them.

"Okay. We'll go by weight if we get the same. That suit you, Jerry?"

"Good enough. Just let's not stay in the woods all day. I got business I need to take care of later."

So they went into the woods and separated.

Ralph found a good spot to wait in the center of a grove of hickory trees. He sat down and propped his back against a dead log, then began scanning the branches overhead, waiting.

He felt fairly comfortable. By some clever maneuvering and dodging he'd managed to get through the bogs without getting his tennis shoes wet. His body had adjusted to the air, though it was even colder in the woods than it had been in town.

A Coke bottle out in the underbrush caught his eye for a moment. He idly wondered who had left it there.

Those woods were pretty heavily hunted. A lot of hickory and sweetgum had grown in when they logged out the cypress years ago. Good hunting, usually. Used to be good fishing, his father had told him, before the poachers started using dynamite on the river and they put that dam upstream. But the woods were still good.

He tried to concentrate a bit more on watching the trees. Good squirrel hunting takes a delicately balanced state of mind. Just stare at every leaf and twig and seconds seem hours. The mind blanks out. But get wrapped up in a fantasy, sit drifting in dreams, and you also fail. The squirrel will be gone before you or anyone can leave the dream and lift the gun.

He listened intently to the jays screeching and brush snapping off to his left, downstream. Another hunter. Maybe Jerry. Lloyd had cut off upstream. Besides, Lloyd never made that much noise in the woods. Always smooth and quiet. And no one could sit silent and perfectly still for as long as he could. Not that he made a fetish of woodcraft. He was just good.

Hunters. Goddamned hunters. Ralph remembered a time several years ago when they'd been hunting. Afterward the three of them had gone into town. Jerry had a check he wanted to deposit. So they went to the drive-in bank, all dirty and scruffy with a load of guns all hanging out of the car practically. Jerry had that .22 that he'd had to nearly fight his father to get. But they drove up and the lady teller's eyes had got real big. She took a long time getting the electric box to extend to the car. Then a man opened the door behind the woman and looked at them. "Just some goddamned hunters," he said loudly enough for them to hear through the glass. And the woman had blushed and the man looked angry when the three of them laughed.

The wind rustled leaves. Ralph looked around. He heard something else besides the wind. There. A squirrel was leaping along in the small branches overhead. Then it stopped, wrapped itself around a tree trunk in that maddening way squirrels do, playing peek-a-boo with the world. It inched around the trunk, then ran out along a long branch.

Still sitting, Ralph flipped off the safety, led the squirrel, and pulled the trigger. The gun blasted, tossing out a wisp of smoke in the cold air.

It fell! The squirrel and a piece of the limb fell together.

He ran to where it lay and picked it up to admire. It was quite dead. One pellet had caught it in the eye. Lucky shot. The body was warm, soft, but firm to the touch; a plump gray female, young but fully grown. A kind of gamey smell emanated from it, blood dripped out on the leaves. Ralph had to spit the saliva out of his mouth.

He cut a slit in its belly with his pocketknife. He began to squeeze with both hands, crushing the vitals down out of the chest and stomach. He took the squirrel by the forelegs and swung it against a tree, popping the innards out in a mess of liverish brown and gray and red. He scraped and cut, finishing the field dress. Then he pulled a Baggie out of his pocket, wrapped the squirrel in it, and pocketed it.

It was nearly noon when Ralph gave up and headed in. The one squirrel was the only shot he'd made.

As he balanced on a log, crossing a backwater puddle, the sound of shotguns being fired reached him. It grew louder as he pressed on toward the car—the quick "kroom-kroom-kroom" of Jerry's automatic, the slower louder shots of Lloyd's big pump gun; the fading rush of afterblast, like the sound of a distant jet, the torn air whirring through the woods. He believed they had sense enough not to be firing in his direction. But he walked slowly and cautiously.

Coming out from among the trees, he found them standing side by side in front of the car. They were shooting at targets they'd set up against the levee: bottles and old tin cans hauled out of the trash heap.

They stopped to reload and as Ralph drew near he could hear Jerry saying ". . . how did that calf get killed if the panther was really toothless?"

"Okay. How?" Lloyd said.

"It was *gummed* to death. I swear my daddy told me that. And you know he never lies much."

Lloyd grinned and shook his head. Jerry laughed at his own joke and stumbled once as if he were half drunk. Then Lloyd turned and noticed Ralph, just as Ralph himself ruefully saw that there were four dead squirrels laid out on the car, two on the hood and two on the trunk.

"Well, Ralph. What'd you get?"

Ralph produced his one plastic-wrapped squirrel and laid it on the hood.

Jerry laughed in triumph. "Looks like you owe me."

"You were lucky," Ralph said.

"Lucky hell. I was skillful. Best man wins be it huntin' or lovin', fightin' or high-low stud. Ain't that right, Lloyd?"

"I guess so, Jerry," Lloyd said coolly. "I guess that's right."

He turned and cut down on an oilcan with his next shot.

The thermos was there on the hood too. Ralph leaned his gun against the bumper, pushed the squirrels out of the way to sit down, and poured coffee.

There was less than a cupful left.

"Who drank up all the coffee?" he complained.

"We did," Jerry said. "You shouldn't have stayed in the woods so long."

The tone of voice he used pissed Ralph off. He'd been looking forward to getting a buzz on when the hunt was over and here they had gone and hogged all the schnapps. But he swallowed the words he could have said, and leaned back on the windshield, sipping what was left, watching them shoot.

After a while, Lloyd stopped and came to sit by Ralph.

"I've got more at home," he said, apologetically. "We can all go there and clean the guns and drink some more."

"Good idea," Jerry said.

Ralph nodded.

After one more shot, Jerry lit a cigarillo and put his gun and squirrels in the car. He was humming something loudly. "Easy Lovin'" it sounded like.

"He sure acts pleased with himself," Ralph remarked.

"Yeah. I guess he is." Lloyd was idly pumping, sighting, and snapping his empty gun at things: a couple of crows flying overhead, a rock on the levee, a crow in a treetop on the other side of the levee.

"A lover and a fighter and wild bull rider, that's what he thinks he is," Ralph said. "And what are you doin'? Want to ruin your gun?"

"Shut up, Ralph."

"Oh," Jerry called, "Ralph is just sore 'cause he lost. Some people can't stand to lose."

"Some people can't be stood when they win," Ralph said.

But Jerry just laughed. And Lloyd scowled and turned to get into the car. They drove back to town.

There in the woods or by the levee, there were Lloyd's chances if he had wanted to get Jerry outright or fake an accident. But he didn't and he hadn't.

Goddamn Jesse Sloat for looking at bits and pieces of facts, thought Ralph, letting his mind blank out.

II.

## Goddamn That Gwyn

"Ralph. Ralph, wake up. There's someone here to see you."

He awoke, trying to remember why he was at home instead of the dorm. Then he remembered, sorry he had.

His mother was shaking him by the shoulder. "You need to get up, Ralph, if you feel like it. Gwyn's here and she wants to talk to you."

"Gwyn? Oh Lord. What time is it?"

"About nine," she said.

"Day or night?"

"Why, night. Are you sure you want . . . ?"

"Yeah. Just wait a minute. Then bring her on in."

He got up and put on his bathrobe. Everything in the room seemed vaguely out of focus. The desk and chair were too large. The light was too bright. Too much space between the books and the edge of the shelves. He sat down at his desk, turning the chair away from it.

The doorknob turned, clicked open. Gwyn slipped into the room, and he pointed her to his overstuffed chair.

She sat down silently, demurely tucking her skirt. Pensively, almost sadly she looked at the floor, giving Ralph no choice for a few seconds but to survey her there: all crisp and fresh in a knee-length gray dress. She'd had her honey-blond hair cut in bangs in front, but she still wore it to her shoulders in back. She looked almost like she had dressed for a date, except she was wearing no jewelry or makeup.

Then she looked him in the face, her slightly bulging gray eyes conveying alertness, mourning, bravery too, all in one graceful if slightly stylized expression of concern. Gwyn still had her style—even in the way she started to speak, lightly taking hold of her own collar with bent wrist, accenting her full breasts with the movement.

"Ralph, I heard what happened," she said gravely, dropping her hand to her lap. "I thought I ought to hear from you . . . just how it was."

Ralph nodded and crossed his legs. "How it was?"

"With Jerry. And Lloyd."

"It was just dumb luck."

"But how?"

"Okay." Ralph drew himself up in the seat, pulled the belt of the robe tighter. "We'd just come in from hunting and we were sitting around goofing off. Lloyd was snapping the trigger on what he . . . what we thought was an empty gun. He fired it, must have been a dozen times, and it was empty."

"Then how?"

"It sometimes happens with those old tubular magazine guns. A shell sticks up in the magazine because the pump just opens the chamber. A weak spring drops the shell. So if a shell sticks, you won't notice until you load it again. Or it jars loose. There's no defense but counting rounds loaded and fired."

"So the shell jarred loose," she said.

"Yes. And then . . ." Ralph snapped his fingers loudly. "Jerry was in the line of fire."

Gwyn grimaced, hunching her shoulders up.

"It could just as easily have been me," Ralph told her.

"It . . . disfigured him?"

"I guess you could say that. Yes. He took it in the face."

"But you say it was an accident?" she asked quickly.

"Yes. Lloyd, well he was damned near cryin' and he did talk a little crazy. When the sheriff took him back in the room, to show them all how it happened, they say he freaked on them. Started to put another round in the gun."

"But why was the sheriff there?"

Ralph shrugged. "Maybe Mr. Jones called him. Maybe the cops did. But there was a cop, the sheriff, and the coroner too, all there askin' us questions before it was all over. Lloyd, he ended up goin' with the sheriff to break the news to Jerry's family. But he acted like he'd rather someone would just haul off and beat him to death."

"But they aren't going to hold him?" The way she said it, rhetorically, made Ralph realize that she'd been talking to someone else already.

"No, I don't guess so," he said. "There's going to be a formal inquest. They took my statement this afternoon."

"Are you going to stay for the funeral?" she asked.

"I don't know."

"They're going to have it Monday. You'd just miss one day of class."

He thought about it. It would probably be lousy. With a lot of people who'd barely known Jerry trying to tell him that it really touched them too, grieved them, made them wonder too. Gwyn, would she wear black? Not hardly. But she'd be there, in one of the pews. She knew how to handle herself in such a setting.

He said, "Maybe I'll stay. Sit with Lloyd. He needs the moral support."

Gwyn nodded sadly. "Yes. I know how he feels."

"Do you?"

She sighed. "I feel, I feel . . . you don't know how I feel. It's really my fault too, some ways. I don't think this would have happened otherwise."

"Oh, bullshit," Ralph dismissed her.

"No. If I hadn't started going out with Jerry."

"Gwyn, it was all accidental. They had made up. Jerry as much as told us that he wasn't seeing you again."

"Then Jerry lied."

"What?"

"Jerry was supposed to have picked me up this evening. We were going to Poplar Bluff. That's how I found out. I called his house when he was late."

Ralph felt sick at his stomach. But he said, "Could Lloyd have known?"

Gwyn shrugged helplessly. "I don't think so. But he could have suspected. He suspected all along, I think, when I was seeing both of them."

"Wait. Wait," Ralph said, holding up his hands.

"But maybe then Lloyd didn't even realize on purpose. Didn't know he knew, or was careful not to. But somehow, somewhere there, I think he did."

"Wait." Ralph was still waving his hands, trying to back her up, stop her, slow it all down. She just sat looking at him earnestly. So many things from sometime back there were, that she could tell him, things she could build into a regular little horror story.

"But not now," Ralph said. "He wouldn't have waited until now to get Jerry, if he was that hurt about it."

"I'm not saying it was on purpose. But somewhere there, maybe

. . . subconsciously, Lloyd knew that gun was loaded. Ralph—" Gwyn half rose—"it was over me. And God, I feel like, like such a stupid . . . a whore; that's how I've acted." Painfully, she finally got it out.

"Ralph." Abruptly she stepped over and touched his arm, held his elbow.

"Ralph, you know me," she said and her fingers were moving in a way that reminded him of a cool touch on his face and a gentle pardon one clumsy night when he had failed at something neither one of them had been old enough to be sure of.

"You do know me," she said.

And for a second he wanted her, wanted to take her and give her the one thing that would make her feel better, brutally or gently—a penance or a pardon. That was the judgment she wanted.

He shook her hand loose, slapped the desk.

"No," he said. "No. Guilt, guilt, here pass the guilt. Gwyn's gonna feel guilty. Lloyd too. Well shit on your guilt. It ain't mine and I don't want it."

She fell back into her seat and tears welled up but did not fall. Then she looked up at him again, in a hurt, softly baffled way. For an instant he had an insane flash, almost a hallucination of her as a squirrel standing on its haunches. A hurt squirrel; all she needed was a tail and she could do away with speech.

"It *was* an accident," he told her.

"I'm sorry," she said. "I don't know what to do."

"Neither do I, Gwyn," he said apologetically. "I'm not the person to talk to, Gwyn. Maybe you should see a preacher."

They both looked at each other and it seemed to him that she was still asking. But he knew he had nothing to give her and so he said nothing.

"I guess I should go," she said, at length.

"Good-by, Gwyn," he said, trying not to sound hopeless.

He turned to the desk and sat for a long time, after she had left, nervously playing with an old broken pencil that was lying there.

What was Gwyn after? What good could she do by trying to see herself as a cause for murder? Subconscious be boogered. Why should she want to feel guilty?

Because Gwyn was Gwyn. Maybe Gwyn was too good-looking for her own good. She believed having been prom queen really meant something. That she was a real factor in things. That she had moved a man to murder could almost make her feel good.

It was almost the same as high school. Saturday night, go do the works: dinner, movie, out to the sticks, and lock the car. And, oh, I will have just a teensy bit of that Southern Comfort. Doesn't taste bad in Seven-Up. But not too much, Ralph, it might go to my head. Then Sunday: church, morning and night. It was almost a package deal. Take Gwyn out Saturday and take her to church Sunday. Many, many awful Sunday evenings with Gwyn, sitting on a bench in that little country church out where she lived—the smell of chalk and faded stalks of iris by the pulpit, old women's cloying perfume, while listening to some old foot-washing Baptist drone on and on. Make Saturday right with God.

So there was the guilt. Murder, how thrilling. But how awful. Gwyn gotta pay for her thrill. God's chastising rod.

God's rod. Ralph laughed out loud. Goddamn that Gwyn, that's what she wanted. God's rod.

He stopped his laughter abruptly. It wasn't that funny. He'd spooked himself with his own laughter.

But Gwyn and her women's magazine subconscious, and her dream of herself—the tragic, romantic Gwyn Stacey. It just wasn't that way.


The three of them had been sitting in Lloyd's room listening to records. Lloyd had his gun partly broken down on the table, swabbing out the barrel and holding it up to the light, looking through it and swabbing at places he'd missed.

Across the room Jerry sat on a chair by the bed, sipping schnapps and waiting for him to finish with the cleaning rod.

Ralph had his gun cleaned already. He was leaning against the wall at the foot of the bed, drinking and looking around Lloyd's room: the pinups and Remington prints on the oak-panel wall, empty picture frame on the desk, the bookshelf stuffed with science fiction and *Field and Stream,* some Hardy, Hesse, lots of novels. There was Seagrave's book on Haitian voodoo. Ralph had forgotten he'd loaned it to Lloyd.

Ralph yawned contentedly, feeling warm and worn and strong from the hunt. His legs were a little stiff. But it was a good stiffness.

The Red Sulvine album finished playing and another record

dropped down. "Solitary Man" it was, Neil Diamond moaning and groaning along with a lot of crappy brass to back him up about how bad them women did him.

Lloyd was nodding his head in time with it.

"Why don't you get that thing off and put on some real music?" Ralph said.

Without looking at him, Lloyd reached over and hit the reject button. Satisfied with the barrel, he began reassembling the gun.

"Black Oak, Arkansas" dropped down, the sweet, electric, acid-country guitar and raspy crazy voice of Jim Dandy Mangrum. Ralph shut his eyes to listen. He could relate to those people and their music. Take some young rednecks and jack them up on LSD, where else could they go but the halls of Karma "to talk to both the devil and God?" And how to tell it but with an organ and a choir and the amped up sound of pissing in a bucket of water? Oh, Neil never had such problems getting laid. But Jim Dandy must have gone some hard rounds with God one time.

But just as Ralph was beginning to get goosebumps from those absolutely correct chords, as rightly spooking as blue gaseous light hanging over a tombstone in a midnight country churchyard, as a wild dog's clawed foot scratching rock somewhere out in the dark, just then Jerry broke it by calling to him:

"Hey, Ralph. When you gonna pay me that five?"

Ralph said, "I'll have it tonight."

"Oh. Well I'm goin' to Poplar Bluff tonight."

"I can get it when you take me home then."

"No rush."

"No, that's okay. I may go back early tomorrow."

Lloyd passed the cleaning rod to Jerry. Then he took his gun and drew a bead with it on one of the wall pictures.

"Snap-snap." He pumped the gun. "Click." The hammer fell on an empty chamber. Then he did it again.

Ralph and Jerry both looked mild askance at him. It was not a good idea to wear out a weapon by firing it empty.

"Blew that horse soldier away," Lloyd joked. Then he pumped and pointed and fired at Ralph.

Ralph started to protest. But then Jerry got into the act too, clicking his empty gun at Ralph. So he took it in humor, staggered around in a comic routine trying to cover half a dozen wounds with two hands. He fell at Jerry's feet and jerked convulsively, finally lay still as the record went off.

Jerry and Lloyd were laughing. Then only Jerry was laughing.

"Don't flinch a inch, pardner," Ralph heard Lloyd pump the gun.

"Looks like you got the drop on me, pardner," Jerry mocked back.

It was like a dynamite blast inside the room, like the clash of spheres, planets stripping gears when that .12 guage went off.

Ralph lay frozen, believing that in a second he would come out of shock, feel the pain, open his eyes, and see the blood he felt on himself. Then he wiped his face and convinced himself that it wasn't his own. He stood up.

Jerry lay crumpled back on the bed; his shotgun dropped on the floor. His face was just awful pocks where the pellets had torn in, broken flesh draining blood that soaked the covers, bits of spattered stuff sticking to the splintered wall. It smelled of burnt hair and powder in the room and something fecal too. Then Ralph knew that Jerry had shat himself when he died. And for a second that seemed the worst of it to him; that was the worst, corrupt indignity of it all.

Lloyd was kneeling on the floor, holding his temples with both hands and staring at Jerry. The recoil had tipped him out of the chair, and he'd dropped his gun too.

Then footsteps came running through the house. Something hit the door and the knob turned. Ralph started for it, but Lloyd's mother threw it open.

"Don't look," he said.

But she did, at him, then Jerry.

"Oh my Goah . . ." the word was choked off in a gagging noise.

Lloyd's father pushed in. He took one look at Jerry.

"Are you hurt?" he asked Ralph.

"No."

He grabbed his wife by the shoulders and hustled her out.

"Stay with him, Ralph," he called back.

Ralph stayed. He wiped some more blood off his face with his sleeve, and stood there feeling numb and stupid.

Lloyd was still looking at Jerry. Then he turned and looked at the drawer he kept his shells in, looked for a long time.

"Oh," he said, long and low, like someone fighting with himself out near the ragged edge. "Oh, nothing's ever going to be the same again."

*Vaughn D. Brown*                                                                 29

Then he looked hard at Ralph, asking silently for Ralph to blame him or not. Ralph just shook his head.

Then Lloyd's father came back and Ralph stumbled out.

Like a sleepwalker he moved into the front room and sat down on the couch. He sat for a long time staring at the coffee table and the cut-glass ashtray on it; staring without words, memorizing the exact translucence, shadow, and form of that ashtray. Not thinking any words because he knew words would crack him open and there wasn't time, yet, to break down.

From the room he could hear insistent but unintelligible talk as Mr. Jones went at Lloyd. He could hear Lloyd answer, but not what he answered. It might have been a different language for all he could tell.

Soon the police would be there. There would be many questions. So much to say. Keep the words away. But damn the luck. We all knew better, but damn the luck!

He came to himself, realizing as he hit the coffee table with his fist, that he'd been speaking all he thought.

The police came, one policeman. But he brought the sheriff and the coroner too, along with two deputies and the funeral home ambulance. They took pictures in the room where Jerry lay and led everyone, one by one into the kitchen, politely and efficiently questioned them, took statements.

After the body was carried out, the sheriff made Ralph go with him into the room where Jerry had been. He had Ralph go through it all, demonstrate what had happened step by step.

"No," Ralph told him, "they weren't angry, either one of them. Yes, sir, it was very stupid. A little kid should have known better than to play with guns that way. No, goddamnit. I was Jerry's friend too. If I thought Lloyd . . . but it wasn't that way. Yes, it was stupid."

When they took Lloyd in the room to walk through it, there was a scuffle that ended with Lloyd being brought back by his father and one of the deputies. They took him in the room and his father and mother both talked to him while Ralph sat in the kitchen and wondered what had happened.

Finally it was decided that strain or no strain, suicide attempt or no, Lloyd ought to go with the sheriff to break the news. Ralph offered to go too, but the sheriff said no. One of the deputies drove him home and let him off at his front porch with his gun and all five of the squirrels. Lloyd's father had insisted that he take them.

Ralph walked in and found himself alone in the house.

He washed. Then, though it seemed somehow vaguely improper to him, obscurely wronging to Jerry, he changed clothes and took the bloody hunting clothes into the bathroom, put them in the washing machine, set it, and turned it on.

After a while his father came back from uptown. Ralph told him what happened, explained all the details as they drove to the state line for liquor. Later, when his mother and little sister came back from town too, Ralph let his father explain to them why they were drinking so early in the day.

Goddamn that Gwyn for believing in all-mighty dreams.

III.

*Goddamn You Too*

Sometime after Gwyn left, Ralph persuaded himself to get up from his desk. His stomach was queasy and his head felt light. It occurred to him that he hadn't eaten since breakfast.

In the kitchen his mother was sitting at the bar reading. She looked up as he came in, then turned back to her book without speaking.

He opened the refrigerator. There were the squirrels, all skinned and dressed out: headless, footless, just naked hunks of pallid flesh and bone with raw wounds all over them.

Ralph shut the refrigerator door.

"Do you want me to fix you something?" his mother asked.

"No. Not right now, thanks."

He went back to his room and dressed. While he was in there the phone rang. When he came back out his mother said, "That was Lloyd's mother. She says Lloyd is comin' over here to see you."

"Oh?"

"She wants to be sure he gets here. She says they're still worried. Lloyd's daddy has taken all the guns and sharp knives out of the house."

Ralph met him at the door. "What's up, Lloyd?" he asked.

"I just wanted to talk," Lloyd said.

"Well I was just goin' out to eat. You want to come with me?" Lloyd nodded.

"Who's there?" Ralph's mother called.

"Lloyd," Ralph called. "We're goin' out for a Coke."

He plucked the car keys from the top of the TV set.

"Oh. Well, Lloyd's welcome to come in."

"No. We'll be back before long."

As they walked out to the car, Ralph noticed the taillights of a car parked up the street.

"That's Jesse Sloat," Lloyd told him. "He followed me over here."

"Screw him. Let's go. Here, you drive." Ralph handed Lloyd the keys.

They drove right past Jesse, and Ralph waved to him as they went.

"Well, how you doin'?" Ralph asked.

"Lousy," Lloyd said. "I'm all revved up. Tried to sleep this afternoon. Took a handful of my old lady's Libriums, but I still couldn't close my eyes. I can't help thinkin' about it and the more I think, the worse it seems."

"Oh hell. No one blames you, Lloyd. Bad luck."

"I don't know," Lloyd said. "I just don't know."

They stopped at the A & W. Ralph got a hamburger and Lloyd got a Coke. Jesse Sloat parked across the street and watched them. Ralph didn't know whether to laugh or cry, seeing Jesse there. Maybe he thought that somehow what they ordered to eat would give him clues for whatever weird theory he was working on now.

When the food came they drove out of town, toward Chalk Ford again. But they stayed on the highway. They were too many important places on all the gravel roads: Gwyn's parents' house was out on one, and the drinking roads too, and the roads that led to places they'd been so many times with Jerry. They lost Jesse Sloat when they crossed the state line, and he didn't pick them up when they slipped back into Arkansas on the Poplar Bluff road.

Lloyd kept trying to tell Ralph how bad he felt about it all. Ralph tried to tell him not to let it get to him. They both agreed in every way they could that Jerry had been a good man.

When they came back to Quantril they joined the Saturday

INTRO 8: THE LIAR'S CRAFT

night parade of cars making the circuit from the court square to the A & W and back; kids with their dates, drinking buddies, a few longhairs looking to score dope. The people drove up and down Main Street honking and waving, pulling off into parking lots now and then to huddle their cars and match notes on what was going on. It made Ralph weary to see them: a few new faces, a few new cars but doing the same old things. Drive around. Drive around. Who's with who? Who's got dope? Who's got beer? Hunt some pussy. Hunt a party. Hunt up something to do. It's gotta be here somewhere; though we've driven these same streets a thousand times each this one night. Maybe just around the corner, maybe just up the street. Gotta catch it. Go catch it.

"How'd Jerry's family take it?" he asked Lloyd.

"Bad. Of course. His mother had already heard. I think mine called her. Anyway she and Jerry's brother were gettin' ready to go to the funeral home. She said she didn't want to talk to me. And Jerry's brother, he was cold too. I tried to apologize, explain, but there wasn't any way. It just made her mad and she said a lot of hateful things."

"Oh?"

"She didn't say murder. But she meant it. 'You feel bad?' she said. 'I should guess you would. It should weigh on your soul. Before the judgment throne, it must weigh on your soul. And goddamn you too,' she said to the sheriff. 'There's no justice in this world.'"

"She was hurt," Ralph said. "When a person's hurt that bad, they just lash out without thinkin'."

"Maybe. But it was worse the way his old man took it. Sorrowful. He came in from workin' at the mill and it was him, it looked like, had cried. 'Another one,' he kept sayin'. 'Another one. Goddamned huntin'. Goddamned hunters and guns.' He acted like he blamed himself as much as me . . . you know."

"Yes," Ralph said. Jerry had told them many times how his father hated for him to have a gun. Jerry's uncle had been killed hunting. Crossing a field he had touched an electric fence with a loaded deer rifle and it had blown up.

Much later that night, after the Saturday night parade of cars had disappeared, all gone home, Ralph and Lloyd parked by the court square and sat on one of the benches.

"But what really gets me, Ralph, what really gets me is that right as I pulled the trigger, right then I thought, 'This is for takin' Gwyn, you bastard' and squeezed . . . not like when I shot at you. That was play. But I felt serious. And when it went off. God. The first thing I thought was that now I'd better find a shell and kill myself. The only way I could get out of it all would be to kill myself."

"That's nuts, Lloyd."

"Yes. Now I can see that too. I mean, I saw it the minute I started to and stopped myself. They couldn't have stopped me."

"I'm afraid you spooked your people already," Ralph said.

Lloyd ignored that, just sat looking blank for a second. Then he said, "When I saw Jerry dead, right then I thought, I knew, that I would rather he was alive and him and Gwyn hunchin' there before my eyes. But it was too late."

Ralph just shook his head, staring at the brown grass on the ground. That tore it. There wasn't anyway to get around it now— Lloyd had known. He started to ask Lloyd for all the lousy details of what he had known of Gwyn and Jerry and all that had been going on. But then he closed his mouth. What good would it do?

They sat there and it was so quiet that they could hear the buzz of the transformers and neon lights, dogs prying at a trashcan in the alley, a car rushing along out on the highway.

Across the street, the night marshal saw them and stopped short. He muttered into his walkie-talkie and it muttered back. He slid the antenna in and walked on.

Something rumbled like a chain being dragged across stones. Their heads turned and they saw that it was the street cleaner grating and scraping with a shovel at the sand in the gutter, the sand that kept fighting its way out from under the concrete, breaking the streets and seeping out of the cracks.

There were just the two of them on the bench, the sand and the cleaner battling in the gutters, the dogs and the night marshal contesting the alleys. That and a train rumbling out along the ridge like some act of God building up momentum to slide into the world.

"I've talked," said Lloyd. "Maybe I've talked too much. I know that some will think I did mean to kill him. That doesn't matter so much. If I could just get over the feeling, if I didn't think that my wanting made it so." He paused. "What do you think, Ralph? What do you really think?"

"You can't blame a person for wanting."

"But, I mean I *wished* him dead. Doesn't that have anything at all to do with it?"

"No," Ralph lied. "I don't think so. I know it didn't."

"Okay." Lloyd sighed. "I guess I'd better go home."

They got back into the still-warm car and drove to Lloyd's house.

When they had stopped, Ralph, scooting across the seat to the wheel, asked, "If I came back next weekend, would you go hunting again?"

"I don't know," Lloyd said.

"You aren't gonna be like Jerry's old man?"

"I don't know. No. I know I'll hunt again someday."

"Yeah. You can't let things throw you."

"I guess that's right," Lloyd agreed halfheartedly.

"Shouldn't go from one . . . mishap to the opposite extreme," Ralph said. "You know it. Don't you know it?"

"I guess you're right."

"Good man."

Jesus, but it was inadequate. So totally inadequate, Ralph saw as he closed the car door. Everything he'd said, probably. But it was too late then, Lloyd was already opening his front door.

But what else can you do? Ralph asked himself later that night. What else can you do but carry on? Why cry to God that it's all unfair, or call on the world that it is unjust? What if Lloyd did know, oh he must have known somehow, felt that shell slide into the chamber or just the weight of it. Like when you get into a car and can tell without looking at the gauge, just by how it handles, that it has a full tank of gas.

Unable to sleep, he got up, put on his bathrobe, and went into the kitchen.

He took the squirrels out of the refrigerator and stepped out the back door into darkness. He sat on the edge of the porch, dangling his bare feet in the air to keep them from contact with the cold porch. He listened to the brittle scratching sound of the wind whipping dead leaves across the asphalt street, the quieter sound of leaves blowing through the grass. He felt the stiff, cold rigidness of the squirrel in his hands.

Ralph called and the cat came bounding up the steps. He held the squirrel under its nose. It sniffed avidly and made a lunge for it, but Ralph dropped the squirrel on the ground. The cat leaped down to it. Ralph dropped the others beside it, one by one, noting the dull thud each made hitting the ground.

What else can you do? He asked himself again. For it was everyone's fault or no one's that Jerry got killed. If Lloyd had any inkling that the gun was loaded, then Gwyn was partly right. And Ralph himself, he could have stopped it. The second Lloyd pointed the gun he could have, should have, called him down for it.

His feet were numb, he realized. But he continued to sit.

He listened to the noise of the cat feeding below him, the greedy tear and gulp, crunch of bones, the faint stir of a squirrel being turned over and worried.

But finally, Ralph decided, finally it was true that even if all the others were correct, if Lloyd was responsible in the final sense, accountable before God's throne for Jerry's death, or even if it were true that all men and women are ruled by murky mumbernumberish were-things in their damned subconscious selves—free will merely one weak vector in the field, like a shrew hanging to the ear of an elephant; even so, even if, then still there was no reason to try to tell the sheriff that. There was no reason to let Gwyn believe it or Lloyd, much less to speak to Jesse Sloat. Why cause more pain to come out of pain, more evil out of evil?

He sat for a long time in the darkness and the cold, listening to the crunch of bones, faint tear and swallow from below.

Never to tell. Just to know, Ralph decided. To deny what he knew. God knows, someone had to tell the right lies. Someone had to have some mercy and stand up to lie to the rest.

*John G. Bryan*

## SOUGH AWAY, SWEET CY

Cy.

See? He lies there on the cot beneath the windows harboring his trinity of discomforts: bloated, constipated, the arthritic spirit moving stealthily from joint to joint. Cy?

*Who is there?*

I.

*Mime?*

As every afternoon, of course. I come to find you as a child in the forest. And I come to speak of those matters that would only pain you were you to speak of them yourself.

*Leave me.* His lips barely parting to speak, his massive head immoble. The silhouette of a reclining Alfred Hitchcock—it is fitting.

And what gratitude is that? I, who give you new life each day. I, the kind of man who tells your tale.

*The dwarf, the liar. I will tell it this time.*

No, Cy. You are not able. You would wet your lips, close your eyes, and begin to mutter about me and Siegfried and Toto and Dorothy, but it would only be an unwitting parody of the fine tale of your adventure.

*Then you will tell it?*

Don't I always tell it?

Cy. Clearly he is in pain. But that is typical: It differs little from what has passed every afternoon since he returned from Topeka in mid-June 1957.

I concede that there are at least three aspects of his history which might deserve whatever little pity you may wish to offer on this clear autumn day. First, his birth, a joy to none—even then he had to be cut from the warm depth of his mother's belly.

Second, this town, this small dim room, the umbilicus of Cy's existence. It has always been so: Nash, Kansas, in the northwestern segment of Pottawatomie County, twenty miles east of MayDay, twenty miles north of Manhattan.

Finally, his name: Cyrus Luther Grim—a fictitious name, you suppose. Perhaps he thought so himself: Cy still believes himself to be a cryptic allusion to a number of folk tales, those of Jakob Grimm, Frank Baum, Richard Wagner, and others.

What Cy would tell you would be a series of fantasies, of myths. But Cy's adventure, while fantastic, is not myth. If Cy could tell you what is true he would probably speak slowly, calmly, with measured rhythms, saying:

"My name is Cyrus. Grim. I was born in 1919, two years after my parents, Gunther and Greta, were married. The same year my papa built this building to house Grim's Feed, Seed, & Hardware. I married in 1945, after coming back from Guam. Her name was Ernestine Fraser, from Junction City. By then Papa had changed the name of the store to Grim & Son and made a lot of money. When he died in July of the next year, 1946, Mama took the insurance money, bought the Homeland Grain Mills, and turned it all over to me.

"We couldn't have babies so we adopted a girl. Henrietta was already three. That was 1947. She was awfully big for three and bit me on the finger the second day we had her. I wanted to take her back to Salina, but Erna said 'No.' And Mama said 'No.' Erna and Mama were always on the same side. It went on like that for a long time."

There is reason to believe that Cy was not a happy man.

"Miserable."

*A weak man.*

He had no courage.

*I had no heart.*

He was small and confused and afraid.

*A man made of straw.*

He must always interject, must always try to qualify what I say for him. Close your eyes, Cyrus. I will speak your lines.

"My name is Cyrus. Her name was Erna and the girl was Henrietta. She was awfully big for three."

The acquisition of the Homeland Grain Mills had created various problems for Cyrus between 1946 and the early fifties. The transition had precipitated an unusually high rate of office turnover, the initial unionization of the millworkers (followed by frequent disputes with the Amalgamated Butchers and Meatcutters of North America), and several violent acts against the Mills (including arson).

Grim & Son still showed good profits each year, but his brother-in-law had come from Junction City to manage it while the problems of the Mills remained the burden of Cyrus alone.

In 1952 he considered re-enlistment in the Navy for the Korean police action, but at age thirty-three he was fat, married, and well-anchored in Kansas.

*Caught in a whirlpool.*

He likes that. He plays the spiral bit to the hilt. Did even back in 1957.

"I am Cy. I live in this house with Em and Henry and my little dog."

*It is so.*

"I met a man, Wortley, one day, who was passing through, looking for work; a migrant, a lettuce picker, a store sweeper."

*Wanderer, his guise.*

"He showed me what he could do with a broom. He winked at Em's brother, Milo, and I thought they were in league."

*Traveler, his name.*

"But he obviously had experience, and Milo didn't like to sweep the store."

*Wotan, dark and cunning, short and lean.*

"So I hired him and paid him in advance, a hundred dollars for the month to come."

*A weak man.*

He had no courage.

*I had no heart.*

He was small and confused and afraid.

*A man made of straw.*

"But in the evenings when I would lie here under the windows, after closing, before going home, Wortley would come sit on that very stool and tell me about grape picking in Napa Valley and orange picking in Florida, and about how, lying here, I look like his son who was knifed in the neck creating a goitrous-like swelling with a narrow red slit at the summit of the mound. He had died lying there on the boardwalk between the Atlantic and Neptune, New Jersey, at the end of the tomato-picking season."

*Siegmund.*

Be wary, I warn you. He is not a well man, this Cy.

"That was the middle of April. The weather was warming and jimsonweed was beginning to bud. I would lie on this cot in the evening with this small room darkened, with only the light from the alley showing the details, the walls and scant furnishings, the shotguns, hunting knives, and duck calls hanging from eight-penny nails."

For seven days the migrant floor sweeper had been there cleaning up after the store closed at five-thirty, sweeping and then going back to the small office at the rear of the building, his trouser cuffs lined with the yellow dust of grain, his shoes leaving yellow traces in the path to Cy's office.

*Like a voice in the wilderness. Prepare the way.*

Later he would finish sweeping and leave the store clean and darkened.

*Like a child lost in the forest. The birds have taken my seeds and are puffed up with the food of my wanderings.*

Cy would lie there as he does now, a large body with its massive head, bloated, constipated, arthritic—even then, in 1957.

"Cy. Then and now. And I barely breathe in this little house in Kansas. Uncle Henry scolded me for sassing him. And Aunt Em put my right hand on the wood stove because I was scratching where it itched."

*That's so.*

" 'If your hand be a temptation,' Uncle Henry said, 'cut it off and cast it into the fire.' "

*I told her that I didn't want to be cooked.*

Late in April 1957, Greta Grim, Cy's mother, suffered a massive stroke. She died a few days later, on May 2, a Thursday.

*She was going to save me. She was going to push the old woman in the oven. And the woodsman was going to come and take us back home to Kansas.*

"When she did that to my hand, I screamed. 'If you can't stand the heat,' Uncle Henry said, 'don't never touch yourself there again.' I went out and started to running but it was getting dark. And came back."

*A weak man.*

About five forty-five Cy heard the sweeping begin. It was slow but steady.

*Like the fall of a smith's hammer.*

Usually in May the store's skylights provided enough light for a man to sweep; but the day was overcast, and the yellow light from the several incandescent bulbs on the ceiling shone through the narrow door of Cy's darkened office. He lay there as always, listening to the methodical swish. The fine yellow dust whirled in the stream of light spreading toward Cy.

Most days in a Kansas May warm up enough that Cy would open his three windows and enjoy the breeze.

*But it turned to wind. The gold to straw. My wife to a pillar of salt. Water to dust. Dust to dust. And from the lump of clay—a man.*

The day was prematurely dim at six o'clock. Cy felt the wind streaming over his bloated belly. The temperature was dropping quickly, and the wind had switched from southeasterly to southwesterly. He considered closing the windows since his joints were already stiffening and he assumed that within minutes the rain would break and come spattering through the screens. But he waited.

As the wind became stronger he listened and heard that the sweeping had stopped. Slowly he became aware of the diesel-like roar which he had heard about but had never himself heard before. The farmers said it sounds like a locomotive in a roundhouse.

He tried, with only vague decision, to rise; his joints refused. Out the end window he could see the gray curtain with its girdle of debris.

*On the altar, bound, hands and feet. My father's spear raised above me. A circle of fire around me, the flames licking at the rocks. Who will free me from my sleep?*

"The noise had gone when I was able to get up. The tornado had not touched my room except for the grain which was sprayed through the door giving the walls and floor a yellow coat. But the front of the store was blown in; pillars split; bricks scattered and broken; hardware piled on the floor.

"I walked up the length of the store and looked out the open front. The other side of Fouth Street was nearly all wrecked. By then the civil defense siren was going.

"The migrant wasn't buried except for his feet which were covered over with birdseed. Part of his shirt was still on him though most had been blown or cut off. It wasn't the wind that had killed him—hadn't snapped his neck, I don't think, but the flying glass. He must have been standing by the front window when the twister blew it out.

"His hand was still wrapped around the broken broom handle.

"He was dead though. Dark with blood. Small, curled up in the middle of scattered grain."

*Wotan. Dark and cunning. Short and lean. Master of tempests.*

"In that still minute of standing over the old man I felt invitation."

*The voice of a bird.*

"It asked me to leave that place, that house where the torments grew by day and night. To go to a new place with nothing, not even my name, with nothing but myself."

*Notung with me.*

That was May 3, 1957.

"Aunt Erda slept. The spinning went on as Nash was eaten up by the winds. And for all that wind I could hardly breathe, but I stood looking at Wortley's body, and I could hardly breathe with all the dust still flying."

And what did you do, Cy?

"I stood scratching my eyes, rubbing out the dust."

*That's so.*

And what did Uncle Henry say?

"Cut it off; throw it into the fire."

*He did.*

And did you?

"No, it was too hot, and he said, 'If you can't stand the heat get out of the kitchen.' "

*So I did.*

What?

"I ran out, didn't take anything, ran like hell, right down the road, kept running."

*Right into the darkness, by God.*

Where were you going?

"Just away."
*No, to the mountain, to the ring of fire.*
Cy?
*With Notung, with the ring.*
Why?
*To save fair Brunnhilde.*
How noble! How kind! A strong man.
"With courage."
Cyrus the lionhearted.
"A giant, clear-headed, fearless."
A hero!
*Siegfried!*
And did you? Save her?
*Cy. I am he.*
Yes?
*I am Cy.*
And?
*And I live in this house with Aunt Em and Uncle Henry. It can-
not be helped. It comes fully round and I must take a new breath.*

Cy. He lies there as he did in June of 1957. After returning
from Topeka. After six weeks, almost seven weeks, of living with
a blond dancer named Toots LeChien in the Sherwood Forest
trailer park just east of Topeka. You laugh, but it is true. She
worked at the Continental Comfort Lounge on Droll Avenue.

"I hadn't ever been to a place like that. Not since I was in Hong
Kong anyway. She was up behind the bar on a platform with the
lights shining up at her. Hot damn she could move!

"When she got off work I followed her but she knew it, and
when she got to her car she didn't get in. She motioned to me. So
I went over and said could I help her, you know, acting like I
hadn't been following her. She said, 'You scratch my back—'"
*I'll scratch yours.*

The army reserves and local ROTC directed the immediate
clean-up of the county. American Red Cross inspectors and vol-
unteers set up shelters, distributed medicine and food. The Methodist church, Nash's only large building not heavily damaged by
the tornadoes, became the headquarters of the disaster relief
agency. The smaller churches and the schools not destroyed

served as food and medical supply areas and as temporary housing for the four hundred left without shelter.

The commerce of the town remained idle for three days while power and water were restored, while the seventeen dead were buried, and the search for the four missing people continued.

The people of Nash believed that Cy had been buried in the rubble of Fourth Street or had simply been blown into too many ragged pieces to recognize the whole.

None of Cy's family had been injured. Ernestine had slept through the storm. Her brother, Milo, had been in Junction City talking to the John Deere parts distributor.

Henrietta had locked herself in her bedroom away from her mother. She always did so when she sat down to an evening of trimming her bangs, studying herself in the mirror, listening to her records. She was thirteen.

When Ernestine awakened around six-thirty that evening, she found Henrietta still locked in her bedroom, Milo still away, Cyrus unusually late (his standard was six-fifteen, maximum deviation of five minutes), the evening uncommonly dark. When the civil defense siren sounded once more to signal the passing of danger, she began inquiries. By nine o'clock Wortley's body had been found by lantern light in the debris of Grim & Son. At midnight most searches for missing people were suspended until morning. By then a dozen bodies had been found.

Cy had taken the week's receipts from the store plus some cash he found in the pick-up he had stolen when he left that night. In Nash it was assumed that the money had been taken from the store in the scattered looting and that the truck had simply been lifted away by the tornado and perhaps dumped in the reservoir. It was not too hard to believe. Tornadoes have always bred portentous events.

It would not be correct to say that, as the days went on, Cy was not missed. As owner of Grim & Son and the Homeland Grain Mills, the Nash business and social communities could hardly ignore him when he was there and could hardly dismiss his absence when he wasn't there—though they tried. However, even the extremity of Nash's trauma failed to bring much remorse over the loss of Cyrus Grim.

Much of Pottawatomie County was declared a disaster area and federal aid slowly began reaching the state relief administration. The process of reconstruction had begun.

"I hadn't been to Topeka but maybe a dozen times in my whole life. The first time was to a convention of the FFA. Must have been about fifteen then. In 1948 I went to a Rotary convention there but left a day early—sickness at home, everyone had the German measles.

"Most the other times were to meetings at the capitol, mostly on ag business.

"And then came the tornado and I woke up in Topeka, hardly sixty miles west of Kansas City, with McCain's pick-up I stole and a pocket of money and later my own pick-up, Toots. So I took off the license and dumped McCain's in a ditch just south of the trailer park—beyond the grove. First I stripped out the seat so nobody would want to take it. Later I went back and took out the carburetor."

*And fan belt.*

"And fan belt. And got the flashlight."


The eulogy at the services held for Cyrus Luther Grim, born 1919; died in a great wind, 1957; the only child of Gunther and Greta Grim; the husband of the former Ernestine Fraser of Junction City; father of one daughter, Henrietta; owner of the Homeland Grain Mills and Grim & Son; veteran of the Pacific theater, World War II; prominent Nash businessman; member and trustee of the Nash Methodist Church; member of the Lions Club; survived by wife and daughter; the eulogy was delivered by the Reverend Bob Lupus. From the May 11 issue of the Nash *Plain-Talk:*

Cyrus L. Grim, missing since the tornado of last week, for whom hope has been hanging these many days by the slenderest threads, has apparently yielded to the fell destroyer. The iron constitution of his beloved family carried them through the hours as they refused to turn their faces to the wall until the last searches through Nash's perdition were complete.

Services for the prominent Nash businessman and civic leader were conducted by Reverend Bob Lupus under the auspices of the Booth Mortuary. A marker was placed in the Grim family plot at Rhine Memorial Cemetery.

Reverend Bob, long-time shepherd of the Methodist flock in Nash, delivered a moving eulogy which touched all those present and was said to have brought tears to the eyes of many.

The minister spoke first of the many contributions which the deceased had made to the welfare of all the people of Nash, of Pottawatomie County, of Kansas, and of America, citing his military service, his service in community functions, and the many less conspicuous benefits conferred upon us all.

Next, Reverend Lupus spoke of the fine example of family life which the Grims had set for others in these times of declining moral stamina. In the Grim family, he said, the strength of our Savior could be seen at work.

Finally, the eulogist called to the minds of all within earshot the significance of the passing-on of Cyrus Grim, of the destruction visited upon Nash like unto that of Sodom and Gomorrah, of the sin and weakness which must be put out of our hearts, and of the restoration of our souls to a single purpose and that the attainment of our salvation is tribute to the goodness and greater glory of Jesus Christ.

Honorary pallbearers were Silas Alberich, Junior Ernst, David Dark, Herbert Frank, Lawrence O'Connor, Eddie Blag, Hugh McCain, C. G. Sigmoid, Gus Tiemann, and brother-in-law of the deceased, Milo Fraser.

The service, which began yesterday at ten o'clock, was the last of the many rites which have come out of the tragedy of what is already being called the "Great Kansas Tornado of 1957."


"I am Cy. Irrevocably, like the quickest fugitive from Pandora's box, like the soul fleeing the body of a dead man. Cy, loosed upon the world."

Cy?

*It is so.*

"I am he. Held in the hand of Melinda Brown, a woman of shocking purpose and strength and cunning."

*The issue of Wotan.*

"On the altar of dance with her blade and rubber gloves. She took ahold of my hair and dragged me back to her. She was insatiable."

*Abram had great faith.*

But did the boy?

"Hadn't known what I was bargaining for."

*She never stopped.*

"She went on, never to tire of pulling me back, to tire of pulling me back to her."

*Rocking, cradled in her sheath.*

"And in four weeks she made of me a child once again. June 16th."

The proper gestation for a turkey.

*Whimpering, pulled from her oven, shocked by the sudden realization of the cold and my nakedness.*

It could have been no harder on Adam.

*Eve no more cunning.*

Nor her child more savage. For the child rose up his body still wet with mucus, saw the man with his mother and slew him without a lost breath of effort.


Six weeks and three days had witnessed the reconstruction of Grim & Son, the first of the tornado-damaged stores to feature a "Grand Re-Opening."

The store front had been rebricked, the roof given new and better support, the interior restored but improved with modern shelving, subdivisions, lighting, stocking arrangements. Milo had overseen the construction; the widow, his sister, had overseen the expenditures. Probate on the Grim estate had not been settled, but there seemed to be no possibility of contests, and credit in Nash was readily extended. The Homeland Grain Mills had not been damaged in the May storm and its profits were still regular and considerable. Further, the state authorities had encouraged the extension of easy credit until federal aid could be filtered down to the community level. It was an effort to encourage reconstruction and discourage businesses from leaving Nash.

As the first of the Grand Re-Openings, the town looked upon the dedication of the new-old Grim & Son as a reaffirmation of faith in the future of Nash and its economy.

The Nash *Plain-Talk* sent a reporter to immortalize, in the word and on film, the green ribbon cutting ceremony. Green because it represented the fertility of Nash, of Kansas, and of the Grim business. Later the *Plain-Talk* would submit the story to UPI by sending a reporter to Manhattan to use the teletype sender—they could only receive wire stories in Nash. The copy submitted:

Mayor Eddie Blag, semi-retired owner of the Nash Ford dealership, joined Mrs. Ernestine Grim in cutting a Grand Re-Opening ribbon today. The rededication of Grim and Son (sic) by the widow of the late Cyrus L. Grim marks the first such ceremony after the devastation wreaked on this Kansas community of 6,000 by the Great Kansas Tornado of 1957. That tornado claimed the lives of twenty-one people including Mrs. Grim's husband whose body is still missing but presumed dead (sic).

Shortly before ten o'clock this morning Police Chief Morris Shifflett directed the cordoning-off of one block of Fourth Street in downtown Nash so that the crowd might gather to witness the event.

General Kenneth Sprouse (Kans. Nat'l Guard, retired), who had headed the local Tornado Restoration and Rehabilitation Operation, sped through the blockade in his jeep just as the ceremonies were commencing with an unexpected message from President Dwight David Eisenhower.

General Sprouse read the President's personal message to an estimated crowd of 300 people. The missive commended the people of Nash for their courage and determination in rebuilding their city, in renewing their faith in Kansas and the United States, in not fearing to dream once more.

"The people of America," the President said, "join you in mourning your dead and in praying for your prosperous and peaceful future."

When General Sprouse concluded, the enthusiastic crowd cheered the President's words.

Before cutting the bright green ribbon to the front doors of Grim and Son, a hardware and feed supply store dating back to 1920, Mayor Blag made a brief speech, entitled "The Phoenix of Kansas," to the gathering.

Mrs. Grim thanked the mayor, General Sprouse, and the people of Nash for their faith and help in the weeks of trial since the semi-destruction of the store and the loss of her husband.

She closed by encouraging her fellow Nashites to rebuild and rekindle the fire of community spirit.

The assemblage then beheld what they had all come to see, the cutting of the ribbon and the opening of Grim and Son to hopefully another thirty-seven years of business.

UPI edited and carried the story which a Topeka radio station broadcast that evening, June 17, 1957.

Monday evening Melinda Brown (or, professionally, Toots LeChien) was called by the owner of the Continental Comfort and told that she would have to take the place of the lounge's other dancer, Corrine Coosman.

"She left the trailer at about seven o'clock. Before that she shut me in the bathroom and put a chair under the knob. 'Wash yore filthy sef,' she said."

*That's so. Wash the corn outen your ears.*

"'Got no corn in my ears,' I says to her. 'I'm tarred of eating nothin but corn cob,' she says. 'Too damn hot to bear,' she says."

*Don't you shut me in this bathroom.*

"'Flush your filthy sef,' she say to me. 'Wash yore body good and I don wan see any of that sticky jujubeez on your fingers when I git home.'

"'I'll suffcate in hyere,' I says. 'Take cold shower,' she say back at me."

*Lemmeouten hyere.*

"'Don you dare poun on thisere door, boy,' she say.

"'Ah caint breedth ind ear, year?'"

*Too hot to breathe.*

"'Giddown, beau,' she scream at me.

"When she left I pushed on the door but it wouldn't go, so I kicked my foot through it. Trailers are like that, built of balsam and construction paper.

"Then out. Down the drive past the Sherwood Forest sign on the county highway and over the dirt road leading south.

"No money left. Just a yellow cotton shirt and khaki trousers and the remains of McCain's pick-up.

"But I forgot the parts to make the truck whole."

*Don't make me go back.*

So Cy returned to the trailer, found the carburetor and fan belt, and ran out again leaving the door open, the living-room light spreading in the summer night.

When he reached the ditch where he had left McCain's truck, he opened the hood and looked down into the darkness. He could feel the parts of the engine but could see nothing. No moon, no stars. He reached into the dark body but it bore no familiarity.

"You'd think I'd never of been under a hood before."

*Stranger.*

He sat on the running board and cried.

*Not fair.*

Take heart, Cy. You got up and began to reach in and feel about. True?

*Yes.*

And for two hours you tried to put the carburetor back on the engine, back in the dark, feeling for wires and holes. But with no luck. So once again you walked back to the trailer, found it still empty, the yellow light spilling out the door, found a flashlight, and returned once more to the site of the pick-up. And right way you saw the mechanics of the mystery and put the carburetor to the engine. True?

*Yes.*

And the fan belt.

*Yes.*

And when you were done you tried to start the engine. But you see, Cy had failed to notice that there was no battery. It had been taken. Then, Cy?

"Ran. Down to the county highway, then west toward the city."

But there were cars in the trailer lot, Cy. You could have stolen a battery.

*No.*

You stole Hugh McCain's pick-up.

"West, into Topeka, to the ATSF rail yards. West, in the freight car, toward Manhattan and Junction City and Salina. West from Melinda Brown and her dancing legs."

Cy didn't go all that far. He didn't tell himself why, but he jumped from the slow-moving train as it passed just south of a small town, Nash, Kansas, small surprise indeed.

He knew where he was and ran up the rows of corn, north, to the feet of the co-op grain elevators, through nigger town, right into the heart of Nash. It was seven-twenty, the morning of June 18, 1957.

Cy. In name and, yes, you know, in other ways. Convenient, you suggest. And you protest that coincidence is not very believable. That Cy could hardly have returned the day after the Grand Re-Opening of Grim & Son. But Cy knew. He listens to the radio. He reads the newspaper. He would have you believe that it was the cycle of fate which returned him to Nash, Kansas, forty-six days after he had left. So why not forty?

No, it was Cy.

Cy, the self-fulfilling allusion.

But we are not yet finished with our friend, Mr. Grim. For all his embarrassment at returning from Topeka, from his failure at making it stick with Toots LeChien—for the embarrassment of running from Nash—all that is nothing.

*Notung.*

Quiet, Cy. It is nothing when one compares it with what has passed since June 18, 1957.

Nash labors on. The efforts of General K. T. Sprouse at reconstruction were beginning to pay off. The Grand Re-Opening of Krummer G. E. Appliances was to be held on Friday. The dedication of the new Nash Central Baptist Church was scheduled for August 31, though the groundbreaking ceremonies had not yet been held. "The Lord will provide," said their pastor, Reverend G. C. Chancroid. His associate pastor, Vaughn Wasserman added, "He works in strange and wondrous ways."

Heed these words: Cy was returning to a town of optimists who were reborn, revitalized. Even the priest at Slaughter of the Holy Innocents Catholic Church had adopted the popular Protestant phrases to describe the spirit in Nash: "born anew," "saved in the Lord," "true believers."

To all this Cy was coming, running through the cornfields from his six-week debauch in Topeka, panting with his stale lungs in the light mid-June air of northeast Kansas. He could hardly wait to enter that back office of Grim & Son, to sleep or lie still in the mild summer evenings.

As he panted along Third Street he said to his pained body, "Gracious to God, I'm glad to be back. Gracious to God."

*To sleep, to sleep, per—*

Yes, to lie there as he does now. Cy. On the cot beneath the three windows, to harbor his bloating, his constipation, the arthritic spirit—the silhouette of a reclining Hitchcock.

*To suffer the slings—*

Yes, and do nothing.

*Notung.*

Yes, the magnificent transformation of Cyrus Luther Grim. From nothing to—

*Notung.*

And enjoy the comfort of being called a madman. By the people of Nash? No, not by those sensible people, not by those people of reason. For when Hugh McCain saw Cyrus Grim bumping along Third Street at half-past seven that morning, he knew damn well that Cy was as sane as Hamlet, and then some. And he wondered where his pick-up had got to. And he shouted at ole Cy Grim, that mass of resurrected civic leader stumbling on through the wide-eyed folks of Nash, Kansas.

*Lazarus, he called out.*

No, "Cyrus," he shouted. "Where's my truck?" Because after all these weeks Cy and the truck were the only objects weighing over two hundred pounds that weren't accounted for. With one back, Hugh felt singularly cheated by the wind.

But Cy tumbled on down to the intersection of Third and Tuttle, crossed over and then up to Fourth Street. The end of his grand adventure was near.

At the front of Grim & Son, Milo Fraser was directing the placement of sale lawn mowers on the sidewalk. The new store sweeper, Milo's cousin, Dwayne, provided the muscle.

" 'Jesus,' he whispered when he saw me."

*O Cyrus!*

"And I stopped dead in front of him, then pushed past him into the store. It wasn't the same. Brighter, shinier, new linoleum, new shelves, new merchandise, no more feed sacks piled in the front.

"Behind the counter she stood looking at me, me in the same shirt and trousers from the day I'd left, standing there panting, arms hanging down."

*Notung with me.*

"She said nothing, but gave change to the customer with the barrowgelder and closed the register.

"But I was thinking fast by then because I could tell words were coming first before any hugging or tears of joy at seeing me. And I was right. Real quietly she said, 'Where've you been, Cyrus?' She had the nerve to ask that first. 'What've you been doing for the past six weeks and four days?'

"Well, I looked at her and Milo had come in behind me and I could see McCain, Junior Ernst, and Eddie Blag getting out of a shiny new Ford pick-up out front. Lavern Ralston and C. T. Odell were crossing over from the other side of Fourth. Gracious to God.

" 'Well, Cy?' she said. 'What happened?'

"So I was panting like mad and I went over and sat down on a low shelf and put my hands on my knees. I couldn't seem to catch my breath. 'Been running,' I said. My windy exhaustion failed to impress her. 'I can see you've been running,' she said. 'Where you been running from?' That would take time, I knew.

"By then old man Burnett was standing over me with his hand on my shoulder. 'Where you been, son?' he said. 'We thought you was dead.'

" 'I thought so too for a time,' I said. 'Thought I was a goner, sure enough.' Then Blag said, 'You mean you weren't covered over in all that rubble?'

" 'You're right,' I said. I'd caught my breath by then. 'Straight right. I wasn't covered over at all. You see, I was standing here just looking out the store window when I heard a great noise and gracious God I knew what it was and I fell to my knees. It sounded like forty diesel engines, like the belly of a thunderhead. I closed my eyes with all the sky falling in on me.'

"I paused there to let them picture me and recall the force of the tornado. 'Then,' I said quietly, 'then as I felt all the clothing on my back whipping around me and the seeds peppering my cheeks, the whole store seemed to be settling downward and I felt as light as light can be, light as nothing.' "

*That's so.*

" 'Light as the wind—because that's what I was then: part of the wind and good lordy I thought I had been hit on the head and killed and was making my way to some underworld. Thought I was dead and a goner. Lord help me.'

"Well Eddie Blag looked down at me sitting there and just gave a low, long whistle. But the rest of them didn't say nothing; just looked on.

"By then there must have been a score of people jammed in the store, listening and whispering. I was going to go on but we heard a siren in front and then the general came pushing through the crowd. 'What's going on here?' he said. 'What's this about, Grim?'

"When he got through to where I was sitting on the shelf, old man Burnett said to him, 'Kenny, Cy here says he was taken off by the twister. Says he got blowed away.'

"'Blowed—blown away, where to?' Kenny said.

"'Well,' I said, 'wasn't real sure at first. I stayed up in the wind for what seemed like the longest time and I thought that I was dead and that was eternity though it didn't seem at all like the churches feature it.'"

*Carried on the back of a horse.*

"'So I floated on and on till I could tell I was falling.'

"'It was the strangest feeling, falling through what I thought was the space of eternity. Or is it infinity? One's time and one's the other. Don't recall.'

"'Sounds like one of those Rod Serling things,' old man Burnett said.

"'Anyway, when I landed it was light so I figured that either it was another day, me having been up and flying so long, or it was China where it's light when it's dark in Kansas.'

"Right about then Eddie Blag whistled again and the general said, 'Where were you?' But some girl over near the door called out, 'How'd you land without breaking your neck?' Then the General said, 'Yeah, how'd you come down without being killed?'

"But Hugh McCain spoke up, 'Where's my pick-up?'

"'Shut up, Hugh,' the general said to him. 'Your truck hasn't got nothing to do with all this.' Then the girl by the door called out again, 'How'd you land?' And I realized it was the girl, my girl, that is, who was saying those things.

"'Well, I'm getting to that now. Just you listen to your father and he'll set you straight as right on this here matter. Yes I will. Now—'

"But she called out again, 'You people don't believe him, do you?'

"'Why, child,' I said. 'You just hush up now and let your old man, who you thought was dead and gone all these weeks, you let him tell the folks the truth of the matter.'

"But she was a sticky girl. 'You're not my old man,' she said. 'You're not anybody's father.'

" 'Let your daddy talk,' General Kenny said. 'Cy, how'd it happen? How'd you land? That's what I want to know?'

" 'Well, I came down in shallow water.'

" 'On your head, Cyrus?' This time it was the woman. 'Do you expect us to believe all that? Look at the shame you're bringing on our family with all these stories of yours. Mercy knows I've tried to make you a good home.'

" 'Now, Erna, just let me finish what I'm saying.' But she has a will to match that of any man.

" 'Don't you know when to stop making a fool of yourself. You people get on out of here and leave us alone. This man's sick.'

" 'Where's my truck?' McCain said again.

" 'Erna, I'm talking now. I admit I was feeling a bit winded when I first come in here, but I'm doing okay, yes I am.'

" 'Go on,' she said. 'Get on out. You can see plain enough he's mixed up so just get on out and let me put him to bed.'

" 'Erna, I won't. I won't. These folks want to hear about what happened. Just let me finish what I's about to say.'

"The people were leaving but she couldn't move the General or Eddie Blag. 'I want to hear,' Eddie said. 'Let him finish.'

" 'What's this all about here?' The general moved over to me and looked down. 'Cy? What is this, boy?'

" 'Get on out, Kenny. This is no matter of yours.' Then the girl came over too.

" 'Em,' I said, 'I don't want them to go.'

" 'You hush now, Cy.' "

*But it's too early. I'm not sleepy.*

" 'I don't want them to. I just got here.'

" 'Don't argue with me, Cyrus. I've had just about enough out of you.'

"The general turned around to leave. 'Well, I don't know what's going on here, but the people here have got a right to know and I plan to find out for them.'

"But Aunt Em wouldn't let him stay because she didn't want it. And Uncle Henry was sitting looking at me and shaking his head."

*Like Papa.*

"And when she took the mayor and the general out she stayed and talked to them for the longest time but I just sat there with the old man tapping his foot. 'What'd I tell you about telling stories to people?' he said. 'What'd I tell you about lying? Hmm?'

"I thought about it but couldn't remember just what he'd said.

" 'Child, the Bible says liars burn in everlasting fire and damnation where thar is wailing and gnashing of teeth and a giant worm eats at you but doesn't never consume you. And it grabs aholt of your tongue, this monstrous big worm, cause that was the instrument of your wickedness, and it chews on your tongue and forces you to tell and retell all the filthy lies of your life till you can't stand the untruth of it, but it won't never let you stop but makes you keep on telling them over and over. So don't you never ever let that evilness in you get spilt out in words again or by the justice of Almighty God I'll take aholt of your tongue with fire tongs and pull it straight out of your head—tongue, tonsils, and all.'

"And when he finished saying that, he stood up over me and told me to stick my tongue out so I did and he hit my chin with his palm so that I bit into it and went off to the back room crying and gurgling blood."

*A weak man.*

He had no courage.

*I had no heart.*

He was small and confused and afraid.

*A man made of straw.*

But that was years ago, that day when the whole of Pottawatomie County heard of Cyrus Grim and his flight.

*To the mount of the Valkyrie.*

To Topeka, as they later learned through the courtesy of his daughter, and to the Continental Comfort Lounge and Melinda Brown.

*Into the circle of fire.*

It is a striking fact that although his story of being swept into the clouds by the Nash tornado was found to be less interesting than the truthful account of his adventure in the Topeka wonderland, it is his tale which is recalled by the people of the area today. Its detail has endured and has been fed to a new generation.

Since that June in 1957 Nash has swollen with another six hundred people. They and their children have heard all there is to

hear and have retold all there is to tell with remarkably little em-
bellishment. Still there is in the oral tradition the license of demon-
stration and there is rarely a day that some group of children does
not pass in front of Grim & Son, their arms outstretched, their
trunks twisting as they spin on small feet, their lips whistling the
sound of the wind. Fourth Street witnesses the flight of the children and tolerates the mockery of Cyrus Grim. He spent the last
of his social indulgences on June 18, 1957.

Cy?

*I am he. Irrevocable—the world loosed upon me. Spare me.*

Cy? It is done. Told.

*Again?*

Yes. Today as every day. We have it nearly perfect now.

*One would think so. By now.*

He stills lies there upon the couch, beneath the windows in discomfort.

*In distress.*

But he is about to move. Because it is done for today and tomorrow is a new day. Truly it will be a sign of change in this
town.

Skeptic, be silent. Cy wears the sign of his treasured spiral, not
I. And tomorrow, for the first time in all these years since his
scandal, Cy will participate in the annual "Barnwarming Daze" parade. It is change.

Look, now he moves—more than those fleshy lips. He moves
his eyes and arms. He rises. Through the darkened store he moves
slowly.

Standing in the opened front door he watches a small girl, six or
seven years old, spin past him, arms outstretched and flying. She
whistles up a wind. She mocks without knowing the word mock.
Cyrus watches but knows the many meanings of mockery without
having to watch.

Tomorrow he will ascend the steps of the float, it near the end
of the parade, preceded by the Lions float and followed by the
Shriners on their Harley-Davidsons.

A commemoration of the devastation of the Great Kansas Tornado of 1957, this float has been a Barnwarming Daze fixture
since the autumn of that year.

Each year it bears the names of those killed in the storm and
displays a small scale model of the business district which was

built out of the ash and debris. At the rear of the float a gray papier-mache tornado in its familiar funnel form rises up in a properly menacing fashion.

But it is a new tornado this year, built after Cy had quietly agreed to participate. "That's the cost," Ernestine told him this morning. It is the price of buying back social indulgences from the community. "People can't twit you if you do it yourself."

So Cy will step into the mock twister, will put his arms through the provided side holes and head out the top, and will ride through the thirty blocks which, on the parade route, circle and bisect the heart of Nash.

*Jane Butler*

## THE GAELIC SNAIL

The silver box has broken, and I'm going on a trip to Ireland. It's an Irish box. I taped it together and put it into my dufflebag. The box broke one afternoon as I was packing. It seemed to throw itself from my hands, and then it landed easily on the carpet, so it shouldn't have broken. The box belonged to my grandmother and then to my aunt. I've kept it with me for five years. The cover is decorated with Gaelic serpents winding around a tree. The box was made to hold cigars, but I kept old coins and safety pins in it. It makes no sense at all to me that the box should have broken. When it landed on the carpet, the box exploded quietly into three fragments. Still, I'm taking it with me.

Flying bores me. I want to meet someone, and I don't. Dublin is a dirty city. Old women sleep on the bridges here, with their shoes next to them and their muddy ankles in the gutter. Across from my hotel there is a potato store. The store consists of a counter and a grimy window displaying a pile of potatoes. A light bulb on a long wire hangs over the potatoes. I haven't seen anyone go in there. Many of the storefronts on this street are empty, and I can't find a shop where they sell silver boxes. The store people say maybe I can find one in the countryside, or maybe in the west, where some Gaelic crafts are still being done.

I don't feel well. There's nothing good to buy for dinner. In the cafés they sell Lipton's tea and sandwiches of cheap white bread and processed cheese. The tea comes in an old white teacup. Most of the cafés are like snack bars. People track mud on the floors.

I've seen such dirty tile floors only in the tackrooms of American stables. For breakfast, my landlady gives me bread and tea and cold eggs. No wonder everyone is so pale. I'm going to take a train out into the country. In front of the train station a poster on a kiosk says, "GUINESS WELCOMES YOU TO DUBLIN." The photo shows a healthy-looking Irishman with his sleeves rolled up, raising his glass to the camera. In a vacant lot next to the station a little carnival has been set up. A young priest sells raffle tickets to the crowd there. Then he introduces the band.

There are baskets of flowers hanging from the rafters in the station. That's nice. My ticket will take me to the center of Ireland. The train pulls out of the station, and we pass little farmhouses and schools. From the window, I watch a boy pouring soapy water on a draft horse.

I have changed my ticket so that it will take me to Galway, on the western coast of Ireland, because I am talking to a tall Norwegian man who is going there. I had thought perhaps we could spend some good time together, but when I asked him his name, he was lighting a cigarette, and he set the whole box of matches on fire. It exploded on the table between our seats. He said his name was Arnie, and he started a fire. I can see that we're not meant for each other. At Galway, we share a room for economy's sake, without making love. Arnie falls asleep first, snoring softly in the next bed.

So I begin my walks and teacups, and I talk with the people in the teahouses. Yes, I am an American, but I am not the Vietnam war. I didn't want that war either. I can't answer all these questions. Didn't you hear about the antiwar people in the States?

But why don't you talk about *your* war? Ireland is the same size as Indiana, yet the war in the North isn't part of your life here. You don't want to talk about it. All right. You want to sleep with someone, I know. Because I am an American, I am not a virgin. Irish girls won't sleep with you. They do everything else very well, but finally they back off. Irish girls want to be engaged. Those are used condoms on the wash line over there, bought on the black market. Leave me alone.

Do you have a silver box like this one? Well, then, can you tell me where I can get one? It's Irish, but you don't make things like this anymore. Perhaps it was British money that paid for the making of this box. It's an antique. Now you've got some British soldiers, but nobody's money. You say you don't want the British to leave, though. There might be a bloodbath in the North if they did. You don't like needing them here, but you do need them.

In the dance halls in Dublin there are no more Gaelic dances, only country-western dances. You speak some Gaelic here in the West. In the villages there are a few Gaelic dances, ceilaghs, but they are dying out. Cracken is a little town on the shore north of here where the fiddlers come to play on Sundays. I can camp there for a while, and hear some music.

What a lot of nuns live in this town, Cracken. The convent is a huge chicken coop of nuns, white and black. They sun themselves on the rocks in the afternoon, pulling up their skirts to expose white knees. In the morning, a strange boy is outside my tent. He throws a rope with something tied to the end of it and then pulls the rope back in. Again and again he throws the rope. When I crawl out of the tent, I see that a falcon is circling above his head. The boy has tied a piece of meat to the end of the rope. The falcon lights on his gloved arm, and he walks away. The beach is quiet now, except for fathers taking their children for Sunday morning walks. To me they say, "Luvley marnin', issen t'it?"

On a peninsula, the ruins of a bombed Protestant church are crumbling into the sea. Crimson interior walls can be seen through the arches. The roof is gone. Two chimneys rise above the empty peaks. But I thought the war was in the North? It must be coming. Perhaps the people here are too poor to be afraid.

A stone monument as tall as I am stands next to the water. It commemorates a sea tragedy. A tablet at the bottom explains the deaths. It reads:

ALEC AND SEAN
AND PETER BRA
NDEN DEPART
ED THE MONTH
OF JANUARY 18
11 AT SEA. GOD
REST THEIR SO
ULS

I am sitting on a scratchy boulder. Perhaps all my life I have been on my way to this sand and this boulder. All the rocks on this beach are covered with green and black lichens. Fat brood mares graze between the rocks. Their yearlings follow just behind. Behind me, the fields rise back to where the poor people live in the hills. They made the fields by pushing back the rock by hand. In some places near the sea where there was no dirt, the people filled the cracks between the rocks with seaweed to make soil. The fields are tiny divisions of pasture marked by erratic lines of gray fences. The fences are just broad piles of rock that have been there for centuries. There was too much rock to carry it away.

Near the boat landing the waves wash up against the base of another monument. A man is feeling the surface of the monument with his hands. I'm walking toward him; the gravel bites into my feet.

"You canna' read it," he says. "They haf hacked away at t'it wit' axes in the night. 'Tis here in honore of two boys from Boston who came over inna rowboat. They haf hacked t'it up because the boys were Protestant."

The fiddlers will not be here until this afternoon. I'm walking away from the sharp whiteness of the ocean, toward the villlage, past more nuns and fathers. The nuns on the rocks are like holy blackbirds. They've got to go to Mass in a little while. A donkey stretches his neck over a stone wall to be petted, and there are dogs sleeping on top of the whitewashed fences. Under a buggy, a black kitten plays with a tabby. Some people are on the way to the church, up ahead on the main street. In front of the church four men in worn-looking suits are drinking beer and talking. The roads that lead away from the ocean go to the farms of the poor people, the people who never got over the famine. I can see some of them walking down those roads now. They don't lift their feet far from the earth.

It is still Lipton's tea for breakfast. Why is that? I always thought that the Irish were very fastidious about their tea. In a novel that I read at home, an Irish woman said that the American tea bag was like a dead mouse in the teapot. All the tea here is made from tea bags, but this is a very clean tearoom. A man and his wife sit across from me. They're worried about my traveling alone, but I want to ask them about the war. The woman doesn't say anything.

"The southern Irish are not Nort' minded," the man says. "They are sympathetic, but canna' get involved. The West here never got over the famine. It reduced the population so much. From seven million to three million. Soon we will be four million, and we will knock on Indiana's door." He smiles, and the teeth are yellow in his red face.

I want to buy an Aran sweater, a fisherman's sweater, but they are as hard to find as a silver box. They're the ones with the intricate designs on the fronts, very warm sweaters. Each design belongs to a family, like the family plaids do in Scotland, but they're not designed for beauty. They enable the families to identify the bodies of dead fishermen when the faces have been eaten away by crabs.

It's time for the fiddlers to come to play in Hughe's Pub. Inside, an old porcelain bar runs the length of the room, and long tables fill the center. The beer is served in pint glasses; a lot of beer is being drunk. We are singing "The Nightingale," and everyone is drunk at one o'clock. Under the tables, stray dogs climb over our feet, and there are children drinking and singing, too. They drink the strong cider, and they have come to the pub from Mass.

Another round for the musicians. They're playing wooden flutes and mandolins, bagpipes and fiddles. Over and over again they play the refrains, faster and faster. We beat our feet on the floor. One young fiddler with blond hair and crooked teeth is asking me if I am Irish. I have an Irish name, yes.

"Ah," he says. He knows some history. "They were from the Sout'east. Always very loyal to the crown they were. First they lost their religion and then their language. Language is the more important, I say, for 'tis the spoken wort' of religion. The damned communists they say, 'Religion is the opiate of the mind of man, and we will obliterate it from the face of the eart'—so help us God.' Ha! Ha!" He is advising me with his arm on my shoulder. He reeks of stout. He doesn't want me to go to Belfast.

"The Nort' . . . 'tis noa-where fer ye ta go un yer oane, luv. Nut a loane garl. Nut un yer oane." And it has become late.

The fiddler lives in a thatched house with ten brothers and sisters. His mother is dead and his father runs a store in Cork, so he takes care of the kids. There is no electricity. In the kitchen, he fixes me a cup of coffee. His brothers and sisters are asleep; they mustn't know that I am here.

"Why do ye ask me of the war?" he says. His name is Pat. "Ireland is dying of itself. Our boys leave fer Dublin ta' work, and many cross to England, niver comin' home. We'll niver get over the famine, and the war will niver end."

But what will you do?

"We'll drink and we'll go ta Mass."

We climb the stairs to his room. Next to the broad windowsill, we undress each other. He is whispering in my ear that he has never made love to a woman before. Making love to him is like holding a child. We dress quietly. I follow him out into the hall, and his brother stumbles into us at the stairs.

"Holy Mary Mother of God!" The brother crosses himself.

"I 'tink we give the maan a fright," Pat says, and Pat is someone to remember, not someone to see again.

In my tent late at night, I feel that the wind has turned and is blowing in on me. As I untie the ropes to turn the tent around, I see the moon hanging white over the ocean, and I seem to see myself at a great distance, a small person, a little cold, in a yellow tent at the edge of the sea.

So, I can't sleep, and I light a candle, propping it up between two rocks. I start to read in the circle of light. But something is moving into the edge of my vision from the right. It's a huge land snail, a gray one, moving slowly toward the candle. After painfully crossing little rocks and leaves, the snail reaches the rock that supports the candle. It taps the rock twice with its antennae and grips the side of the rock. I'm watching the snail crawl slowly up the side of the rock. It takes a long time. Now, it is reaching the top of the rock and moves more quickly to the side of the candle. It seems to sniff the candle and then grips it to climb the waxy surface. When the snail slips a little, it stops and then starts to climb again. Finally, it reaches the top of the candle and halts there for a moment. Now, the snail is pulling itself up so that only its rear part still holds on to the candle. It stands up next to the flame, facing me, with the shell behind the candle. Slowly the snail rears back from the flame, and, suddenly it dives forward, falling into the flame. The soft gray flesh of the snail shrivels and turns black. The shell falls lightly and bounces off the rock next to my arm. I tap the dead snail out of the shell and put the shell in the silver box.

Raymond Cothern

# THE OTHERS HAD NO GIRLS

The first minutes were a cautious probing of each other's strengths and weaknesses. Our aging football team (my brother Harold and I, John and J. C. Angelo, who were also brothers and future heirs to the only slaughterhouse within miles of Traveller's Rest, and lonely Joe Marino, a whiner) quickly found our Saturday afternoon opponents (Mert and Vernon Tullier, seasonal crayfish trappers, with the addition of Ernest, the stuttering co-owner of Andy's Esso station, and Ernest's mammoth friend whose name, at first, some of us couldn't remember) had a staggering amount of strengths and practically no weaknesses at all. Each team eyed the other's progress by the four large oaks that lined the field—the two end trees marking the goal lines.

"Bastard practically tore my ear clean off," Joe whined, his voice shaking, the unbroken line of his bushy eyebrows pushed down over his eyes. "What's his name? The one with the ape arms."

"What you gonna call, Harold?" J.C. asked.

"Call time out," Joe said, hand over his right ear. "For Chrissake, call time out. I think it's bleeding."

"Let's get the first down," Harold said, clapping his hands together. "Huddle up."

"Oh, man . . ." Joe grumbled. "Get that guy's license number."

"Listen," Harold hissed, "pitchout to Robbie, to the left, on two."

"Let's do a little blocking for me this time, hunh, fellows," I said. "I realize the age of thirty is a factor and all."

"Yeah," Joe said, "this time somebody else take the big guy."

I carried the ball for a respectable gain halfway between the first two trees. "First down," I said as I got up, pleased (even though there were five of us) that we were holding together against four guys that had played high school ball.

From the other team, begrudgingly, the big guy said, "Yeah . . . yeah . . . first down, studs."

"Who the hell's he talking to?" Joe asked. "Who's Studs? And what's *his* name?"

"Boolus Rabalais," John said. "He was a year ahead of us. Y'all don't remember him? Nicknamed Boo Boo. He was kicked out of school one year."

Joe said, "Kicked out? Lord, I believe it."

John nodded.

"Huddle up," Harold ordered.

"He's the guy that sneaked in before the Senior Dance at the VFW Hall and tied inflated 'nipple-tip' rubbers along with the balloons."

"Huddle up . . . come ON!"

"Ask Mr. Mulhman, he'll remember."

"Why should I ask him?" Joe said. "Look at my ear. I know how crazy he is."

We began moving the football. "Let's go, guys . . . not far now," I kept saying. "Not far now." Harold hit J.C. with two quick passes. We tried to reverse but John was trapped for a loss. In the huddle, wheezing from aging lungs, streaked faces dripped wet like duck backs.

"Bomb to Robbie, on two," Harold said. "Let's go."

As we broke from the huddle, Gorilla Man jeered us. "Come on, studs. Let's see what you got for us."

"There he goes . . . calling somebody Studs again," Joe said. "Guy oughta be in the zoo."

"Go ahead, let him hear you, Joe," J.C. said.

Joe smiled slyly. "I didn't say anything. John, did I say anything?"

"DOWN!" Harold called.

"I didn't say a word," Joe said.

"SET!"

"I ain't got no quarrel with—"

"ONE!"

"Everybody hear? No quarrel at—"

"TWO!"

(Joe, who raised flowers for decoration—primarily chrysanthemums around All Saints' Day—could be amusing despite his annoying habit of whimpering while jabbing for attention with his bony elbow that he spent hours honing on bar tabletops.)

I started slowly, then cut to the right. Mert, who was guarding me, fell down. Amazed, alone, I waved like a berserk windmill. *"Chrissake!"* I screamed, my voice breaking the windows of a passing automobile. *"Throw it! . . . Throw it! . . . Thrrrrrrrooowwww it!"*

Harold lofted a wobbler and, hey, see that, I caught it neatly over my left shoulder but fumbled moments later when Mert, cursing, pissed because he slipped down, tackled me from behind. The football rolled end over end across the goal line.

*"Get it! . . . Get it!"*

"WHO the hell *clipped* me!"

*"Jesus Gawd!"*

*"Fall on it!"*

J.C. did, quaking like a water bed as he smothered the ball for the first touchdown of the game.

*"All right,* J.C.!" I yelled. "Way to go." Since we didn't bother with extra points, the score, surprisingly in our favor, was 6 to 0. "That was *Great!"*

"Yeah, great. What I call a well executed play," Harold said. "Let's call that the bust-your-ass-for-a-TD play."

"I think he clipped me," Joe said, followed by a long sigh. "My ear wasn't enough. . . . He's going for my legs."

"Maybe it's feeding time," I said.

Joe rolled his dark eyes; his elbow jerked at his side.

"Time out, time out," Harold said. "Let's celebrate or something, hunh? What say, fellows." Hell, odds were we'd lose, but since a guy had been running his ass off most of the game, why not imagine: the leaves rustling nearby, faintly like applause.

"Shit with celebrating. . . . I'm getting too fat for this," J.C. said, his legs dissolving under him. "Why can't we play poker like civilized people?"

"Somebody check my ear," Joe said. "Feels like a firepopper exploded in it."

"Looks like somebody's been gnawing on it," J.C. said.

*Raymond Cothern*

"I knew it," Joe said. "I'm suing if I go deaf."

John, quieter, less forceful than the rest of us, plucked idly at the slender tongues of grass. "I dreamed the other night," he said, "that the grass—. Hey, somebody's blowing at us."

"See there," Joe said, "I can't hear a thing."

John pointed toward D Street. "There. In the Ford."

"Teen-agers," I said.

"Fuckers got nothing better to do than ride around, blowing and waving like idiots." Joe blew air disgustedly, then shook his head.

"Yeah," Harold said, one side of his mouth drawn back, "they need something constructive to do."

J.C. shielded his eyes. "Somebody go tell that blonde with 'em to come do a little cheerleading for us. You're good with words, Robbie; go talk her into it. Tell her we need . . . unh . . . some cheering."

Roaring off with a last blast of the horn, the Ford, sagging to one side, then fishtailing in the gravel, rounded the corner and disappeared. Dust began settling on already coated bushes.

"You're too slow, boy," J.C. told me.

"A bit young, hunh?" I said.

"Naw, it's like this," J.C. said. "When I was that age I was still playing with model cars in the dirt for Chrissake. Hell, these young things now are having *affairs*."

"Must be all that dope they take," Joe said. "Gets 'em all hyped up."

"Might be, Joe," J.C. said. "Just might be."

"You two are so full of shit," Harold said. "God."

J.C. turned to say something, but instead stretched his legs with a sigh. "Who's the finest girl you been involved with?"

"You asking me?" Joe said.

"Yeah, I guess."

"No bells," Joe said. "Ask somebody else."

John propped himself up on one elbow. "As I was saying," he continued, "I dreamed the other night the grass was burning. What's that mean?" Harold, on his back studying the empty sky, said, "It means you have funny dreams," then continued chewing pensively on the single blade in the side of his mouth. Between complaints about his ear and his recent leg injury, Joe tried to place a blade between his thumbs for a whistle.

"Like this," I said, stretching a blade until it was held tautly, dividing the slender opening between my thumbs. "Listen," I said, blowing softly, vibrating the blade of grass. The low-pitched sound pleased Joe immeasurably; he smiled broadly and shook his head slowly in admiration of my feat.

I laughed.

"What the shit's so funny, Robbie?" Joe asked me.

There weren't too many guys in Traveller's Rest I could impress by extraordinary achievements like grass whistling. Take J.C. and John—being thirty years or so old and rich boys, they weren't as easily impressed.

"That right, J.C.?" I said.

J. C. Angelo, fleshy guy, who had to use money as clout with the women around, stared, his puffy eyelids dropping watchfully to halfmast. "Screw you, Robbie. Don't try baiting me."

"Go get Boolus," Joe said, a smile flickering at the corners of his mouth. "Get him to gnaw on Robbie for you."

Harold turned from staring vacantly at the sky. "Delia Breaux," he told J.C. softly, "you were asking; well, she was the finest." Then, his tongue pushing the limp blade of grass to the other side of his mouth, my brother smiled privately at me.

I smiled back, letting my thoughts slip to my father's partner in carpentry, Paul Breaux, and Delia, his daughter, the contortionist.

"She made me want to do *any*thing to please her," Harold said. "Lord, she was fine."

Delia, supple at fourteen, spindle legs, long blond hair like the springy curls of lemon-wood shavings. Harold and I had banded together to tease her, her acrobatics, and prim attitude when performing the Visitation Special. I remembered one time . . . But that was after the change in Harold, when he no longer tormented her.

How long ago, I wondered.

"She was pretty, anybody remember?" Harold said. "But since she got stuck on Merrit Davis in high school, she never did me any good."

"Introduce Joe to her," John said, winking at Harold.

"Yeah, I could do that, I guess," Harold said, "if I hadn't lost track of her."

"He needs a good woman," John added.

"Now that I don't know," Harold said. "Some good women

have a habit of running off." Harold turned and looked at me, his tongue still working at the limp blade between his lips. "Or around."

Not some women, I thought. Just two. Or three, if you count the contortionist, your first love.

I closed my eyes.

One time when Paul Breaux and family had visited . . .

Harold's voice droned on, extolling in his drawling way the virtues of his women; at first particularly Delia, like wifey Reba, lost to him now.

I imagined Paul Breaux's deep voice. Once the grown-ups were gossiping between sips of boiling coffee, he had demanded Delia to *"Do* it, honey, for the boys."

"Neighbor down the street from my sister has got the sugar *Diebee-tees,"* Mrs. Breaux had hissed suddenly.

"Hmm . . ." my father commented, then sipped. "Hmm . . . hunh."

"Hmm . . . unh-hunh." (Mother's contribution.)

Delia had curtsied, then knelt; her sculptured knees and shins and the top of her feet, all pressed to the floor, she proceeded to perform the Visitation Special.

Delia *did* it, honey, for us, the boys.

Back arching, backward she went (bent), her tiny breasts following her chin as her head came over and through her legs until she was facing forward, her palms and elbows now also pressed to the floor.

"Now *that's* a *stupid* thing to do," I said.

"Shut up, Robbie," Harold whispered, "just shut up."

I glanced at Harold, then to the contorted mass of Delia. There, plainly outlined by tight blouse, were Delia's breasts, pointing downward like tiny cannons ready to blast the dirt from the cracks in the worn floor.

Sipping her Coke leisurely, Delia remained in her position for twenty minutes; occasionally she squared her shoulders (mustn't have any wrinkles across the blouse front). The wet from a clenched Coke bottle dripped on my hand. Interesting, privates pointing earthward, but I marveled how the syrupy Coke made the journey upward from mouth to stomach.

Harold had elbowed me and whispered: "First place in *any* talent contest."

The change for me, when privates pointing in any direction was exciting, came two years later, with Linda.

"How long you fuckers gonna lay around?" Mert yelled from the other end of the field where his team sat huddled, waiting, telling jokes. "Come on, hunh? Let's play ball."

"Ten more minutes," Harold yelled back.

"It's half time," Joe added. "Y'all march around like you're a band." Joe cracked his knuckles, stopped, probed at the skin behind his ear, then looked up. "Anybody want to come to the house tonight? Got some beer needs drinking. Like to hear some more about what's-her-name. Delia. Was that your wife's name?" he asked Harold.

"My wife's name was Reba," Harold said. "You dumb ass."

I rolled over on my side and examined D Street.

How long ago? Running, keeping close watch for any sign of Linda, envisioning the pleasing prospect of someday skimming with rocket packs over the countryside. Like Rocket Man, the Saturday serial hero, flying at vast heights over the patchwork earth.

(Sometimes disguised as a skinny boy of thirteen, Rocket Man had a rival: Arrow Boy—The Human Pogo Stick.)

I was winded, I remembered, and dove through the fence of Ryan's Wrecker Yard and made my way through the automobile skeletons. Summer-tree green grass bugs leaped upward around my ankles, clinging briefly to my faded jeans. That was okay. On days when the disfigured automobile bodies became a tank battalion, wasps were the threat, and battled against as much as the enemy in the next tank.

Slowing, then pausing, I waited. Hubcaps like round mirrors hung on the side of the tin building, a pile of bumpers haphazardly ringed a large beech tree. Where was she?

(Harold was saying, "I started dating Reba after Delia moved to Memphis. Rebound with Reba.")

As I emerged at the front of the building, I saw her gliding along North Street in that walk she had. Linda. Linda. Tall; dark hair teased high; skin like burnt honey.

"Engine's busted up good though."

"Yuh wanna see somethin', Mr. Ryan?" one of the Negro workers gathered near the tow truck had asked. "Guy's face hit the dash . . . yuh can see it."

"No shit?" Ryan asked.

"Fellow had no chance."

"Bloody inside?" Ryan asked as he joined the group at the truck.

"Yes, suh."

"Seats, too?" he asked, the damp cigar stub working in his stained teeth. "Just the front one, hunh? Yeah, I see. Go on, get it out back now," Ryan ordered.

"Yes, suh."

Linda, honey, there, headed for the store?

Making a note to tell my brother about the Cadillac, death-mask dashboard, the ideal place for flashlighted stories at night-time, I quickly skirted the hot sidewalk, passing Linda, honey, there, an arm's length to my left, headed for the store, clear pearls of wet clinging above her lip. Oh, God, look how close. Just reach out and . . .

Show her your arm?

God, give me strength, yes, muscles, too.

Fingering the quarter in my pocket, I stopped and glanced through the fly-specked screen door of the grocery. I could see pimply Jason Streiffer behind the counter busily stacking packages of cigarettes.

"Excuse me, sonny."

Sonny? Oh, God, no. I've followed you all summer. Back in July, when you had that date with Willie Lee, I was arrested as a Peeping Tom. (Well, actually, I wasn't officially arrested, just roughly hauled out of the bushes and questioned while this two-hundred-pound police dog sniffed me cautiously and then appeared not at all impressed that he had taken part in the apprehension of a thirteen-year-old klutz who had been spying on his honey and her date.) Sonny? Oh, God, no. I love you, Linda.

Disturbing the flies on the screen, she swung open the door, calling out, "Hello, doll," as she entered the store.

"Hey, how goes it?" Jason asked.

"I'm okay, you know."

"Hot enough, hunh?"

Linda sighed softly. "Ain't it the truth?"

"What can I do for you?"

"Three packs of Lucky Strikes, bread, half a pound of butter, and how's your meat today, Jason?"

His jaw working up and down like a pelican gulping fish, Jason turned to interpret her meaning. "My . . . meat's fine."

Linda nodded and studied Jason until he dropped his eyes.

(Harold was saying, "Robbie called it my falling Redwood imitation. I was so nervous first calling on Reba, I got dizzy and fell off the steps—swear to God.")

After entering the grocery, I waited several moments for my eyes to adjust. The cramped walkways between the six double-sided rows of grocery-ladened shelves all funneled back toward the white enamel meat counter. Behind the counter there was a small receiving room with stacked boxes of canned goods surrounding the table and chairs the men of the neighborhood used nightly for card games and bull sessions. Many breezeless summer nights the freezer door stood ajar, making it cooler and easier to get at the stacked cans of beer inside.

The sweet rolls on the bread rack were inviting, but cost more than I was willing to part with at the moment. The quarter was the last of my money, but it was past six in the evening and my stomach rumbled and knotted in hunger, demanding that something tempting be thrown sacrifically down to it. Let's see. Definitely something cold to drink. But what else? My eyes darted to the candy counter. A chocolate marshmallow moonpie. Yeah. My stomach grumbled its consent.

"Spareribs are good," Jason was telling her.

"I don't know. Mama's so damn particular when I cook for the two of us."

Licorice—aaahh, no—gum balls, peppermint.

"Pork chops, rump roast."

Peanut butter cups, peanut brittle, peanuts.

"Ham, T-bone, ground veal," Jason continued.

Jawbreakers, candy cigarettes, Baby Ruth.

"Hog jowls, horse butt."

"Now, Jason, you're pulling my leg."

"I wish I was," he answered. "I just wish."

"Hmmm," she hummed coyly. "HmmmMMMmmm."

Wax lips. My love doesn't even know it, I thought. An exact replica of her pouty lips was smiling at me from the third shelf of the candy counter.

"Hey, kid, stop fingering the merchandize."

"I was just getting some candy," I said.

"If you're not going to buy the wax lips, leave 'em alone," he ordered.

"Jason, honey, give me some of those pork chops," Linda said. "Four ought to do it."

"Right away."

Calling me "sonny"—then caught drooling over the candy counter like some ten-year-old. Look at me, Linda; you're just three years older. When I'm eighteen, you'll only be twenty-one. Age doesn't matter, and I could learn all I needed. She'd be impressed if I bought a beer and downed it like a cowboy in a saloon throwing a shot down his throat.

Jason expertly finished wrapping the pork chops in waxed paper. His voice bright, he slapped a piece of tape on the outer fold with a flourish. "Ready and waiting for your pretty hands."

"Oh, Jason."

"Loaf of bread and . . . unh . . ."

"Half pound of butter and cigarettes."

"Got you."

I ran my hand along the icy inner edge of the cold drink box. Root Beer, Orange Fling, Strawberry Dew. Marshmallow moonpie and—

"Butter and cigarettes. What else, Linda?"

"That's it."

Which drink had ice crystals in it?

The bell clattered on the cash register and Jason said: "Out of five." In all the time I had seen Jason ring up a sale, he never failed to drop several pennies from the register into a slot on the wooden counter. Harold said it was tax money and he kept it separate that way. I didn't know, but it seemed an excellent way of saving money; a large barrel, I imagined, standing under the slot, brimming with copper coins added to by several more on each sale.

"Thank you, Linda. You come back soon."

"I'll just do that." And with an enticing flutter of her fingers, she smiled and turned away, her shoes clicking, carrying her out into the evening sun.

"That all for you?"

"I don't know," I said, staring at the empty bottle in my hand, trying to remember how the drink had tasted.

Ripping open a carton of Camel cigarettes, Jason began placing the packs in the wire racks. He started humming "Wabash Cannonball"—tilting his face up for help on the high notes. His sweaty blue workshirt clung wetly to his back; occasionally he pulled at the back of his collar, but each time he released it the shirt plastered itself back between his shoulder blades.

"You like her?" I asked.

"What's it to you?" he answered.

I narrowed my eyes, hoping Jason would go on and answer my question.

"Well?" Jason said.

"I . . . I don't know," I said, crafty manner slipping away with the flush on my cheeks.

Without hesitating more, Jason said, "It's maybe worth it to her to escape Momma. High price for somebody though. She lives over by you, hunh?"

"Unh-hunh."

"You like her?"

"Naw," I said, noticing Jason turn to study me.

"Good thing."

I opened my eyes.

Crickets chirped incessantly, fireflies blinked and flitted in the warm dusk air, and soon nighttime bugs would be batting against taut screens along D Street, punctuating porch talk.

I studied Harold. His profile pinched in thought against the line of a scrub pine near the field reminded me of my father, who was quiet, usually, until his day off when a swallow of Jax beer (or less, perhaps just the wet of the clenched can) loosened the talk.

Hey, Harold, look at me. We had some good times together, hunh?

"Be dark in thirty minutes," Harold said. "Let's play ball."

"Oh, God, my legs are stiff," J.C. said.

Like the time we had that supper double date together, remember? That was the night Linda told me she thought she was pregnant. I remember that night. And I remember your Reba in the yard, clasping and unclasping her hands, and smiling, eyes dreamy as she watched you lighting the candles on the white wrought-iron table. Flickering light played over waxy green leaves, over wisteria hanging in grapelike bunches, over white and yellow honeysuckle blossoms patterned like petite trumpets.

"Looks fine, doesn't it?" Reba whispered as she inspected the yard during a leisurely turn. "Candles give the place a festive air."

"Sure does," you said. "Like a stupid garden party."

You and I had laughed, remember?

Reba inhaled deeply, then turned to Linda. "At night I keep my bedroom window thrown open as high as it'll go, and the attic fan going not so much to cool the house, but because it pulls in smells of things blooming here in the yard." She sat at the table, glanced at you, then was still. "I'm happiest when I'm out here," she said quietly.

Good times, gone with disquieting wizardry, all too quickly.

"My legs are stiff," J.C. said again. "They feel like rifle barrels."

"Yeah," Joe said. "But you should've been clipped by Boolus like I was."

"Come on," Harold said, "up, UP! Let's go. Come on, Robbie, wake up." Harold pounded his heel into the ground and teed the football. "Y'all ready?" he called down the field.

"K-k-kick the ga-ga-gawddamn thing!" was the answer from Ernest. "F-f-fuckers been layin' around for t-t-twen-ty minutes."

"Can't you see Ernest at quarterback," John said, then mimicked him. "D-d-down. Thir-thir-thir-thirty t-t-two!" John shook his head, then added, "Talk about some offside penalties. Fucker talks like a machine gun."

Mert and his brother, Vernon, and their formidable friends goofed off for three downs—showing us boastfully in that manner that our touchdown had been a fluke. Mert punted for his team. (Since he had stout legs, and the field was only sixty-five yards long, our end zone usually marked halfway on the flight of the ball. When he played high school ball, Mert used to come out for pregame warmups and intimidate the other team by just showing his legs.)

A short gain running the ball and two missed passes and we lined up to punt.

It was a beautiful spiral snap from center. But the football sailed two feet over Harold's head. An outcry rose full-throated as every man on their team rushed passed our faltering line. Harold made a valiant dive, grunting as he hit the ground, managing to get only his fingertips on the ball before being swarmed under. Like a flopping pile of fish out of water, legs churned as flailing arms searched roughly for the football. Someone gave out three

INTRO 8: THE LIAR'S CRAFT

short croaks of pain—"Aaahh! Aaahh! Aaahh!"—and began moaning loudly as though he expected whoever's foot or knee or hand was indelicately placed would get the message.

Vernon Tullier (who once during a high school game, while rolling a runner out of bounds, managed to jar Norma Rickles' knockers out of her cheerleading costume) recovered for a touchdown.

Ernest started machine gunning. "T-t-tie game, t-t-tie game!" he yelled.

"All right, all right!" Mert encouraged his team. "Now we looking good."

Walking to the other end of the field, Harold asked, trying to regroup us in time to receive the kick off, "What the hell happened?"

"I misjudged the snap," Joe answered.

"Damn, you might say that," J.C. said disgustedly.

"Keep 'em lower," Harold instructed. "Roll it to me if you have to."

"I want to *know* . . . who the hell *kneed* me . . . in the *nuts?* Hunh? Which one of you . . . *bastards* did it?"

We turned as a group and watched as Boolus came toward us, his ape gait more pronounced than usual.

"C-c-come on, m-m-man," Ernest said.

"Naw, I want to know."

"C-c-come on, B-B-Boo."

"Fuck you, Ernest. Get off my back," he warned.

"Let's play ball," Harold said.

"Naw . . . naw. I want to *know.*"

"It was an accident probably," Vernon said.

"Like hell."

"Either play or shut up," I said. Realizing Boolus had turned to me and was standing there glowering, nodding his head slightly, I pressed on: the prospect of different action was exhilarating. "If you're such a pussy, Boo Boo, just don't bother to come next Saturday."

Boolus stood there smiling crazily, nodding occasionally for emphasis. "Well, well, well," he said, "I'm ready now. Let's play ball." Boolus turned and jogged away.

"What happened to his limp?" Joe said. "Wasn't he just limping?"

"Yeah," J.C. said. "But he sure looks ready to gnaw a few ears."

"Watch your legs," Joe said. "He'll go for your legs. He clipped me a while ago."

The game got rougher. Well, Boolus got rougher. Same thing. He came charging toward us on the kickoff, ignoring J.C., the ball carrier, hurling his body at me as though he had been catapulted suddenly off his feet. I timed my maneuver and side-stepped at the right instant.

"That guy's crazy," Joe whined, elbow flailing, as we moved downfield in blocking formation. "Stay away from him."

"I can't do that," I said.

"Then *you* stay away from me. I ain't letting him clip me again."

After the kickoff, when I ran the ball or went out for a pass, Boolus followed, striving (amid elbow shots and leg tripping) to do disservice to my body. And the prospects of Boolus giving up weren't in sight; finally, after hurling a barrage of threats and curses, he said: "I'm gonna bust you open like a melon, you tightass you!"

"Hey, Robbie," John said before we huddled, "a tightass, hunh? That anything like calling somebody's wife a 'mattress-bumpin' bitch'?" John laughed, but sudden concern at his remark twitched at his brow. "I . . . I . . . didn't mean—"

"Tightass?" Joe said, his laugh hollow as he tried to cover John's embarrassment. "Tell him to go blow up some funny balloons."

"Well, there ain't any tightass in this town," Harold said. "Not since my Reba ran off."

"Runs in the family, brother," I said, winking at John.

Harold laughed thinly. "Runs in the family . . . yeah."

"Sorry, Robbie," John said, "I didn't mean anything."

I thumped John on the back and nodded.

On the next series of downs we began to use Boolus' anger to our advantage. Harold told me to be the permanent end on every play. "That suits me," Joe said. "Anything to get that maiming hulk out of the way." Harold's strategy took care of Boolus in the matter of tackling or rushing him—which was an intelligent move on the quarterback's part. If one of the other guys rushed Harold, whoever was centering the ball would block and then go out for a short pass, giving us three pass receivers; if no one rushed, and Mert, Vernon, and Ernest guarded J.C., Joe, and John, Harold had all the time he needed to throw the ball. It stood to reason that one of us would get open sometime.

Then it happened (it had to), though not to anyone's surprise. Or you had to be fairly oblivious (Joe might qualify) not to realize that something, some incident, had to settle the matter between Boolus and myself. I remembered the time Harold and Merrit Davis struggled in the heat like slippery bears over some point of honor concerning Delia. I watched from an automobile hood and heard the hollow thud of blows landing amid grunts and curses.

John jogged over to me before we hudded. "Let's try a double-end formation. I'll hit him with a quick block, enough to give you a step on him."

I grinned, acknowledging in his offer any intended further atonement for the remark that had embarrassed him.

"Let me call this play, Harold," John said. "Robbie and I cooked something up."

As it turned out, the play easily stood out as the decisive point of the game—since the game ended moments later with Boolus' nose pumping blood and the score still tied at six points apiece. (Our first non-loss in six games.)

"It's to spring Robbie," John told Harold. "Get the ball to him."

"All right, huddle up," Harold said. "Quick pass over the middle, to Robbie, on one. Let's go."

The pass came in low causing me to stumble. Boolus, reaching out, grasping with his paws, grabbed my shirttail with every intention of taking his frustration out on me. Fearing my annihilation, I did the smart thing. I gave the ball to Boolus. And in my desire to get the football to him, to divert him, *before* he had a chance to get me completely in his grasp, I added force behind my fumble. The football landed with a thump on his nose. And it did divert him—at least momentarily. Blood spurted out of his nose. Amazed, Boolus watched the blood running over his cupped hands, and the blood dots appearing on his shirt and pants. I felt the tingle of fear weaken my knees.

"What happened?" Mert asked.

*"Damn* . . . look at that," someone said.

"It was an accident," I lied (badly).

*Raymond Cothern*                                                79

"What happened, Boo?" Vernon asked.

"That bastard threw the ball at me!" Boolus said, his blood-filled nose dulling his words with a hum. (It came out: "Tat basterd throo da ball at be.")

I backed away (on my toes, like a defensive back.)

"What'd he say?" Joe asked J.C.

"You b-b-better lay d-d-down."

"Just . . . just wait," Boolus warned. "Game ain't over, not yet!"

"I didn't mean to," I lied again.

*"Gawd . . . damn . . . you."*

"Easy, Boo."

"He's *lying!*"

"Hey, come on," Harold said, "we don't need more trouble."

"You gonna *stick* up for little brother, hunh? Look at my *nose!*" Boolus said between clenched teeth. "Accident, hell!" Then stumbling around, one hand holding his nose, Boolus grabbed the football and hurled a hard pass toward me.

The football bounded once off the ground and came up into my stomach. Carried away with the distance between us, I screamed back "YOU SIMIAN YOU!" and watched as all heads snapped in my direction. Boolus frowned—not quite sure he had been insulted—then menacingly pushed his way through the arms of Mert and Vernon.

(*The charge of the rhino, Tambanemba. Give me the rifle and stand back. Quickly. Quickly!*)

"YOU . . . WHIMPY BASTARD!" Boolus said, then took a deep breath, a different tact. "Your honey girl screws anything around."

"Tell me something I don't know, Boo Boo," I said evenly.

Long before the arching leather missle reached Boolus, I was gone. But not for home to wifey Linda, my honey girl.

Running, laughing, I saw again, clearly: football was one of our flights. Take your choice: life in Traveller's Rest was dull, monotonous, uninteresting, vapid, boring, commonplace, wooden, well-worn, deadened. . . .

And painful.

The others had no girls.

*Tama Janowitz*

## *MAGGIE, ANGEL*

"Yuh," she said. "Sure. You think I like this?" I can't believe I'm really talking to Angel, she thought. This isn't happening to me. Maggie turned down the sound on the TV. "Taking this kind of crap from people." Am I boring him? "Living in a place like this. *Sure* I like it, Angel. Sure I like going to school. My father won't even give me any money. You know what my father does, don't you?"

"Mmmm," Angel said, "hang on a minute." There was a long pause. Maggie turned the sound up on the TV. A receptionist from the Paterson Lumber Company was up to bowl for the Jackpot. . . . My father is a spy for the FBI; my father is a gunman in the Mafia; my father is a jeweler with a silver monocle who gave me an engraved heart-shaped bracelet for my birthday. No really my father is a businessman. He says, you are running around chasing all these men in the city, you are making a fool of yourself. Of course none of them want you. Your clothes look cheap and in you is a bad streak of smut. A thread of laziness, Angel, that must be it. . . . Angel coughed into the phone. "Hello," Maggie said, pulling the word out like brown taffy. At least I can sound sexy, she thought. "I'll call you back later," Angel said. Maggie leaned back in her chair, looked at the secretary on the show, dancing for joy and kissing Al Brockett, the sportscaster. Oh, Angel, I love you, she thought. I just hope I didn't ruin everything. I know I've done it this time. Why bother with French, I feel too terrible. A flow of magma exploded over her city, covering everyone, orange and black. Parts of the gray scrapers were left covered with ash, tephra. The survivors slowly crawled out. Angel's blond hair would be covered in soot. He would be forced to live off the cooling lava. The crust would be cold, crunchy, and glistening with the white of egg. Underneath it would be moist, still warm, like raw dough.

Maggie couldn't seem to concentrate on her work. Did she care? Why should she? Nobody cared about her. No one liked an ugly person. In the mirror she was a tree, her face an onion. The peel of the onion was so thin you could see through it, to another layer below, and below that. Angel's hair was rich, thick, but hers fell in dying leaves around her face. People would perhaps love her if she didn't look so raw, exposed as if her bark had been stripped, and carefully Maggie painted on a delicate wine-colored mouth, thin and pouting. She licked her white teeth. Who could she fool? In class if anyone said anything to her she would have to defend herself, her reason for being there. They would never include her. Even Angel didn't like her. He didn't even exist; she had invented him. Quite a joke. But now it seemed more important to think of him than of classes that she hadn't been to, out of fear, in weeks and weeks. The days had blurred into soothing half-hour and hour shows. No one touched her. She must be in love. Still, she didn't feel as secure in her fear as she had felt only a few weeks ago. It used to be fine; she had been happier alone. Then, just when she was getting used to it, Angel had appeared, ruining everything. She could never think of things to say to him. She worried he would treat her as he treated everyone else, or leave her. She was as helpless as a dog with a wet nose. Fur streamed into air. The words floated across the pages of her French book like tiny stitches or lumps of cheese. Maybe she could forget how to speak; when Angel called she wouldn't be able to talk to him. That would get rid of him. She thought of Angel in bed, hard but smooth as ash. Her finger traced the scar up from the corner of his mouth. "A knife fight, wow." "Nah. I was wondering how long it would take for you to ask that. I got it playing soccer, this guy came up, wham! Seventeen stitches." The clock said one-thirty. She was already asleep.

Angel in a bar, high on cocaine, talking to a girl he had just met. "Well, I used to play baseball in high school. I was real popular then. I played pretty good, but that was before I knew better

I mean, that was back in Kansas. Those were good years but I wasn't happy. Do you think anyone, even the most popular or elegant, is ever really happy? When I was in—well I'm talking a lot, I'm high. Well, I could always get anything I wanted. Once in high school there was a girl, this Italian chick. It was after a dance. I took her back to my room, grabbed her, shoved her to the bed. I knew she had already screwed half the football team. Then *they* started coming after *me*. I could have had anything I wanted. There was this coach, this is pretty typical or a cliché. After a shower I was drying myself, he grabbed my shoulder, slid his hand down. I didn't even care. I can just accept that; I can do it with anyone, a definite advantage. I got in, started at the acting school, H.A. I'm attractive to everyone; I seem to be a type. I look for an inner vibration I would say. You can tell the ones that are different. I'll survive."

She was watching a game show. The fat woman was wheezing; thick tears fell from her eyes onto the emcee's toupee. The woman was dressed in the ears and face of a rabbit. How nice, Maggie thought, she doesn't care how she acts. Maggie knew Angel would never care if she acted dumb. He wouldn't tell her what to do, say she was chasing him. He would love her. He would be everything to her. In the dark she didn't hear him come in, just felt his hands molding her flat body like clay, pushing her mind out of its warp. She would become like him, a boy, tough and slinky as a cat. He would be her best girlfriend, giggling and laughing with her. Or Angel was debonaire, he had stepped out of the pages of *Esquire* to be with her, gay, so cold and charming. He was English, working as a clerk in a bank, wearing a cheap suit and eating steak-and-kidney pie. Once Angel walked in, his hair dyed Spanish. He grabbed her, danced the Hustle with his crotch swinging into hers, his black satin pants studded with spikes. Maggie started to laugh and felt her loneliness coming to the surface like a blister. We're all orphans, she thought, but why am I the ugliest, the least likable? On the TV the woman dressed as a rabbit wept on winning a trailer, a refrigerator, a trip to Hawaii, an operation for her little boy, her angel. . . . But of course Maggie knew Angel was made up, would never come. She wasn't that nuts yet, ha-ha! . . . She imagined the whole city filled up with different versions of him, some Swedish, others Indians wearing one good earring. They walked across the city in soundless rows. One said something to

Maggie in a language she couldn't understand. She grabbed his arm, tried to stop him and find out what he was saying. But her father was watching her with binoculars from a window. She began to cry, knowing her father would say she was failing in school, that her jeans hung on her like a sack. She was unfeeling, bad, a sick drag on her father's life.

Someone knocked at the door, but Maggie didn't feel like answering. Her hair was dying and her lipstick had worn too pale. After they had left, she found a phone message taped to the door. It had been cunningly abstracted to say nothing, but she knew it meant Angel was coming to see her. She figured he would be on his way now, entering the insides of a Chinese dragon, a gray animal steaming red, breathing hard, and turning in its track, bringing Angel up to her. People got in and out. They were dead, some naked. Her father had hired them as extras on the scene of her pornographic film, a film where the sighing of the subway, its shrill screaming, was the only noise. Maggie tried to look at her French book. It began to make a little sense. The edges were filling in like a puzzle. Maybe she didn't really want Angel to see her. But she waited for him, walking on the back streets of her city, the alleys twisting and falling into craters, a city with a dark cover. She came on a section where the storefronts were hung with meat, heads of pigs, the ears black and hairy. A small dirty goat with little devil horns was being led in to be slaughtered. She wondered if it was Angel. Against the door of the subway was a pile of intestines, the walls were hung with the hides of jackals. Small Arab children ran near her feet, noses running, yelling in a language she couldn't understand. Gypsies with eyes like goats brushed her crotch with a scarred hand that reached at the same time into her pocket, removed her wallet. The walls of the subway were covered with bright advertisements in the wrong shades, people with green faces, speaking words made only of letters. . . . Maggie scowled to herself; it was Angel who was on the subway, not she; she would never have gone on the subway. She'd take a cab. Because she wasn't interested in people staring, saying it was love while stinging her spine like bees. Greasy oil filled her stomach when she thought of the terrible things she had done, that had been done to her. That was why she wanted to stop thinking, to free herself from things that failed.

Angel got rid of people when he tired of them. He needed no

one. Crawling out of the volcanic ruins, he was the first to find the mutant killer dogs, train them for his protection. Soon he lived in one of the remaining skyscrapers, surrounded by the last art objects. A small Degas, an Ellsworth Kelly. The view from his apartment showed nothing but broken black shells. Angel lay back on a bed covered with pink silk. The walls were stacked with Libby's green beans, La Choy chinese noodles, Chef Boy-R-Dee. The last of the jet set sat admiring him. "Angel, teach us how to survive," they said—Mick Jagger, some gay artists, Princess Radziwell, André Malraux. Angel didn't answer right away. He sipped his champagne, lifted some weights while reclining. One of the artists accidentally knocked over all the cans while trying to get to a bottle of Grand Marnier. Something glass broke. "O, how boring," Angel said, "I think you'd all better go now." "But Angel, we'll die out there." "Yes," Angel said, "or survive. But not at my expense." He tossed a baseball in his hand. Outside the packs of dogs and young boys ripped apart the last of the Élite. I break things too, Maggie thought. Even if they were boring, at least they were his friends. But already Angel had made new friends with the killer boys, trained them to worship him, bring him cans. Everything changed quickly in the ash. Maggie was afraid. Angel needed no one. She could cover herself in lava too, in animal hides, learn not to feel. No one was really supposed to be happy anyway.

It was eight-thirty. She switched on the "Today" show. Oh for the brittle hardness of Barbara Walters. There was still time, she thought, to change.

*James Knudsen*

## MY MISSING YEARS

When Meta had been gone for three weeks without a word, I decided that she would not be coming back. I sublet our apartment to another couple and moved in with my retired parents. My mother, with Meta's help, had replaced or rearranged the furniture since the last time I'd lived there and I found myself bumping into something with every step. The lights in the house seemed impossibly bright, so I wore dark glasses. "You could be a celebrity," my mother suggested, "think of it!"

One evening, my father and I sat in the kitchen, ripping our thumbnails on pistachio nuts. "What gives, Spence?" he winked as he handed me a beer from the refrigerator.

"Don't know." I got up and turned the radio on. Every song was my favorite! I began tapping my toes. When I turned around, my father had left the room.

I lived at home nearly two months, subsisting on the routine of my job at Chicago Steel and Wire and my parent's suggestions for a better life. "Take in a movie," they'd say. "We'll go with you." A crisis-line phone number appeared propped against my morning coffee. Some time in November, my mother woke me for work with something on her mind. She sat on the edge of my bed playing with the catch on her charm bracelet. "It's time you went after Meta," she said finally. "She's probably bored too."

"No, Ma," I protested. "I'm twenty-four."

"And that means you know what you're doing?"

"It should."

That afternoon, I moved to Clear Lake Apartments. Though my parents were mystified by the rashness of my decision, they drove out with my clothes and my stereo components wrapped in newspaper.

My father sat uncomfortably on the floor making a map of escape routes. "In case of fire," he explained. I had moved in with the young singles and my father knew about their sundecks, wet bars, and cookouts in the dead of winter.

Shortly after we were married, Meta began playing the victim at ambulance-driver exams. I wanted her home on Saturday mornings eating french toast and watching the cartoons with me, but she was always off at some forest preserve or swimming pool. She was working as a bookkeeper at a Chevy dealer in those days and said that helping the ambulance drivers "blew up her self-image." Besides, she was learning about first aid.

One particular Saturday, she came home ecstatic. "I was great in the auto accident," she exclaimed. "They got this tangled car from the wrecker and fitted it up next to a tree. I was lying out on the hood with my foot still in the car and a putty gash on my forehead. They squirted me with this red stuff—just like blood and from a squeeze tube!"

I could see traces of it on the collar of her blouse. I threw up my arms and screamed in a falsetto imitation of her voice, "Save me; save me!"

"There were seventeen of us that had to be saved this time," Meta continued. "It was a very big deal—forty ambulance drivers. One guy was told to pretend that the roof of my car was smashed down to the dashboard." Meta began pacing the room. She cupped her right hand and held it up to her mouth. "The monitor had a megaphone. He told the guy who was saving me, 'Now, okay, pretend you're a grandmother opening a sardine can. Very, very delicate with that crowbar now.'"

After the testing exercise, when all the victims and ambulance drivers gathered for coffee and doughnuts around the monitor's station wagon, they had all sung camp songs. "I felt so close to those people!"

*James Knudsen* 87

I grabbed my arm as if I were in great pain and began limping around singing, "Down by the old mill stream, not the river but the stream . . ."

After I moved out to Clear Lake, I dated many girls. My habit at that time was to start phoning at six o'clock on Friday night and take out the first one who was in and interested. I had heard of Leslie through my mother—she was her hairdresser or a friend's daughter. She lived at Clear Lake and laughed nearly all the time.

In the space of two days, we went to three parties, a drive-in movie, and a hot dog banquet given by her sorority's alumni group. "I may not be in love with you," she confessed, "but I sure feel like it!"

Suddenly, I felt obligated to tell her about Meta. "My wife left me," I said, beginning in the middle.

Leslie curled closer. "No problem. You're still recovering and now that I know that, I can handle it."

Later that night, I heard her inch quietly out of my bed. She dressed in the bathroom. Now when I see her, she is driving a snowmobile, waving madly in the direction of my window.

Meta once told me about two guys she had almost married in high school. "We never got around to it," she disclosed. She was lying on the floor making her right arm look dislocated in practice for another first-aid exam.

I wondered why she had "gotten around" to marriage with me, but I didn't ask her about it. "I've been in love a couple of times," I said. "Big deal."

"Greg and I were going to take a night train to New York with a suitcase of champagne."

"What happened to him?"

"We were going to spend our money on food and places to sleep and trains—that's it."

"Don't you think I'd like to do that if I could afford to?"

"It's not a question of affording it," she said, closing her eyes. "It's an attitude. You can always think of reasons not to do something. Spence, you don't have ends in mind—that's no fun."

I got down on my knees silently. Her dislocated body was arousing. I moved closer.

Since my father and I have never liked to play cards, my mother always cornered Meta when we visited for a hot game of hearts. They sat on the living-room floor with tumblers of soda pop and played for hours. "I'm gonna kill you this time," Meta would say as she dealt out the cards. "You're dead already!" my mother laughed.

My father and I sat out the games in the kitchen with the portable TV. "You and Meta fought in the car on the way over here," he accused me one night. I couldn't deny it. "She's the kind of girl whose cheeks burn when she's mad." I couldn't deny that either. I waited for him to continue. He seemed so jolly. "You fight in the early years," he winked, "so there's nothing to fight about later."

I nodded, hoping that he was finished. We stared at the television. "One more game, Mother!" I could hear Meta call from the living room. "I can't stand ties."

"Yes sir," said my father, not taking his eyes off the set. "That girl will be a breeze to live with one day." When he realized that I was looking at him, he turned to me—smiling.

I haven't seen Meta in at least a year, now, yet she has insisted on keeping in touch. When she first arrived in Reno with divorce on her mind, there were letters of loneliness. I could barely read her handwriting. Then she wrote that she was dating three men simultaneously.

I decided she was inventing stories to make me jealous. Then Ramsey came along and all of her letters were filled with him. Ramsey was on the '56 Olympic water polo team; Ramsey could order dinner in six languages. I wanted to ask Meta if there was anything that Ramsey couldn't do, but she would have said "No."

A couple of months ago I received a postcard from Meta that pictured a spaniel peeking out of a top hat. The message scrawled on the back was simple: DIVORCED. The postmark was Hawaii so I imagine she and Ramsey were honeymooning at Diamond Head when Meta finally got around to dashing it off.

My mother called recently and sounded as if she were reading a prepared statement: "The fact that Meta remarried has hurt the chances of you two getting back together, but don't rule it out."

*James Knudsen*                                                          *89*

I told her that she was becoming a ridiculous old woman. "Meta is out of the picture!" My mother hung up.

When I went over for Sunday dinner as usual, I found the house deserted. I waited in the living room for three hours. Snow clouds were gathering overhead and the room grew darker and darker, but I did not turn on any lights. When I heard my parents' car pull into the driveway and stop, I picked up a magazine.

"You'll hurt your eyes," said my mother, entering the room and turning on a lamp. Then she went into the kitchen and fixed me a couple of cheese sandwiches.

I should have seen the end when Meta turned to me after our wedding ceremony, laughing under her breath, "Is this really us?"

At the rehearsal, I had joked with the best man about having a car warmed and waiting with a plane ticket in the glove compartment. "It will be embarrassing at first," the best man answered me earnestly, "but she'll thank you later. Believe me."

I just smiled. I had already questioned myself as to whether the marriage was right. I had even taken instruction in Catholicism. At the reception, when I realized that I had left my top coat in the confessional, I apologized to the priest with lowered eyes. "Young people," he said, shaking his head. I kept hoping he would laugh.

Even after the divorce, my parents referred to me as "you two." "What have you two been up to?" "Will you two be dropping by on Sunday?" I corrected them time after time.

When I was going with a girl, I would always say something nice about her. "There's a head on her shoulders" or "She really has both feet on the ground." My mother would become curious and ask me to bring her home. "That's an idea," I'd say, "maybe sometime soon." But I never did. I knew they would compare her to Meta and that wouldn't be fair to the girl.

I laughed when Meta sent me her wedding picture. It was quite a shock. In memory, her face had become anonymous, a composite of common features. Now, she disarmed me in a long gown and a crown dripping orchids. I would write her a letter telling her this, but I remember one of our last fights too well—a mess of fists came at me and her voice crying, "I'm tired of your compliments!"

Meta enclosed a note with the picture that asked for suggestions on how to handle her major problem in life, Ramsey's nine-year-old son, J.R. J.R. hated her guts and had stuck a gob of Pep-o-mint gum in her hair.

Hearing this made me realize how glad I am that Meta and I didn't have children. When I was a kid, my best friend had so many stepfathers that he could blockprint his Father's Day cards.

This afternoon I had dinner with my parents. My mother said that when we were married, she had thought that Meta and I looked like brother and sister. "Now," she said, while examining Meta's new wedding picture, "you don't look a thing like her. Here," she handed the picture to my father. "She looks kind of like that Ramsey fellow now."

My father slid the picture half under his plate and began to stir his coffee. "In our day, we married forever. . . . It was all we knew." He looked at me. "You think you know different."

*Thomas A. Kriksciun*

## GOOD KING WENCESLAS AND THE BENGALI BEGGAR BOY

Citayram
Jay Ram
Jay
Jay
Ram—
—Chanting over the loudspeaker. Eight weeks straight now. It can't be the same person, can it? Perhaps some holy man *sadhu* propped up by his disciples, taking a bit of sustenance during a tabla interlude. A gulp of *Ganga pani* through parched *sadhu* lips, and the beginning of another week. Perched above the Ganges, begging Shiva to rise out of the mud water, from among the half-burned bodies and twenty-foot carp, who know.

Arise from opium dream sometime in the half-light. Dusk or dawn either, but of course dusk, dawn having sounds and smells of its own. Throw back the shutters, and it's *Kicheree*—the Festival of Kites. Some boys stand on the roof of the cinema down the dirt alley flying homemade kites. Strings slick with glue and glass shards for aerial fighting. Also, tribe of baboons, on the marquee, cornered afraid to move, or on the marquee, playfully grabbing at the kite strings when they dip low enough. Warriors only— females huddled behind. Babes in arms. Boy moves in with stick wanting to put an end to this, but stops short at sight of yellow fangs. Cornered baboons kill leopards, which boy realizes he isn't even. Then a change in temperature from the West drops strings to within monkey grasp. He lunges and takes hold. Boy runs now up to monkey to hit him with stick. Monkey senses attack on his tribe, pounces and lands on boy's back. Friends drop kites and shouting run to aid. No avail. Fangs sunk in back of neck, boy delirious screaming running. Kitestring tangle of *babu* and baboon fall over the edge of the roof, both leaving this incarnation in a pool of blood in front of the Nisham Talkies.

I walk out the door of my hotel into the alley. A woman is beating clothes against the side of a wet rock. She sees me, and covers her mouth and nose with her hand. I pass by, then stop to turn around. She has taken her hand away and returned to her washing, but no footsteps have startled her. Frightened now, she covers her whole face with her *saree* veil and turns away. I continue on my journey. A moment later, I hear again the sound of cloth being slapped against stone. I turn back and watch her for a second. Nothing has changed.

I pass the drivers sleeping in their rickshaws, moaning to the wives they will never be rich enough to buy. I turn onto the street, and walk toward the River. My enemy, the hot-milk seller, is stirring a huge cauldron of milk on the sidewalk, and ignores me as I pass.

Little white *kuta* dog rummaging around brick pile doesn't like the smell of *Sahib,* and he barks and growls and guards his unearthed treasures. Holycow ambles by and stops to see what the disturbance is. Looks at *Sahib* with either all-knowing or ignorant eyes—but liquid with girllashes. *Sahib* pets him as he passes, the skin on his back flinching when he does. *Kuta* is barking and growling now. Holycow lowers his head and points his horn at the dog. *Kuta* realizes that he is finished unless he retreats, backs off the slag heap, and continues barking from a safer distance down the street.

Little girl in rags stands before *chapati*-maker. She carries naked child propped up on her hip. Looking up at man leaning over *chapati* oven. Throw me a *chapati* for my little brother. We have not eaten in three days. Go away, for if I feed every beggar girl in Benares, I will be a beggar myself. *Chapati*-maker yelling and waving spatula. Holycow ambles by and looks up at shouting *chapati*-maker. Throw Me a *chapati,* for I am Holy. Flatbread *chapati* blowing in the breeze from the heavens, lands on Benares sidewalk. Little brown girl bends to pick it up, but cowtongue snakes around and swallows it without effort. Little girl angry and ready to cry. Holycow senses her agitation and turns around as if to leave. But no. He drops his dung all over the sidewalk. Smiling girl grabs passing *Hindustani Times* and scoops up excrement into it, and trots away to somewhere. Holycow ambles off in the other direction. Shiva the Provider.

I follow Holycow's path with my eyes. The cow passes by Bruce not twenty feet away. My eyes meet his.

"Hey, man," he says. "What's happening?"

"Bruce! I can't believe it. What are you *doing* here? I haven't seen you in three months. *Four* months! I haven't seen you since . . . Kandahar!"

"Uh . . . yeah! Kandahar!"

"Where have you been?"

"Oh, hanging out, mostly. After you left, I went to Kabul and dug the scene on Chicken Street for a few months, till they kicked me out. They wouldn't renew my visa after three months, so I moved on to Pakistan."

"How did you like Pakistan?"

"I couldn't stand it. Too many Pakistanis, too many hassles in the street. I finally got sick of it and flew from Karachi to Delhi yesterday."

"You just got to India yesterday?"

"Yeah, and I'm leaving tomorrow. I'm leaving for Kathmandu in the morning. I've got a 6 A.M. flight from here."

"You mean you're going to be in India just one day?"

"Well, I have to meet some people there tomorrow. We all plan to come back here and do it up right in a couple of months."

"I should hope so. I've been right here for three months and could stay the rest of my life."

"Yeah? What do you do with yourself here for three months?"

"Oh, I've been staying down by the Ganges most of the time, talking with the Holy Men. I have some friends down there. Little kids who row their boats on the River for a living. I sit down there with them at night and talk."

"Oh, yeah?"

"As a matter of fact, I'm on my way down there now. Come on with me. You're not doing anything now, are you?"

"Nah. I was just out walking around. It's not far, is it? I've got to get up pretty early."

"No, it's just down the street."

"Sure, let's go."

*Dhal* is the Hindi word for lentils. *Kicheree* is a mixture of rice and *dhal*—starch and protein—which is the staple of the poor Indian's diet. *Kicheree* is also the name for the kite-flying festival in Benares, the Holy City of the Hindus. On the festival of *Kicheree,* pilgrims come from all over India to bathe in the sin-cleansing water of the Ganges River, which winds through Benares on its way to Calcutta and the Bay of Bengal. . . . After bathing in the Ganges, the pilgrims distribute alms in the form of *kicheree* to the beggars who have come to the *Kicheree* festival to receive the alms.

Thousands of pilgrims are gathered in town, sleeping in their hotel rooms or *dharmasalas,* awaiting the day. Thousands and thousands of beggars are sleeping in the streets, eating in the streets, sitting in the streets, awaiting the day also.

Bruce and I wade through a sea of beggars on our way to the River.

Citayram
Jay Ram
Jay
Jay
Ram—

—becomes louder now. We are standing in the street above the Ganges, before the steps that lead down to the water. A loud-speaker blasts out chanting and static. The chanters themselves are sitting in a temple to our right. I can see their shadows, larger than life in flame light. Flame and shadows move, chanters immobile. Five or six voices singing in improvisation. One tires of the rhythm and raises itself, straining to slow down the tempo. Momentary confusion, then an ally joins in, then the others, then the tabla accustoms, and finally harmonium fingers pick out the new melody. A dirge.

eeeeee eEeEE EEE tayrammmmmMMM

jayyyyYyYYY rammmmMMM
jayyyYyYYY
jayyyYyYYY
rammmm

I see a fire down below on the steps, and make out the figure of Ganiela. We walk in that direction. Ganiela sees me and shouts out. All eyes are on us. Bruce holds back for an instant, but I tell him that these are my friends, that we are known to each other.

We join the group by squatting around the fire. I introduce Bruce as my friend to Ganiela the boatboy, who rows his boat by day and sleeps in his boat by night. Ganiela, at twelve years of age, is both father and older brother to Vijay and Rishi, who are squatting down with us. Another boatboy is there. And Ganiela's friend Ramakrishnan, the rickshaw driver, whom I don't care for. I can see immediately that Ganiela and Ramakrishnan have been eating *bhang,* marijuana candy. Their eyes are glazed over and their speech is slurred and louder than usual.

There are two other people in the group, whom I haven't seen before. One is an old man, the other a boy about Ganiela's age. Faces of mud, clothes of dust. I think they must be beggars who have come to Benares for the *Kicheree* festival. The old man is blind. Cataracts cover his eyes, and he stares upwards at the moon. Squatting down like the rest of us, his outstretched arms resting on his knees, he warms his hands close to the fire. He is without motion. Neither speaking nor spoken to.

His companion and guide, the young boy, is trying to communicate with Ganiela as best he can, but speaks only Bengali. He tells Ganiela about having escaped from a refugee camp in Calcutta to come begging at *Kicheree.* I see a difference between his speech and Ganiela's. My boatboy friend asks him questions in a brusque, flippant tone, used by men of means in addressing their social inferiors. He answers quietly, with eyes cast down. He unfolds his arms from his chest to wipe his nose. His left hand is bandaged with a rag, and blood oozes from the spot where his last three fingers had been. I see Bruce stiffen at the sight.

I wonder why these two have been allowed to sit by Ganiela's fire. For some reason, I think the *bhang* candy is linked somehow.

Bruce asks if the Burning Place is near here. I say yes and offer to walk with him. Ganiela says he will take us there in his boat.

The old man shifts his weight and brushes against Ramakrishnan. The rickshaw boy yells "Hup! Hup!" at him and blows at the spot that he had touched. Ganiela sneers at the old man and laughs, telling me in his English that the man is very dirty and covered with lice.

The three of us get up to leave for the Burning Place. We walk down to the spot where Ganiela's boat is moored. From behind us we hear laughter. We stop and turn around. Ramakrishnan has a stick and is bent down, trying to lift up the old man's loincloth without his feeling it. Ganiela's little brothers are giggling. The old man is statue-still, staring at the sky. Ramakrishnan is laughing and shouting. The only word I can make out from is, "*Aloo*. Potatoes. *Aloo*." Rishi, Ganiela's youngest brother, is laughing, his head close to the ground, looking up the old man's loincloth.

I think the old man must be deaf as well as blind.

Where we row, the River is completely still. A mist hangs over it, and the temples and fortifications silhouetted against the light from the city beyond them.

Bruce is silent, and I make no attempt to communicate with him. But the *bhang* candy has loosened Ganiela's tongue, and he rattles on like a tour guide. This, Golden Temple. Mister Thomas good man. Mister Bruce, what are your qualifications? Your emoluments? What do you think of my country? India very poor; America very rich. Our God speaks Sanskrit, yours Latin. Same God. I do not believe, but I partake. I must partake. I am poor boy. My friend Ramakrishnan bad boy with Bangla man.

We reach the Burning Place at the bank of the River. I count eighteen fires. Eighteen souls leaving this incarnation. Three or four mourners are squatting down by each fire, and they watch as the fire tenders throw wood and *ghee* onto the pyres. Smoke rises up and clouds the view, sending an acrid-smelling fume. Just beyond the flamelight wild dogs are howling at the moon.

Ganiela rows his boat up to the bank, and moors it next to a woman's body, wrapped up like a mummy in red swaddling and soaking in Mother Ganges, waiting its turn to be burned.

Bruce asks Ganiela if it is proper for non-Hindus to be here. Ganiela answers, yes, yes. Why not?

Now the three of us are silent. There is nothing to say. Listening to the fires crackling, the wild dogs howling, the fire tenders whispering instructions to each other. There is nothing to say.

Now we hear a popping noise like a small pistol being fired. Bruce asks what the sound was. Ganiela tries to communicate as best he can that the sound was made by an exploding brain case. Bruce shudders there in the damp mist.

Now a fire tender carries the almost-burned body of a child to the bank of the River, a few feet upstream from us.

Now he throws the solidified ashes into the Ganges, the Holy River, next to our boat.

Now *Mata Ganga* reaches up Her Holy, Fluid Arm from the deep, raises It into the air, and brings It down on Ganiela's head.

Now Ganiela, covered with *Ganga pani,* is beside himself with rage. He shouts, *Kuta! Kuta!* Dog! Dog! at the fire tender.

Now the fire tender looks back, shrugs his shoulders and continues walking.

Now Ganiela, muttering Hindi curses to himself, pushes the boat away from shore, and we ride silent through the mist back to our own fire.

I make a motion to squat down again. But Bruce says he is cold, and that it is getting late. So I straighten up and say I am cold myself. Bruce says good-by to Ganiela and his brothers, the other boatboy, Ramakrishnan, and the Bengali beggar boy. He looks at the old man, but says nothing.

I say good-by as well, and start to walk away. But I sense that Bruce is not with me. I turn around and see him standing over the beggar boy. He has unwound his scarf from his neck and holds it in his hand, offering it to him. The beggar looks up fearfully, as if Bruce might be accusing him of having soiled it somehow. Everyone is silent. Bruce and the beggar boy look at each other.

I walk back, and ask Ganiela to tell the boy that Bruce wants to give him the scarf. He looks puzzled, but does, speaking the single word, *Baksheesh.* The beggar boy reaches out and takes the scarf. His eyes are downcast. He holds it aloft for an instant, then drops it onto his lap.

We turn to go. We walk up the steps and away from the River. Although I'm not looking at Bruce, I know that he is crying.

It is late. All the beggars who have come to town for *Kicheree* are asleep in the street, except for one young man, about my age, who rocks back and forth on the pavement, trying to keep off the chill. Wrapped up in a dirty cloth, he watches us without emotion.

I stop and look at Bruce. He stops and looks at me. I speak in a low voice. I ask him what Good King Wenceslas is going to give *that* beggar, and I point to the young man shivering on the street. His coat? His pants? His socks? And what about the other eight hundred beggars we're going to pass between here and his hotel? What's *Sahib* going to give them? Ten dollars apiece? The keys to his Cadillac? I'm standing there shaking, daring Bruce to say something.

Bruce waits a few seconds until he is certain I've finished talking. Then he starts walking again, toward his hotel room.

I catch up to him. We walk in silence.

I see Bruce to his hotel. We make plans to meet in Kathmandu in a week or two.

I make a gesture to open the door of my hotel, but I know that it has been locked an hour ago. I knock loudly, and hear a familiar cough from within. The old man who will open the door for me, has been asleep in the courtyard. Now he is coughing and trying to say something to me in his frog voice. I stop knocking, and have a momentary twinge of conscience. In a moment, I hear his keys rattling on the inside of the door. Then it opens, and we are face to face. He is very small, and wears a loincloth and a sleeveless undershirt. He gives a neutral grunt when he sees me. He knew already who it was who had been knocking.

Then his single sleepy eye lights up. "Opium?" he asks me.

I am confused. I don't know what he means by his question. Does he want to know if I have any opium to give him as a favor for unlocking the door for me? Perhaps he wants to buy some if I have any for sale, or then again, he might want to know if I would like to buy some from him. Would *Sahib* care to partake in a bit of opium I have saved for just a sleepless night as this? Why is Sahib coming home to bed so late in the night? Has he been to the opium house of Mahomed next to the Cinema?

"Opium?" he asks.

"No," I answer to his question. "Sleeping."

"*Baksheesh?*"

I reach into my pocket, and pull out several coins, which I hand to him.

"Yes," he says, feeling the weight of the *paise* in his hands, without looking to see how much is there. He closes his fist and moves it up and down. "Yes."

"Yes, opium," I say.

"Opium," he says, nodding.

"Sleeping." I turn toward my room.

"*Sahib* sleeping." And he fits the key back into the hole to lock the door. "*Sahib* sleeping," he repeats, as I turn away.

I turn the key to my own room, and open the door. I bolt the door behind me. I take off my clothes and lie down on my bed. I can hear the old man shuffling back to his pallet in the courtyard. He is coughing his horrible dry cough and talking or singing or chanting to himself. I hear him reach his bed. He lets out a huge sigh. Which is the last I hear from him.

Silence. Nothing. I try to hear the Shiva devotees chanting at the River, but the wind isn't right. I know that they are still there, but I can't hear them, as hard as I strain my ears.

But now I *can* hear music. Or rather, drums. Very faint, but getting louder.

*One* two *two* two *three*
One two three
*One* two *two* two *three*
One two three—

—like a march, a parade. No sound at all excepting the beating of hand on drum. Getting louder. Now the drum moves into my alley, I'm sure of that. The sound is echoing off the shacks on either side.

I get up from my bed, and lean out the window.

On the street below, I can see four men walking toward my window in single file. The first is an old man, who carries a long wooden stick, from which bells dangle on strings. He carries the staff aloft in his right hand, as if he were a drum major leading a band. The second carries a small copper kettle in both his hands. The third man carries nothing. He marches along empty-handed. The fourth plays *one* two *two* two *three* one two three on a conga drum hung from his neck.

The sound of the drum grows louder and louder, and reaches its peak under my window. Immediately after the marchers pass by, the sound begins to fade. I watch them continue on. The music becomes softer and softer, until finally, I can't even imagine it any longer. A dog barks twice from a distance, and then all is silent again.

I have been staring out the window without moving, fixing my eyes on an immobile *bustee* shack across the alley.

I wonder what those men were doing. I must assume that they did in fact exist, that, a few minutes ago, I did see four men walking down the alley in single file, marching to a conga drum that one of them was playing. But why? For what end? Where were they going? Or is it—where had they come from?

The air becomes chilly. I go to the bed and pick up my loincloth. I wrap it around my shoulders and return to leaning out the window. I stare once again at the shack in the alley.

Those men. Who were they? . . . They must have been *pariahs*. Perhaps the men who burn the bodies at the River, or they might have been simple washermen. They must have been going to the segregated area outside the city, where the *pariahs* live. They do live in segregated areas, don't they? And the drum was to warn all caste Hindus to beware their coming and going. It must have been that.

I feel lightheaded. My head starts to spin. I turn around, and sit down on my bed.

It's the Fourth of July, although it might easily be a warm Memorial Day. I go to the parade downtown with two of my cousins, Ann and Marilyn, who are babysitting me. Whenever a group goes by with the Stars and Stripes, I stand at attention. Someone has told me that this is the proper form of respect for the Flag, so I do it, even though no one else is. The Post Office Bugle Corps marches by, and I stand at attention. The Gold Star Mothers, the American Legion Marching Band, twenty troops of Boy Scouts— they all carry Old Glory at the head of their units, so I stand and cross my heart until they pass. Then the Electrician's Union Pipe Band. I stand up at attention. I feel a pain in the back of my leg. I look around. Ann has bitten my leg and shouts at me to sit down and stay down. I sit, and rub the spot where she has bitten. Then I start to cry. I feel embarrassed because I am crying but I cannot stop, and my tears flow like the River Itself.

*Karen Loeb*

## *RODEO*

Charlie was six years old yesterday. He was sitting on the curb in front of the house where he and his sister had a room, fingering the Indian-head nickel Jack had given him with a hole punched through it and a leather cord that was rough like the inside of moccasins; you hung it around your neck. It had hit against Charlie's stomach until Janice had said to take it off so she could tie it again, and now it came to his chest. Every once in a while he'd give his new tennis ball a kick along the gutter and then he'd stretch out his foot and catch it just in time. He stood up to wave to the ice cream truck, with the umbrella on top, as it passed by because Mr. Wodeka had said he liked to sell ice cream but he didn't like the hot sun on him.

Charlie was wearing a pair of Jack's Bermuda shorts which were tied up with a leather belt around his waist. He went over to the railing of the house and climbed up on it and rode it like a horse, yelling "Giddy up" and slapping its side until he felt a splinter go into his hand. He stopped long enough to pull it out and wipe the blood away. He didn't go to Janice any more to pull railing splinters out. He was too old for that. Besides she wasn't home, so he might as well do it. Then he gave the railing a kick, not too hard because it would hurt and that would make the horse jump up.

He wished he had a real horse. One time he went on the pony ride in Lincoln Park and ever since that he'd wished he had a real horse. Then he could be a real cowboy instead of just a pretend one. But Janice wouldn't hear of it. She said where would you keep a horse in the middle of a city when you just lived in a room and didn't even have a backyard to turn it out to pasture. She said it would be cruel to do that. And Charlie agreed. But then he would go to the railing and ride the horse all over again. Now he could only do it when Janice wasn't home because one time she caught him riding and said, "I thought I told you you couldn't have a horse." And Charlie told her he knew, but that he had made this one, and she said what was he trying to do, make her look cheap? And he said that it was his horse and it wasn't hurting anyone, in fact it helped, because everyone else could use it as a railing and he just took it up a little bit of the time. But Janice wouldn't hear of it and said if he didn't climb down in one second she would take him down herself, and that's how it ended up, only a spanking followed.

Now Charlie looked out over the sidewalk and saw his herd of cattle grazing. He circled his arm with his lasso and roped a black heifer, and struggled to drag it over to him, but after all, being a cowboy wasn't easy. Then he jumped down and tied the heifer to the post, which was the railing horse, too, and he pulled a few logs that he and his sidekick, Sam, had chopped this morning into the middle of the walk and lit them for a fire. Soon he had a bonfire blazing and he told Sam to bringing the branding irons over to the fire. Sam brought them over, one by one, and left them in a row by Charlie, and took a plug of tobacco out of his vest and popped it into his mouth, like a gumball, Charlie thought. He left the irons in extra long to make sure they were heated properly because last time they weren't and he had to do it over again. He looked over at the heifer and it was eying its mother who was standing about a hundred yards off grazing and not too interested in her baby. Charlie scowled at her, wishing she would try to get through the fence because then it would be fun to stop her, but she just stood there eating. He lifted one of the irons out and held it up. It glowed red, blinking on and off, and its tip was white.

"Okay, Sam," he said, "you hold it down."

Sam had been leaning against the fence repairing his saddle, and he looked up and spit out some tobacco. "Which iron you using?" he asked Charlie.

"The one which is like my medal that I got in the rodeo," he said, and he held up his Indian-head nickel to Sam. Sam nodded, and smiled too, Charlie thought, because he wanted the medal, and was waiting for a chance to get it from him. He took the iron over to where Sam was struggling with the heifer. He had tied its legs and was holding down its bleating head. Charlie noticed with satisfaction that the mother was now watching and mooing from behind the fence. He held the iron above the calf's head and watched the waves of heat hit it in the eyes until it screeched in a human way.

"Hold her down, Sam!" he screamed, and he jabbed the hot iron into the flank and watched as tiny flames spurted up from the hide and put themselves out. He threw down the iron and told Sam to leave the calf tied up. He watched as it squirmed on the ground trying to roll over. Then he walked away, mopping his head with the red handkerchief that had been so large Janice had cut it in half and made two out of it. He told Sam he was going to the saloon.

Inside it was damp. Charlie climbed the stairs, counting them as usual, never quite sure if there were twenty-five or twenty-six. He took off his hat and hung it on a peg on the saloon wall which was higher than all the other pegs because he was the tallest cowboy around, and he stopped when he got to Irma's door because he sniffed jam. He always liked Irma's jam because it meant Big Joe was away on another trip and it was the only time Charlie would visit with Irma because he hated Big Joe.

He pushed the door open and walked in. Irma had her ironing board up with a mound of clothes on it. There were other mounds of clothes in the two yellow chairs, and on the couch. Charlie wondered if she ever ironed because it was always like that.

Irma was standing by the kitchen sink which was in the same room as everything else, only you could pull a curtain across and it would be like two rooms then, but she never did that because it was bigger if you left the curtains open. She was shaking something in a mesh bag. Her fleshy buttocks shook when she did. Charlie went up to her quietly and touched the soft flesh. She dropped the mesh bag and red berries bounced out, and she jumped back, looking around and finding Charlie at the same time, and she was about to get mad, Charlie thought, only she changed her mind and smiled instead. She had been crying and she wiped away her tears with the hem of her dress. "I bet you smelled the jam," she said. Charlie nodded. She took a strawberry out of the sink and told him to stick out his tongue and make a wish and then she popped it in and he chewed it up.

She told him the jam would be ready in a minute so he might as well stay because Big Joe wouldn't be coming, so he didn't have to worry about that. "I know you don't like him," she said, "but it sure is bad without him, nights mostly, but you're such a small child—" and she patted his cheek. "Seems like I'm making more and more jam these days." She went over to the cupboard and opened it to show Charlie the neat rows of jam jars, labeled with lipstick covered over with clear nail polish. Charlie remembered the jam because Irma always made it when Big Joe was away and he knew each story about each row of jam especially the one about Big Joe kicking in all the store windows except the liquor one which he passed by and went to the next window.

Irma pulled a deck of cards out of her pocket. They were the cards with the animal pictures on the back and recipes on the front. Charlie took them and began looking at the pictures. He already had hundreds of them in a dresser drawer and one day Janice almost threw them out because she said they were cluttering up all her clothes, but Charlie begged her until she let him keep them. It was when she first met Jack. Jack was like Big Joe, only skinny, and he lived where Charlie lived, so he had to see him every day.

Soon Charlie was eating pieces of damp bread slapped with globs of strawberry jam. He left only the crusts on his plate. Sometimes Janice made things, but it was mostly cakes with cinnamon on top, and cinnamon swirls in the middle, because she said when she was a little girl they had cinnamon coffee cake every Sunday and she had her own dish with her own butter that she could put on if she wanted, so she liked to make the cakes now to remind her of then. Irma looked proudly at the wreath of strawberry around his mouth. "Wanna stay for supper?" she asked. Yes, he wanted to stay, he told her, but he couldn't. He knew that if he weren't home for supper he'd get a spanking because Janice didn't like him eating at the neighbor's like a little beggar. He took up a sausage that was on the table from the morning and began to suck on it, chewing it gently until it broke in his mouth like the soft rocks his friend George had found in the alley and they had crushed with their heels. Irma had taken down a magazine from over the jam cupboard and was sitting on a stool at the stove reading and stirring the last batch of jam. Charlie finished his sausage and found the recipe cards which he had put in his back pocket, where he saw Jack put his wallet. He flipped through them thinking of how many duplicates he had, and how many were new.

Then he left as quickly as he had come, without a good-by because he never said good-by. He went out into the hall, leaving the door open, and walked down a little farther until he came to his door. He put his ear to it to listen for his sister, hoping that she would be there because he didn't like to be alone with Jack but he didn't hear her voice, only the window shade flapping that kept him awake sometimes when he wasn't sleepy. Jack had told him once it was an invisible monster that made it flap, and after that Charlie didn't want to go to sleep for a while, until Janice told him it was only the wind and she even lit a match and blew it out to show him what the wind could do, and she blew against a piece of paper to show him how the wind made noise, and he finally went to sleep, only with his hands over his ears.

He opened the door and smelled the spice cakes that his sister baked, and stuck out his tongue, leaning against the wall, getting used to the gagging which happened every time he smelled the cakes. Janice always shook him to make him stop, because he was always putting on an act, she said, when the door was open and the neighbors could hear; except one time she didn't say that when Jack made him eat the cinnamon cake and he didn't want it, only he shoved it into Charlie's mouth and put his hand over his lips until he chewed it and swallowed it, and he did it again, only Charlie got sick and Janice got mad, screaming at Jack and pulling Charlie along to the bathroom.

Charlie walked across the room to the kitchen and heard Jack snoring on the one bed which was a couch during the day. He prayed a prayer he had learned from Janice that Jack wouldn't hear him. Just when he got to the kitchen, he heard the voice, low and muffled, saying, "Hey kid, where you been?"

Charlie held his breath.

"Hey kid, when I talk, answer!"

"I was out playing," Charlie told him, and stopped, waiting to see if he would go back to sleep.

Jack told him to come over to the bed, fast he said, and slapped his hand against the pillow. Charlie didn't want to go but then was no way out. He thought of running through the door and back to Irma's but he'd only have to come back again. He held up his cards and he walked over to Jack. "Got me some new cards," he said softly, hoping Jack would look at them.

Jack snatched them away. "You save these things, kid?"

"Sure," Charlie told him. "I got some more, only these are a lot of the same ones I already got."

Jack threw them down on the bed and grabbed Charlie's arm and shook him and told him about how only girls are supposed to save these things and how was he ever going to learn to be a man when he disobeyed his sister and went out when he wasn't supposed to, and then went to some bitch's house who fucked every man in the building when she wasn't busy doing it at home. Charlie started to cry and Jack spread the cards in front of him and began tearing each one up individually.

Charlie looked on silently, asking himself why he had shown Jack the cards, and knowing if Janice were home this wouldn't be happening. He would get away as fast as possible and maybe play on the roof and find George and maybe they could play catch before it was time to eat and George's mother screamed at him in a voice like a whistle to come home or else.

After Jack finished tearing up the cards, he made a flicking motion with his hand. Immediately Charlie unlooped the belt and dropped his pants. "Aw, Jack," he said, "come on, I didn't do nothing." But he let his underpants fall in a heap at his ankles on top of his shorts.

Jack sat up and scratched his chest, rolling his tongue in his mouth. "Go get me a beer," he commanded, and Charlie stepped out of his pants and walked to the kitchen. He started crying again as he opened the refrigerator door. He pulled out a metal can and took the opener from a drawer and then held his breath to stop the tears because it would mean a worse spanking.

He brought the beer to Jack and watched as he opened it, slowly, letting it steam and spray in his oily face. He put the can to his mouth and left it there for a long time Charlie thought, longer than he could hold a soda to his mouth, and he watched, intrigued. Then Jack set the beer on the floor with the opener next to it.

"All right, kid, it's time," and he slapped his hands together, making Charlie jump.

Charlie turned around and bent down, as automatically as sneezing.

"Hey kid, what you doing?" Jack asked. He looked away from Charlie for a moment and watched the door when there was a noise. Charlie heard it too, and watched hopefully, but nobody opened the door.

"No, kid," he said, "you got it all wrong."

Charlie looked at him with mistrust.

"You getting to be a big boy now."

Charlie smiled proudly, in spite of his terror.

"So turn all the way around and face me, *now!*"

Charlie turned around.

"Stand up straight."

Charlie stood like a toothpick.

"When you get to be a man, you got to take it like a man." And he let the back of his hand hit Charlie between the legs. A wave of shock worse than last year when a bucket of ice water had been poured on him when he went to the country with George hit Charlie, and at first he could not cry out. He doubled over and let out a screech. Jack pulled him up and yelled that he doubted that he'd play with girls' stuff now, and he struck him again, holding him like a rag doll.

Charlie stooped over and put his head between his knees and held himself, coughing on his tears as they hit his mouth and ran down under his shirt. He heard Jack's footsteps and then he heard him peeing in the toilet and he hoped somehow he would fall down into the water and be flushed away, like his torpedo fish which had died and Janice had flushed away.

He felt the whole room floating around him and he saw himself trying to grab out for something to catch hold of before he floated away. "Better hurry, Charlie, better hurry," he seemed to hear someone tell him, but he felt he could not lift a finger away from himself, for if he did the throbbing would start all over again.

He stayed hunched over on the floor for a long time, he thought. Still Janice wasn't home and his head hurt and he wondered if it were safe to get up. He finally stood and it was dark in the room. Jack had turned the light on in the kitchen and was sitting and reading the paper at the table. Charlie rubbed his eyes because they felt stiff, like the collar on his white shirt that Janice made him wear to Sunday school even though he told her it was choking him, and he hunted around for his clothes and put them on, fumbling for a minute with the belt. He went out the door and walked to the end of the hall and sat on the steps waiting for his sister, wishing she weren't late, because she should have been home by now, and he fell asleep against the railing.

He was awakened by Janice shaking him. He looked up at her and began to sob, trying to stop himself because he knew she didn't like him to cry, and he didn't want her to go away, not when he wanted to sit in her lap.

"Charlie," Janice said, "what are you doing out in the hall? For heaven's sake go back in."

He only cried harder and she sat down next to him wearily, looking around to see if any doors had opened.

Charlie leaned his head against her breast; it was soft against his cheek, and he wanted to push and push to see how far it would go, but he only rubbed his eyes over the material of her blouse.

Janice ruffled his hair and rocked him, blowing on the back of his ear. Charlie felt that he had melted against his sister and would never be free. "Do you love me?" he asked, pulling his head up and looking straight into her eyes, which were shaped crooked like his.

"Of course, don't be silly; you're the only family I got. Of course I love you. You eat yet?"

Charlie shook his head. "No, Jack hit me, so I been out here a long time."

"Look, leave Jack out of it." She pulled some money out of her purse and told Charlie to go down to the delicatessan for a sandwich. "Hurry back," she told him, and gave him a push to urge him on.

When he got to the bottom stair he turned around. "Do you love Jack?" he called up to her, biting his lip.

"Yes," she said, "now go on before I get mad." He heard her walk to their door, which was now also Jack's door, and then he went out to eat.

They had left the door open to get a breeze. Charlie tiptoed in and saw the two figures on the bed, lying naked, with a sheet over their legs. He went over to where he slept on the two chairs pushed together. "It's not going to be the same," Janice had told him when Jack moved in. "That's what happens; things change."

Charlie had slept on the pull-out bed that was attached to Janice's bed, but more often he ended up curled next to her, holding the sleeve of her nightgown. Now he closed the door part way, so the neighbors couldn't see in, Janice had said. Then he pulled off his clothes, leaving his underpants on, and climbed into the chairs.

He dreamt about the calf he had branded. He was riding on an enormous horse which was so large it had a rope ladder attached to the saddle which you let down when you wanted to get off. He had two whips in his hands. Sam had a whole row of calves that he had finished branding. He looked up at Charlie and said, "All right, your turn." Charlie kicked his horse, trying to make it run; such a large, strong horse surely could get away, but it turned into the railing and he was left sitting there with Sam coming with the iron, closer and closer. The whips in his hands came alive and began switching at him. He awoke in a sweat, feeling the shape of his head printed on the wet pillow. He wanted to run to Janice but he knew he couldn't. He stood up, and walked across the room, feeling clumsy, as if he had on huge boots and couldn't walk in them. He went into the bathroom and took a drink of water from the toothpaste glass. He lifted the toilet seat and tried to pee, but it hurt. Finally he managed to make it come out in spurts. He flushed the toilet and held his breath because the noise sounded louder than thunder and tiptoed out of the bathroom and across the floor.

He heard the sheets rustle on his sister's bed and he heard her voice which sounded like crying. He crept under the table and saw the two figures moving on the bed. He had watched plenty of times before, but if Jack caught him out of bed and watching, he'd really get it worse than this afternoon. "I don't like this business of having him around," he had told Janice. But she said he was asleep by the time they started, and besides he was so little it didn't matter.

He saw Jack kissing and biting her on the stomach and between the legs; their shadows were huge on the walls. Flashes of light blinded Charlie for a minute and he blinked them away. He felt his stomach churning and he wanted to vomit but he couldn't. Now Jack was between her legs and his sister was curled around him. The bed was moving, gently at first, but then faster. Charlie knew about how many creaks it would take to stop, and he counted, thinking tonight it took more than usual.

Suddenly there was a bright light in his face and he cupped his hands over his eyes. Jack was pointing at him and he heard him say, "See, what'd I tell you, what'd I tell you? I knew he did this all along." Janice was sitting up, with the sheet pulled around her. "Charlie," she said, "why the hell were you watching?" Jack was going over to the table now, and Charlie darted around and avoided his grab. "Get out of here, you bastard, or I'll kill you, I swear I will." Charlie ran out in the hall, waiting to hear Janice call him back but she didn't.

He leaned against the high wooden baseboard. Whenever he told George what happened at his house, George looked at him wide-eyed and secretly wished he could see, too. And when George told Charlie what went on at his house, Charlie asked if he didn't even get to see them doing it, and George asked doing what. Then they went on playing catch, because grownups were funny sometimes and you didn't have to know all about what they did to be friends.

Charlie crept along the wall and stopped at Irma's door. He peeked in. She was alone, heaving around in her sleep. He could still smell the jam from before and he wished he had a whole plate of it. He walked in, listening to the sticking noise his bare feet made against the wooden floor. He climbed into her bed at the foot and inched up to her like a caterpillar. She awoke halfway. "Here I am," he said, and he pressed his small body against her large round one, and fell asleep with his foot between her knees.

*Sara McAulay*

## THE LIAR'S CRAFT

1. *The Setting: Time and Place*

   She is still meticulous in her work; her attention to detail is as careful as ever. Note the name of the motel: El Ranchito Cadeau. Also note that the number ("3") on her door is tarnished, and that the screws that hold it in place are a little loose, so that it does not hang quite straight. The Taco Bell next door is a nice touch; a quickie-wedding chapel would have been easier, but lacking in the subtlety she prizes. It is sufficient that the heavy clouds that have been gathering since afternoon reflect the neon flash of the casinos on the main street, two or three blocks away.

   A town in Nevada, then, just over the California line at the south end of Lake Tahoe. A "resort area." The skiing has been good. Packed powder, huge boisterous weekend crowds; the lifts were mobbed, but this is of no concern to her. She stands at the window, spreading the grimy plastic blinds with two fingers to watch the after-dinner crowds jostling between the hard-packed dirty drifts that line the curb, and the patches of glittering ice where the thaw runoff from the motel's eaves spilled onto the sidewalk and refroze when the sun went down. She has been waiting since noon, scanning the passing faces through the slits in the blinds. The gun is on the bed, just out of reach behind her.

2. *A Few Words About the Gun*

   She cannot say precisely when or how it came into her possession, and this (like so many other things that have happened) is a source of embarrassment and perplexity to her. It is certainly not the gun she would have selected for herself, had she been given a conscious choice; it is, she feels, at odds with her personality. It looks, with its long, TV-Western barrel and flashy pearl handle, entirely too melodramatic. Furthermore, it is heavy. Unaesthetic: she will have to use two hands. She would have preferred a derringer, one of those old-fashioned pepperboxes, or even a cheap Italian "Saturday Night Special."

His doing, she supposes. Yet another of his little jokes.

## 3. *Introduction of Characters*

### A. *Who She Is*

She would like her name kept out of this, and it is well to humor the heavily armed. Suffice it to say that she is a Liar.

### A. (1) *Digression: About Liars*

Nearly every family has at least one; a cousin, perhaps. They begin as impressionable children, the odd ones, given to fancies; the ones who don't always hear what is said, and often hear what is left unspoken. On stormy nights the trees outside their windows rap with bony knuckles on the glass, and Lord only knows what hides under their beds. These children love the look of stones under water: the soft depth of the pinks and greens, the crispest whites, translucent grays with glinting flecks and veins. They understand the fate of things lifted from the stream and left to dry on the bank or in the hand.

### A. (2) *Digression: Early Recollections*

It seems there was a panda bear; one with a missing eye. Dimly she recalls the dangling double thread, soiled white, at which she used to pluck. That panda used to talk to her. He told of what he had been: soft plushy fabric, sawdust, and before that, a tree. A cedar, she thinks. He leaked a little, left a thin trail, a woody pinkish red, on the hall carpet. Somewhere in her mind a child cried, "he's bleeding!" and a dark face topped by a bandana smiles down from a great height: "hush baby." There was some problem about the color of the blood. Another face, paler, less round, framed in gentle curls on which the lamp lit tiny fires: this face expressed concern for blood that was not red enough. A lack of iron was indicated. Egg yolks and spinach were prescribed, and a foul liquid administered by spoon. She sees, with perfect clarity, her own small dimpled hands holding up the bear: "give him some too." Laughter surrounds her. Humiliated, she flees the breakfast table, and later bites off the other eye—a convex plastic lens, much scratched, and a metal back with a small loop for the threads. The captive eyeball, a shiny black disc, slides from side to side when she shakes it; she can feel its desperation but is unable to set it free. On the bear's face is a circle of clean white plush with the nap crushed down like lawn grass when the birdbath is moved. She fluffs it with her finger. Tugs at the clean damp threads. A cedar most assuredly. His blood smells like the closet where the furs are stored.

### A. (3) *Digression: The Listener*

He was tiny and dark, and appeared on her dresser one day when she was nine or ten, squatting like a frog on the pearl plastic back of her hand mirror, between her brush and comb. He could turn Lies into worlds, he said.

His eyes were bright. They glittered like little suns reflected in a drop of dew, giving off colored sparks each time he blinked. "Go ahead. Lie to me. A Lie is a universe."

She didn't know many lies. "Well, Susie Collins stole a dollar. . . ."

"That is not a Lie," said the Listener. "That is an untruth. Try again."

The Lie came to her all at once, whole and complete—peopled, with a landscape, a history, a code of ethics; gods, demons, beggars, monsters, confections, and machines. A shifting landscape—now desert, now polar icecap; the band of pulsing stars in a blueblack velvet sky. Snow fell on camel caravans. Storms in howling funnels swept across the schoolyard. Benjamin Britten conducted his *War Requiem* on the center divider strip of an eight-lane freeway, stopping traffic in both directions.

The Listener's eyes glowed with a friendly light. Lies could be preserved, he said. Frozen on paper, they would keep almost indefinitely.

## B.  *Villain or Hero:  Who He Is*

He is a fugitive from a frozen Lie; he has escaped, he is at large, and dangerous in his way. She means to get him back.

His was a contrary nature from the first, but she liked that and refused to give up on him, to *write him off* as she has done other recalcitrants: the ballerina who would not dance, the Kansas farmer's daughter who quoted Plato to the traveling salesman, the banker who went to work with dirty fingernails. He was different, somehow; he had a life, a spark, and she stuck with him, labored and wept over him, came to love him, and loved him so much that she tempered his wild beauty with a three-day stubble (which she found unexpectedly sexy) and a chipped front tooth. She yellowed his fingers with nicotine from French cigarettes, gave him a tragic past to sadden his eyes, and then, casting about for the final details that would set him apart, affixed a brown raised mole to his lean cheek, in which she set a single stiff black hair.

He was her best effort, the finest focus of the Liar's craft, and she loved him so well, so deeply, that her love became belief. . . . At which point he dusted the eraser crumbs from his clothes, got up, and walked off the page. Out the door, without so much as thank you or good-by.

## 4.  *The Problem*

It is a question of control. He ought not to have left; she ought to have been able to prevent his escape. His freedom is an embarrassment beside which her discomfiture over the gun fades to insignificance, but that is not the worst. She could survive embarrassment, the criticism of her peers (". . . clever enough, but no discipline at all. . . ."); the worst is that he did not leave with empty pockets.

He robbed her blind. Took what he could in the way of imagination and energy; made off with symbols, metaphors, the tricks and tools of her trade, and damaged what he could not carry away.

Her notebooks, the ones on which she worked for so many years, have been all but destroyed. Her favorite Lies: her dreams and secrets, wishes and predictions. These notebooks are where she kept that part of herself that she most values, and she hid them in the closet, down behind the shoes. He found them anyway, and the relationships between words are no longer clear. Even the physical arrangement of words on the page seems to shift from day to day and is not her own. She refuses to accept responsibility for the isolated prepositions, the of's, to's, unders, and aboves: arrowheads with no shafts, no targets, setting up unresolved tensions, snapping and snarling on the page. Or for the dismal nouns, the catalogue of subjects and objects motionless and dumb as skeletons in a closet, or for the verbs (the Prussians of the language) advancing in columns to rattle the bones.

All of this is his doing. It is because of him that her present Lies take awkward, mutant shapes—part plot outline, part credit application, part nostalgia, and part nightmare—and are (she fears) in real and immediate danger of withering into mere untruths. His motive must be jealousy. He does not want her to create another such as he.

Once she thought that if he would only leave her alone the word-lists in her notebooks would turn back into Lies. But this has not been the case. He claims her attention even in his absence, and when, as happens from time to time, he vanishes for weeks on end, she worries. He has been out of sight for almost a month now, but he is much on her mind as she imagines illness overtaking him, changing him from her familiar hero into a gray and melancholy stranger who grips his belly with white-knuckled hands, as if pain had a reedy neck and could be strangled. Sometimes she dreams he has died, that his escape is final and irrevocable. It is always a relief to see him again, the lei still fresh around his neck.

5. *Evidence Against Him*

He follows her. She feels his presence like a stare, and if she turns quickly she might glimpse his coattail as he vanishes around the corner of a building, into a waiting taxi, down an open manhole; he's a shifty one, no doubt about it, and there is no telling when or where he will show up. Sometimes she turns on the TV and there he is, trying to sell her a new detergent or a chapped-hands remedy. The stubble is shaved clean these days, he has had the tooth capped, tweezed the hair from the mole, and smokes his Gauloises in an amber holder in which, close to the mouthpiece, a tiny fly is trapped. He often wears a camel-hair coat and a responsible hat, and carries an attaché case. She has spotted him occasionally, in holiday crowds or at the wheel of a sober green sedan in the rush-hour congestion on the Nimitz Freeway, pretending preoccupation as he watches her out of the corner of his eye. Once he appeared, twenty feet tall, on the screen of an outdoor movie, in chaps and stetson hat, his string tie held snug at his neck by a silver clasp shaped like a dollar sign. She saw him wet his thumb to peel twenties from a wad the size of his fist. Peeling and peeling, licking his thumb again, the wad of bills seeming magically to replenish itself. She was in that movie too, in a gingham skirt that swept the ground, awaiting the arrival of the stagecoach. She watched herself reach up—a graceful gesture: tinkling bracelets, wide lacy sleeves—to remove the pen from his vest pocket and write on his cowboy shirtcuff. A lovely Lie, simple and yet profound. Lost to her now, of course, with the rest of them.

6.  *Going Through Channels: What She Has Already Done*
    She has tried everything she can think of to win him back. She has offered him riches, power, immortality; walled gardens where virgins and whores ripen among the blooms. Does he have eyes for her husband? Her son? Her mother? She will arrange things; he has but to make his wishes known. She sits for hours on end with pen and blank paper before her: "Tell me what you want." (What he wants is to see her suffer.) In desperation she has sprinkled trails of corn along the ground, as one might for a wild bird or squirrel, and baited traps, nets, and snares. Once, on a limpid summer night she perfumed her hair and breasts and lay naked in a meadow near the road. Legs spread, she waited, set to spring. Dew fell. At dawn the headlights of his Volkswagen raked across her. The horn beeped once; the taillights winked derisively and were gone.
    That was the final straw. It was just about then that she began thinking about the gun.

7.  *The Confrontation*
    Certain details are fixed in her mind. His room, for example. It is next to hers, and has green walls and a short-pile, tweedy carpet, also green, worn thin beside the bed and in front of the bath-

room door. The bedspread and curtains are yellow; the spread is new but the curtains have been much laundered. They have shrunk a little, and hang unevenly from fake brass rods. The bed and dresser are a matched set, some sort of blond veneer. There is an armchair, covered in black plastic that has cracked where it is pulled tight across the arms. The dresser top is protected by a sheet of glass or clear plastic, and the overhead light is reflected there as well as in the mirror on the wall above. The drawers stick a little, because of the damp; they are quite empty, except for the one on the upper left, which contains a telephone book, a pack of matches, and (in a corner where the maid has overlooked them) two dark-brown bobby pins.

Beyond this she is not sure. She can only try to anticipate what will happen, and hope she has prepared herself to deal with all eventualities.

A. *Anticipation*

She sees herself raising the heavy gun, steadying it with both hands while she sights down the barrel, squeeeezes the trigger: *Blam!* Blood and hair on the ceiling. The recoil knocks her down.

Or: she sees the hole in his forehead, neat and black and round as a period on a page. The end of his sentence, so to speak. She sees him fall, arranging himself in theatrical attitudes of death on the green tweed carpet, and sees the instant of surprise and disbelief. His eyes jerk wide-open; they are bright and hard, clear as winter stars, just for that instant. (And will his past—the past she created for him—flash before them?) Then they dull, grow dense and lifeless as a pair of metal balls, absorbing the light and giving back nothing but a sticky surface sheen like a coat of varnish not quite dry. The black puncture, neat and round, wells blood. A red bead bulges, neatly centered in his brow. It trembles, bursts, spreads, rolls in hot and vivid rivulets into his hair.

It is possible that he, too, will be armed. Perhaps it is right that he should be. A duel, then; an old-fashioned shoot-out. The question is, does she issue her challenge in the time-honored way, or does she shout "Reach!" even as she throws herself behind the bed, firing over the pillow to drop him in his tracks?

Or does *he* shout "Reach!" even as he dives behind the chair, firing over its cracked black plastic arm to drop her in *her* tracks?

## B. *Bathos*

The gun misfires. The bullet sticks in the barrel, an unsightly protuberance like an undigested mouse in the belly of a snake. Or, instead of a bullet, a flower or a hanky or a rainbow-colored fish flies from the muzzle. Or the barrel droops; she shoots off her own toe.

## 8. *Resolution*

He is there, in the room next to hers. Motel walls being what they are, she can easily hear him as he moves about, clearing his throat, tuning the radio, flushing the toilet. He seems agitated, and paces restlessly. The bed creaks as he lies down and then gets up again. The weight of the gun drags against her arm like a swift, downflowing current.

His knock at her door catches her off guard, but only for a moment. She should have foreseen this final insubordination; should have understood that even in defeat he would insist on having things his way. Perhaps she does understand this. Perhaps it is the meekness of his demeanor that takes her aback, or perhaps it is his air of general seediness: frayed cuffs, a button missing from his coat; can that be gravy on his tie? She stares, amazed, scarcely recognizing him. But the mole bristles on his cheek and the capped tooth is whiter than the others. He has recently shaved, with a dull razor or unsteady hand. The Kleenex tag on his Adam's apple bobs as he swallows nervously, eying the gun.

All is not well with him, he says. He speaks in an unfamiliar whine and has, apparently, lost his hat. Otherwise he would be turning it anxiously in his hands. His life has not been a bed of roses, he complains; it has been quite a trick just making ends meet. No expense account: "you could've given me a trade, you know." Or turned him loose (turned him loose!) in a more salubrious time, economy-wise. Inflation, taxes, and not even a cost-of-living increase, never mind a raise. . . .

The truth is, he's overextended. His car has been repossessed and the finance company is after his color TV; they'll want his stereo next. He produces letters from the garbage collection agency, the phone company, the utilities: service will be termi-

*Sara McAulay*                                                              *119*

nated unless . . . And Internal Revenue is auditing his returns. He is ·ready to deal: "I don't suppose you'd consider a loan . . . ?"

He turns out his pockets for her. Empty. He lost his last dime that afternoon at the casinos, playing the slots. Once he would have left the slots alone; baccarat would have been his game, or roulette. She sees him at the table, placing his bets with elegant disdain as the ribbed red-and-black wheel spins and the silver ball races in its groove, drops free, skipping and rattling, and settles at last. He signals the cocktail waitress, and feigns indifference to the growing pile of chips before him.

No loans, she says.

And now the girl is pregnant. "She said she was twenty-one!" Indignantly: "Jailbait! How was I to know?" And how was he to know her father stood six foot three and was a colonel in the Marines? "You mentioned something about a garden? Virgins and whores, I think it was . . . ?" He has even brought a pen and a pad of paper for her to use.

Her mind races, sampling from the banquet board of possible conclusions. The gun is superfluous now; she tosses it onto the bed and gives him a mock-rueful smile. "Too bad about that garden. Broken into, you know. Most unfortunate: The virgins despoiled, every last one of them."

"And the whores?"

Incapacitated, she says delicately. The garden itself has been taken over by a group of retired physiotherapists, very nice people, perhaps she could arrange . . .

Immortality then, he says quickly. And how about a few of those riches she was trying to give away not so long ago?

Ah, but her abilities have been curtailed, she reminds him (and smiles to see him wince; he knows whose fault this is). Immortality is difficult to handle convincingly, she explains, even under the best of conditions. However, if he insists, perhaps she can manage a pink cloud and a pair of clip-on wings, or a scythe and white nightgown. And as for the riches . . . She sighs. "Inflation: The truth is, I've been hard-hit myself." Would he settle for a steady job?

He will settle for anything, of course, and be grateful to her for it. He is completely tame now, and a part of her is sorry; a part of her wishes he would bolt for the door, make a grab for the gun, transmute himself into a bear, a storm, a massive sequoia overgrowing the doorway so that she must fight her way free. Instead, he ties on his green apron—a stock clerk now—and steps obediently and with full complicity into the page, where he dwindles swiftly, pushing his hand cart between mountains of stacked boxes, pausing now and again to brush away the dust that obscures the unfamiliar labels. New at the job, and the storeroom is a labyrinth. His boss will chide him: "What took ya?" It will be years before he earns a promotion.

Still, it is not a bad life. It is perhaps better than he deserves, but she can afford a little magnanimity: a hamburger, if not the whole fat calf. He is well-liked; he has stories to tell. One foot easy on the bar rail, he flirts in the mirror with the buxom, brassy blonde. She arrived with someone else but she will leave with him.

He has no need of walled gardens now; a trailer court will serve. It is an excellent trailer court. Petunias in window boxes. A fine view of the mountains, but close to town. Convenient, all the comforts: Ping-Pong table, barbecue pit, bluetick hound pensive at his knee; he is happy there. She has seen to that.

And, having seen to that, she caps her pen. The casinos are still open. Perhaps her luck will hold.

*Lee McCarthy*

## THE GESTURE

The way you did it was to take a place out of the middle of your rice field along the highway and put your house down there. It didn't help to put it on the corner of the field because then you would be in the middle of your rice field and someone else's. Which meant you'd be killing his water moccasins, not just your own. So you put it in the middle and ran crepe myrtles along the sides of the house and silver maples along the back. And all those little bushes established the boundaries for snakes and mosquitoes which never paid them any mind.

The old man my mother brought out to help her with the eighty-two crepe myrtles was shriveled. My mother said, as we waited, "I don't know how old he really is. I doubt if he does."

That shocked me. Because back then my mama knew everything. Like she knew just what house to drive to. And there he was, fully dressed and rocking, waiting for something at five-thirty in the morning but not especially for my mother. He had a piece of clean flannel wrapped around his neck under his shirt collar. His arms lay on the armrests as if they would have been just like that even if the armrests hadn't been there.

George was good for my mother. She wasn't a patient woman, but the immunity that age bestows was so much in George's slowness that it kept her silent. As we waited for his daughter to help him down the steps, my mother said, "Without him, we'd end up with eighty-two dead things." It was her explanation to me for going against her nature. But almost everything went against her nature; she was in the habit of it.

George was too old to be lynched so he talked politics all that day as he worked with my mother. He dug the holes and she followed, putting the bushes in *and* filling the holes, which she always pointed out to prove that she worked harder than George *if anything*. He told her she should have been a slave driver and that he would rather work for my daddy any day.

My mother just smiled because George and she both knew my daddy would have died of apoplexy if he'd ever known George had *any* politics.

As it turned out, we came closer to dying from the rusty water than the bushes, those frail-looking plants my mother and George argued over all day, did of anything. She said he wasn't digging the holes deep enough. He said she wasn't packing the dirt around them hard enough, and that he couldn't be held to blame if they all died on her.

That was November. The next summer I spent my days picking up rocks so my father wouldn't break the lawn mower so much. By August, the starved grass of that yard, stiff and yellow, crackled underfoot. Our house made a treeless rift in the lush green of flumed and diked rice. For the many summers of my growing up, it was that way.

## II

It was August. Dee stood in the middle of the front yard, the grass crinkling under her sandals whenever she moved one of them. She took her right foot and rubbed it back and forth, watched the grass crumble into bits. Pale gold against the white-gray dirt. The protruding clump came out of the ground, then, in her next shove, the thin roots turned toward the sun. Dee's shorts were no longer too big in the waist and legs, as they had been on her as a child. That was about all that had changed. Her size hadn't really changed. Just the way the clothes people made shorts had changed. Manufacturers were more realistic about the size of people than they had been the first seventeen years of her life. She was glad clothes-makers had found it in themselves to change. She hadn't. But then she wasn't in business either. She was in the front-

*Lee McCarthy*

*123*

yard, where nothing happened, not even a snake. As long as you came out in the noon heat and took a straight path to the mailbox on the other side of the road. The post of the mailbox leaned toward the roadside ditch because her father had backed into it with his pick-up once. The post always made Dee miss her father.

Dee stood in the yard, crumbling more grass, and wondered why she always brought herself and her son, Clach, to this place for the summer. Maybe because she was bad at money and was always going broke in August. Maybe because Clach and she had nowhere else to be. Maybe because her mother always wanted them to come. Maybe because Dee thought there was something here for Clach. The knowledge of snakes or something. But she wouldn't ever let Clach play out in the yard.

## III

There were two catalpa trees in Robert's frontyard. Robert was my childhood friend. He lived in town on Hamilton Avenue. We pulled caterpillars off the catalpa leaves and sold them for a penny apiece to fishermen. There were not many fishermen who went by on Hamilton Avenue. Most of the worms died in our empty mayonnaise jars, even though we punched holes in the jar lids. When we opened the glass prisons to throw out the corpses, the smell was awful. The smell was light green. Maybe it was the smell of caterpillar-fear. Juices.

The catalpa leaves were fuzzy on the topside, bright chartreuse on the underside. The leaves were fan-shaped, almost too soft to begin with, a fruity, tropical fatness about them. When torn off the trees, the leaves would go altogether limp, wrinkle, and then dry out like Egyptian parchment.

Catalpa trees were in almost all the yards along Hamilton Avenue because they grew fast, were good at being shade trees. They leafed before the other trees in spring. When the catepillars hatched, though, the puffy bodies moved slowly across the leaves, eating in bold, jagged semicircles. The ravage was steady. Within two weeks, only stalks and a few sheds of leaf would be left on the trees. The desolation following a plague then marked those trees in their ugliness while the more common-looking trees surrounding them were intact, whole. But the common-looking trees were never lush in the way catalpa trees were for that short time in the spring.

Something would happen to the caterpillars in the middle of the summer. They became something else or at least went away. The catalpa trees would leaf again before fall, but it would not be the same as it had been in the spring. The fuzziness of the leaves was only an irritation to the flesh in August. The willow in Robert's backyard was better then. The thin leaves were cool, slick, clean. We could reach the branches easily. We could sit on limbs there. Nobody ever climbed a catalpa tree, the lowest limbs miles above our heads. We always knocked the caterpillars off the leaves with cane fishing poles.

Once I remember we laced catalpa leaves together, making vests and hats. Robert must have climbed the tree to get the leaves. I suppose he had had to do something to make up for his best friend being a girl.

## IV

Dee had picked Clach a catalpa leaf, and had shown him how to hold it like a fan. She had rubbed the fuzzy side of it against his face. He hadn't liked the feel of it; he had considered it some more of her teasing him. She had picked herself a leaf as well. Now, as they stood within the big, empty courtroom, the leaves hung limp, wilted as much by their hot breaths as by the leaves' own weeping stems. Clach still occasionally fanned the air with his collapsed one. She put hers in a spittoon. Dee found the spittoons, placed on each side of the jury box, unbelievable, and Dee could believe almost anything. The spittoons were old in such a Hollywood way that they were unreal. Maybe that was why the county had finally decided to tear the building down.

Dee had not brought Clach for the spittoon part. She hadn't even known about that part herself. She had brought him for the smell of the place. The smell was why she had been so pretentiously a prelaw student her first years in college. The decision had not been personal or serious on her part but simply a gesture to this smell. The skylight was covered with chicken wire. Four dead birds were captured in the mesh wire, their wings still spread in flight. A broken pane let in raw sunlight.

In the Revenue Office there was a small winding staircase that led to the ceiling. There were county manuals placed on the lower stairs. The metal steps reminded Dee of her ridiculous visit to the Statue of Liberty, when she had been too old for such an excursion. She asked the man at the desk; he explained that the steps led to a jail cell on the roof.

"It hasn't been used in years and no one remembers when it was used." The man was not interested in the cell and he considered it unsuitable for Dee to be interested in it. She turned Clach around and backed out of the room.

The stairs changed from marble to unvarnished wood the third flight up. Clach asked, "Why are we going up here?"

"Shhh. This is a secret," she said.

"Let's don't go," he said, knowing her.

"Yes, damnit."

She could feel the years' accumulation of grit in the boards under her shoes. As they ascended, she worked on Clach's resistance. "When I was young, there was a jailkeeper who used to sit in the window up here all day."

Clach stopped on the step. "Are we going to the jail?"

"Yes." She took his hand.

"I don't want to go."

"Come on and let me tell you, Clach."

He came.

"At recess we would see him looking down at us through the bars. Afternoons, my friend Robert and I would walk through the downstairs lobby on our way home from school sometimes. We came for the feel of the marble floor under our shoes. We came for the awesomeness of the high ceilings. Besides, it was the only building in town that had a revolving door."

"You mean you walked all the way to Grandmother's house from here?" Clach stopped again.

"No, no. We lived on Hamilton Avenue for two years. We moved out where your grandmother lives now when I was in the fourth grade. Let me tell about this. Robert and I would always be very quiet walking through the lobby, the sound of our steps loud in our ears. On hot afternoons, the north and west doors would be open and that lobby would be cool in a way no house or store in town was. That jailkeeper would sometimes be down there sweeping on those afternoons. And you knew he was the same man as the one in the window because he wore a neckbrace. And nobody else in the whole town did that. But he didn't ever *seem* the same one. And I always tried not to think about it because it was a little scary."

Clach knew all that was supposed to mean something but he didn't know what. At age six, he just knew she was excited enough to keep them there the whole day. He sighed.

"We'll go right after this," she promised.

"Is that man up there?" he asked her.

"I don't know," she said.

Clach stopped again.

"Of course he's not. That was twenty years ago, Clach. More than twenty."

"You're still here," he said but started moving again.

She knew no one had been in jail in years probably. She had never heard of anyone being there. But from the elementary school playgrounds she had seen the bars on the top windows and so, ever since the third grade, she had known it was there, waiting with the terrible patience of all those places that are set apart.

The only murder ever committed in town that Dee could remember was done by a husband, and she remembered her mother saying that his wife had deserved it and the man wouldn't be convicted. Two wives had had vicious rumors circulated about them when their husbands had supposedly committed suicide, the stories amazingly similar to her as a child. But the town had made no attempt to lock those women up. Gossip from mouths had locked them out and both women had eventually moved away. The town's judgments had been passed outside of court, except property ones, with the whole town the jury. Greece's fluke. All she had learned as a prelaw student was: If a twelve-man jury had come to function as the end-all for the rest of the nation, this town had ignored it and ran rather the risks of pure democracy.

V

A dentist once told me I had an impacted wisdom tooth. I went home and looked that up. "Not able to erupt because of the set of the jawbone." The Greeks named that last molar a "wisdom tooth" because it is the last to come in, during the approach of adulthood. Mine never did. It would grow senstive to the touch sometimes but nothing more. I used to spend a lot of time rubbing my tongue over its hard bulk under the gum. I remember I was feeling it with my tongue the night I decided to stop being a history major. I took on a major even more farfetched the next day.

## VI

When Dee saw the big iron door was open, she hesitated. She had counted on its being locked, she realized. She looked in. The room was as dirty as she had expected. It looked as unused as she had expected, the ticking mattresses rolled up on their bunks. But there was more metal than one could have planned on. The bars closer together than she had imagined—barely enough room between them for a hand to pass through. The stained urinals stood in the sunlight of the closed windows along the east wall. She felt terribly clean and waspish and told Clach to be quiet, sensing the capacity for hate in that room. She went down the aisle as Clach stood in the doorway calling her back. It was only on her way out that she realized someone was watching her. She, upon finding the place empty, had relaxed into her natural self, had been walking with her neck craned forward, sniffing, running a finger over the metal here and there.

She stiffened when she found the eyes that watched her from the other side of the bars. They watched her for a moment from the shadowy top bunk and then went back to something on the bed. The boy, his legs dangling over the side, was playing solitaire.

As if she had come for only one reason and that was to carry on a conversation with him, she began a gush of words. She asked him questions, trying to explain her presence without telling the truth. As if she had known all along that he was there and wanted a visitor. She stood her ground for no reason at all except she could not have borne those eyes on her back in any panicked retreat out the door.

She sent Clach to get Cokes for the boy and for himself. But Clach returned up the stairs saying he couldn't work the machine. She knew he hadn't tried. Afraid to leave her up there by herself too long. Unwilling to turn loose the fatally sick catalpa leaf. So she went down herself, knowing it was the worst gesture of her life. When she returned, she saw the loaf of Wonder Bread on the opposite bunk and thought perhaps the Coke was not enough. But it was at least enough to get her out of there. She had to leave the Coke on one of the crossrails because she couldn't pass the bottle through with her hand around it. The boy took the Coke as if he did not want it, did not even know what to do with it. What he needed was thirty dollars. Thirty dollars for thirty days. His mama was working on it, he told her.

## VII

I'm coming down the steps from the jail when there's my uncle-in-law, Raymond, who has just had a bastard child by a fifteen-year-old. He's coming up the stairs in khakis with badges all over him and a captain's hat on his balding spot. He doesn't know who I am and I like that. I even speak and he is left to ogle me. Then he recognizes who I am, that he is kin to me, although he probably understands very well I'm not kin to him, and it's the handshake and I'm out of his pornographic mind because his family gave up incest half a generation ago—when he was told he couldn't do it anymore because somebody might find out—and I'm glad to be out of his balls even if it means shaking his hand.

I search his face—because you're supposed to do that sort of thing—about his bastard baby. That should leave some mark. But it hasn't and I see then it doesn't matter. Something has led him to become a figure of law which, in a southern town, is some terrible, public admission of giving up all hope. Appropriately enough, he tells me how he is Head of Youth Authority. I think of his three kids all grown up to misery. Such grandeur dazzles me and I wish I had on white leather gloves. If I had known, I would have worn them in spite of my three-year-old, two-dollar Ensenada sandals and dirty feet.

"That's really nice," I say, a little nasal. I always get nasal when words break down like that.

And then comes my triumph. I've put a little hesitation in his style. He says, "Yeah." He's so lost for anything else to say, he almost adds "ma'am." His eyes can't quite make it to mine, just to the dark, varnished banister below my elbow. He touches the brim of his captain's hat when I move one foot to the lower step, but his dandyism comes back to him and he raises the whole hat to give his hair a swipe. That swiping his hair has kept him from tipping his hat to his niece. And there the hat is, back on his head, cockier than ever.

If anything saves him, it will be the uniform, he tells me with his eyes. I look at the starch in it and it's really mournful but the starch tells me that he is absolutely right. There is the look of destiny about him and the fresh crinkles in his clothes.

I didn't really expect to run into Ross and deliver the boy's message: that he wanted to use the telephone. It hadn't occurred to the boy that my being in the jail could get *me* in trouble. And I had said, "Yes, if I see him." Once I reached the lobby, there was Ross, walking right at me. A little fatter than in my childhood, but still the county sheriff. It came to me then that I could tell Ross the whole story and confuse him terribly if I just stuck to the truth. Maybe even get Raymond fired for having such a goddamned relative. Ross would have to take a gentlemanly attitude toward me in the end. Or arrest me. Which he couldn't do, there being no jail for females. Besides, I have a way of looking innocent, even in the face of awful truths.

I said it all fast. Ross hadn't even finished tipping his hat because he hadn't expected me to stop and actually talk to him. That startled him so I had to repeat most everything, which made it harder for him to catch on to any one part of it.

## VIII

"You mean the white man?" Ross asked her.

Her eyes widened. "You mean there was more than one in there?"

He looked at her with a new alertness. "I forgot. They took the white man out to work this mornin'. You mean the nigger, don't you?"

"I'm talking about the only one in there. I gave him a Coke. hope that's okay. It's hot up there. Besides, I had to do something I was snooping around. I didn't know anyone was in there. He was on the windowless side, shadowed. And then I saw him and had been violating his privacy like some kind of Junior League president when I don't even have that much of an excuse and he could have been peeing."

"In a bottle?"

She didn't understand.

"Was the Coke in a bottle?"

She still didn't understand. Did he think she had brought the Coke in a glass from home or something?

"Well, now, ma'am, we try to keep those bottles away from 'em. Sometimes, they hide 'em until the jailer's back is turned."

"Mr. Ross, I can't even get *my hand* through those bars."

"That's supplying prisoners with deadly weapons."

"Sir, not even that boy up there is stupid enough to ever let you kill him *with every right to do so* just because of some illusion about the prowess of a Coke bottle. Neither he nor anyone else is ever going to take on a small town sheriff with anything less than a tommygun."

"Mama, let's go." Clach pulled at her hand. Ross rubbed his stubbled chin, as a way of finding out how late it was in the afternoon.

"I didn't mean to break any rules. I hope you'll forgive me if I did." She said it in her appealing voice. The tone was there to reassure Clach, not Ross.

"What's your name?" He said it as if he had lucked upon a brilliant idea.

"Dee Lampkin." She knew he wouldn't recognize her without her maiden name and smiled as his sorrow over the alien name became visible. "He thinks his mama will have the bail money by tomorrow."

"Miss, they always think that."


IX

When we were outside, I looked at the whole building for a last look. And then I checked out the roof. I could see the solid metal cage on top. It was a cage all right.

I asked my child, "Did you like the courthouse?"

"No," he said.

"Why not?" I asked.

"I don't know."

"But they're tearing it down soon. It'll be gone forever. And there will be only that." I pointed to the new, one-story building to the side of the old courthouse. There was only red brick, steel, and glass to see.

"I'll go with you to the new building sometime but not to that old one again," he said, trying to be nice.

"There is nothing to see in the new one. There's no dirt, no evil, no ghost of injustice haunting it."

He placed himself on the car seat with a patient sigh, fanning earnestly with his dead leaf. There was that lovely disregard for reality in his gesture, as much as anyone could possibly give back to the world. So I leaned over and kissed his sweaty cheek. And got out of the car to pick him a new catalpa leaf.

Lewis Nordan

# JOHN THOMAS BIRD

Aunt Louise got Molly the date with J.T. It would do her good, her aunt said, and in the holiday sunshine of Gulfport it didn't sound bad to Molly either. But the minute she saw him she knew it was a mistake. He was beautiful. Spectacular, in fact. His skin was absolutely bronze and, still more astonishing, his body was bald—not one hair that she could see on his arms or Bermudaed legs or the wide V of exposed chest. He was a magnificent golden statue of a man, blond and even blue-eyed, with strong limbs and a hard, perfect waistline. Molly wanted none of it—or rather all of it and so none. Handsome men scared Molly. Even ugly men were kind of scary if they were tall enough.

It was even worse to see him standing beside Aunt Louise waiting to be introduced. Together, in the low hum of central air conditioning and the intoxicating colors of blue-and-green peacocks woven into the brilliant maroons of oriental rugs—Chinese, as her aunt always specified—Aunt Louise and the bronze young man looked like a scotch advertisement in *The New Yorker*. A snail crept with slow inverted elegance across the wall of a large, bubbling fishtank on the table behind them, a salt-water tank, as colorful and clear and cool as the entire house seemed to Molly. Aunt Louise was forty years old, the image of all that women diet to look like—tall and slim, her arms casually braceleted in thin gold rings; she wore tawny-gold bell bottoms which she referred to only as "bells." A drawstring bunched up the waist so that it almost but not quite covered the deep exposed navel beneath a figured silk halter, and her breasts were girlishly small. Molly folded her arms over her own large breasts to avoid a comparison.

"Molly," her aunt said sweetly, "this is John Thomas Bird—J.T." She was holding his hand and reaching out toward Molly to hold hers as well, smiling.

"Hi," she said, allowing herself to be pulled closer than felt comfortable and unfolding her arms unwillingly. Shit oh shit oh shit. Up close he looked even better. Why the hell had she said "Hi"? Like a goddamn schoolgirl. "Hello," she corrected herself, grinning idiotically for no reason that she could think of.

"Whatchasay there," J.T. said, the skin near his eyes twitching in what might have been a friendly way.

Aunt Louise was happy. She released Molly and put her arm around J.T.'s waist and pulled him willingly along to a love seat covered in a brocade of large, royal-blue flowers on a cobalt-blue background, telling Molly, who trailed behind, that J.T. was the second baseman for the Keesler Air Force Base Special Services team. They met at the Officers' Club, where Uncle Walter still had base privileges, though Walter was, of course, retired, whereas "our Mr. Lieutenant Bird," she said, squeezing his hand affectionately, was just beginning his career. She laughed gaily at this thought, and Molly joined her, immediately hating herself when she saw that J.T. had not laughed. "We only danced the one time," Aunt Louise went on, "but I knew right that minute that I would simply have to have him. For my little niece. Who by the way isn't so little any more." She laughed another silver laugh and Molly folded her arms again.

J.T. and Aunt Louise sat at almost the same instant on the love seat and she snuggled comfortably in beside him, patting his naked knee confidentially. Even sitting so close on the little two-person seat she could seem stretched out and luxurious. Molly took the seat nearest them, a Norwegian string chair which required that she lean back at all times to avoid having it snap shut on her like an oyster.

Having mastered the chair, Molly suddenly realized that it was her turn to speak. Since she'd not been keeping up with the conversation, she raced back to the information about the baseball team. "What position do you play?" she said. Goddamnit! Second base, you dumbass, you know damn well what he plays. Oh let me out of this.

Aunt Louise looked pleasantly puzzled at the question and

across the glass table between them offered her the sherry again. When Molly saw it she took the wine and realized how far off the mark her baseball question had been. She needed a joint more than a glass of sherry.

"Second base," J.T. said.

"Oh." She had practically forgotten the question.

Aunt Louise followed their question-and-answer exchange as though it were a tennis match, looking first at one then the other. Molly's "Oh" had apparently gone into the net, because her aunt kept looking at her. In desperation Molly finally said, "What else do you do?"

"Stay in shape."

This time the ball was out on J.T.'s end of the court. Aunt Louise kept staring at him, her smile broadening remarkably but becoming blanker and blanker, a little wild in fact. For a long ten seconds they sat in absolute silence. Match point. Standing abruptly, Aunt Louise said, "Now. You must please excuse me; I have stayed here too, too long. You-all certainly don't need me, now do you?" When there was no reply, another wild silver-bells laugh leaped out. "So," she said, "you-all just talk and talk and talk without the likes of me around to—"

"Two of the most important things in life are a flat stomach and clear skin," J.T. said, apparently without having noticed that Aunt Louise was speaking.

"—interfere," she concluded impotently, soundlessly, sinking slowly back down onto the edge of the love seat.

I love you! Molly wanted to scream. Take me! Take me now, then kill me and my life will be complete. Forgive me for having big tits and a paunch, don't hate me for my wretched freckles and zitses. Kill me now, J.T., please. I hate myself. Instead she said, "Does that include pregnancy and jock itch or just a fat gut and acne?" Why? she wanted to know. Why did she always say such things around men, such stupid, childish things? Last year at college, when she was a freshman, she told Toby Blassingame that she masturbated. He thought it was a joke—everybody thought she was a great joker. Oh shit. Are all jokers doomed to be virgins? she wondered. She hated herself and loved J.T. so much— even more than she loved Toby Blassingame. And J.T. was right, she knew that. She longed for clear skin and a flat stomach, like Aunt Louise's. How could she be that beautiful woman's niece?

"—interfere," Aunt Louise said again, this time employing

breath and lips and vocal chords and larynx and tongue instead of just teeth, but producing only slightly more sound than before. She didn't try again, but rose from the blue love seat and left the room, still wearing the fading smile which now looked like a light bulb slowly burning out. She might have been a princess or an elegantly trained lady of a queen's court except that as she passed the walnut sideboard by the French doors she grabbed an unopened quart of bourbon by the neck and cracked the seal before her slender figure faded from their sight into the cypress paneled recesses of the house.

Though Molly felt a vague discomfort around her aunt, she envied her grace, her sophistication—but right this moment she was too distraught over her jock-itch remark even to think of her aunt. Where are all the ugly boys in this world? she asked herself. There was not one ugly boy on the entire Gulf of Mexico. Anywhere else you would see one or two. And why did she always have to fall in love? She waited for J.T. to leave in disgust—she hoped for it in a way, longed for him to leave so she could go down to the beach alone, as she always did, and smoke marijuana until her mind was gone and maybe die of sun poisoning. But J.T. didn't move.

He said, "Fish helps," the exact meaning of which was not entirely clear to Molly, but the phrase was offered in obvious friendship, or at least a weird form of generosity, and she felt a little better. She still felt fat and freckled and her pores seemed much larger than usual, but when she politely tried to beg off the date—or rather to let J.T. out of it—he never seemed to understand, so she let it drop. She loved him. Why was she always "like a sister" to boys she loved. J.T. hadn't said that yet, but he would.

Aunt Louise came back in to say that she had made reservations for lunch and to suggest that "an afternoon excursion boat might be just lovely for you-all." Molly was surprised at the extreme relief she felt when her aunt declined their invitation to go along with them.

At the Friendship House, looking across Highway 90 through palmettoes and across the imported white sand by the Gulf, Molly dared the Scallops Meunière and Tomatoes Florentine to give her hives, and they did not—she got diarrhea instead, not bad and not from the scallops and tomatoes but, as always, from nervousness. It was made worse by her unexpected confession of it to J.T.

"Sorry I was so long in the john—got a slight dose of the trots." She had already given up all hopes of dying and just hoped he could stand it a little longer.

"Digestion," he said in response, "is related to metabolism." Though he was looking directly at her, Molly could have sworn he was reading from a book, perhaps slightly above his grade level. "The physical condition of the entire trunk of the body," he continued. This made no sense at all, but Molly was grateful for his strange kindness. "Ted Williams swung a baseball bat one hundred times a day. A weighted bat."

"And never had diarrhea?" Molly asked with interest.

"I really wouldn't know." There was a long pause.

"Doesn't Ted Williams advertise sporting goods for Sears now?"

"I don't think so," he said.

"Hmm." During this long pause a thought came to Molly, like a voice. You are bored, the voice said. Impossible, she retorted, and the voice went away.

"Mickey Mantle sells Bow Wow Dog Food, though."

"I thought I remembered that," Molly said.

Later, on the tour boat coming back from Ship Island, as Molly watched Gulf water rush beneath them and tried not to feel nauseated, J.T. said, "Swimming is a very healthful water sport which is gaining rapidly in popularity."

Who writes the magazines he reads? she wondered. "Really? I'm a pretty good swimmer myself." What the hell did she mean by that? She was not a good swimmer, she was an adequate swimmer, a Red Cross Life Saving dropout.

"Wanta go swimming?" he said. "I heard of a good lake."

"Sure. Great." Oh shit.

Back at Aunt Louise's house Molly changed hurriedly into her swimsuit, a tight green one-piece atrocity with a skirt. For ten or more seconds she stood in front of the mirror looking at herself. Look at it, she thought. Just look at it. The skirt made her stomach look enormous. Shit, I give up. I'm not going back out there. I love you J.T., so please just go away and don't make me come out.

Aunt Louise's voice chimed unexpectedly down the hallway: "Molly, is that you?" Pure silver. Suddenly—for reasons that Molly could not understand at all—another conversation with her aunt was more than she could take. From the closet she grabbed a cabana shirt off a hanger and rushed out the door to the car pulling on the shirt and buttoning it as she ran, praying that Aunt Louise would think she was having too much fun to hear.

In the woods beside the lake J.T. completely astonished her by taking off every stitch of his clothing to begin a set of warm-up exercises in preparation for their swim. He was the first man she had ever seen naked except in pictures. It is much better in the flesh, she decided. Entirely different. And much, much better.

While she swatted mosquitoes under moss-covered trees, J.T. counted knee bends in the nude. It was the only way he ever exercised, he said, and hoped she didn't mind. She didn't, she said, no, of course not. As he went through his knee bends, J.T.'s eyes became glassy, and three drops of sweat hung from his chin. His Bronzetoned chest glistened like waxed oak and hair stuck to his neck. There was no other hair on his body. A living breathing Nair commercial—the thought was inescapable. After fifty knee bends he stopped in the "down" position to allow her to look him over, his back perpendicular to the ground, his outstretched arms perfectly parallel with it. He was beautiful.

She wanted to tell him so. To say, "You are beautiful" or "I want you so much," anything to keep from saying "I love you." She almost took off her own clothes, just to make him notice her. But she couldn't do it. He probably wouldn't notice anyway except that she would seem so incredibly stupid. Why had she been in such a rush to get her own suit on? She would look ridiculous taking it off now. It made no sense. Next time she would wear every stitch of clothes she owned so she could take them all off without embarrassment. Hell no, that was a lie and she knew it. Nothing on earth could make her expose those gargantuan jugs and freckled butt to J.T., or anybody else as beautiful as he. Her real problem was that she was biting her tongue to keep from saying what she had said to a dozen boys—and in her mind to a thousand—and what not one had ever said to her. I love you. She hated herself. She didn't mention love yet but she had to say something. She said, "I brought along a couple of reefers; you wanta smoke some dope?" Was she insane? Why would she say such a thing to him? He would not only hate her, he would probably have her thrown in jail. Anyway, what in God's name made her think even for a moment that he did want dope? He was in training. Shit.

J.T. said nothing and did not look her way. His fixed gaze remained firm as he held the position twenty seconds. Then he stood up and walked to a stump which held his neatly laid-out swimsuit, jock strap, and a clean white towel imprinted with the words Keesler AFB Special Services.

He dried each part of his body carefully and thoroughly—face, neck, arms, chest, legs, using short rough strokes. Then he snapped the towel out to its full length and put it between his legs, pulling it back and forth in a seesaw motion against his crotch. It was too much for Molly. She could think of nothing to do with her hands, which suddenly felt fat. Nothing to talk about. She wished she smoked tobacco. Anything. No not that. Not with an athlete. Then without warning she said, "I understand that masturbation promotes clear skin." Why in God's name had she said that? It was the worst thing she'd said all day. She wished he would strangle her with the towel. Stuff it in her mouth. Her mind was gone. Then she heard a voice say, "I've been masturbating for years and it hasn't helped a bit." It was her own voice. My God, she thought, I said that. Why? I have now told two men, two of the handsomest men I ever met, that I masturbate. Why not just put a bullet in her brain? She wanted to redeem herself, to say something right—anything, as long as it was right. To apologize. But nothing worth saying came to mind.

It didn't matter anyway. He seemed not even to have heard her confession, or whatever it was. Placing the towel neatly on the stump, J.T. stepped into his jock strap and red nylon swim suit, bikini style, and if he noticed Molly there was no indication.

She followed him to the edge of the woods and sat beside him against a log, looking at the water. "Seems kind of far across, doesn't it, Johnny?" she said again, tentatively. "Are you all right?" She tried to see his face. "J.T."

He stood up in one smooth motion, angry, she believed. "Don't ever call me Johnny again," he said. "Not even J.T. My name is John Thomas Bird. It is a strong name." His anger, if that is what it had been, seemed to leave him. "It's a beautiful name. Strong and beautiful. I love my parents for naming me John Thomas." He stood for only a moment, pacing, then sat back down. "Where's that reefer you said you had?" She was glad he wasn't angry any more, ecstatic that he had not been offended by her stupid marijuana conversation. He actually wanted a smoke. Her luck was changing maybe. If only he weren't so beautiful. If only she could leave now, get away and never see him again, before she did or said something else screwed up. She quickly found the joint in her Hawaiian-print cabana shirt.

When it was lighted he took it and toked deeply and reflectively, not handing it back right away. In fact he smoked more than half of the joint before Molly got it again, and she felt a little irritated for the first time today. She'd been needing this joint at least as long as he had, longer probably, and worse. At last it came back, she hit it and felt better. They relaxed against the log and listened to the forest hum.

The late afternoon sunlight broke into timid dappling around him and over his shoulders as it filtered through long gray beards of Spanish moss on the trees above. Molly watched a mosquito settle on Johnny for an instant then fly up and up and up until she lost sight of it. When she looked down it was on her thigh. He finished the joint and swallowed the roach, as she lighted the second.

The head of a small turtle winked through the glassy surface of the lake before them and stood still—so still that Molly thought for a moment she had imagined it, that it was a stick instead. Then the water blinked again and it was gone.

J.T.'s voice broke the silence, his tone and manner serious. "Turtles," he said, "are weird." That was all for a long time. Nothing else. What did it mean? It was almost funny, almost frightening. Then he said it again, even more slowly than before, splendidly: "Turtles—are"— he looked directly into her face— "*weird.*" Satisfied, apparently relieved of a burden, he turned and stared again across the wide expanse of water, the mirror-flat surface of the lake. Now taking the joint from her once more and stretching himself contentedly, he said in a distant dreamy voice, "Turtles are definitely a little strange." Molly wanted to say something but all that came to mind was "I love you," which sounded as odd as the observation on turtles, so she said nothing. He said, "They are ashamed of their bodies," then before she could close her gaping mouth, he stood and walked into the water, which seemed to sink beneath his foot like a pillow before it parted, a million speckles of rotted matter bubbling up around his leg in a brown fog.

Taking off the shirt and dropping it behind her, she entered the water too, her legs becoming suddenly warm, too warm. The lake bottom was not sandy but soft with decay at first, then a little sticky when her foot had sunk as far as it would go. With each step leaves and brown stringy things that looked like tiny root systems floated up from the bottom and brushed against her legs. He seemed already to be a mile ahead of her, still wading. She almost caught up when she saw him raise his arms and dive forward and become a long green submarine beneath the surface of the lake. She dived behind him and felt the lake swallow her up warmly then release her. Swimming behind his steady measured motion with her face down in the water, she pulled two strokes and turned her face out to the side for a breath and pulled one, methodically establishing her rhythm, feeling her feet kick steadily behind her. On each breath-stroke she watched her right arm rise streaming from the water as though it were lighter than air, and then her face was back down in the warm and she was plowing two deep furrows of tiny bubbles into the dark liquid beneath and around her.

Suddenly—she couldn't say exactly how she knew—she felt that something was wrong. J.T.'s strange movements in the water must have attracted her attention. She stopped swimming and looked across the water at him. What the hell . . . ? Was he drowning? No that was not exactly it, though it might be. He seemed not to have gone under but to be stunned, floating vertically in the water—she couldn't tell. "Johnny," she called. Near him she saw for an instant a flick of black, like the tail of a deformed fish, as J.T. hung there, his short hair undulating against his neck.

"Johnny!" she called again, more frantically. "J.T.—what the fuck is going on?" Green-black water lapped softly into her mouth and out again. He did not answer. If this is a joke, you bastard . . . Probably it's just a joke. She hoped so.

Approaching cautiously from behind, calling his name and hearing no response, she reached over J.T.'s right shoulder and took his chin firmly in her hand. As soon as she did, he fainted and sank like a stone. Dead weight. Molly went under with him, tightening her grip on his chin. Through the sudden boil of tiny bubbles she thought she saw the strange fish again, but before she could think of it she struggled her way back up to the surface and air, feeling J.T. stir slightly, floating perhaps instinctively even in semiconsciousness.

"J.T.," she said, her face streaming with water. "Wake up." He was heavy and slick but not as hard to hold as he had first been or as she had imagined he would be. "You fainted," she said, laughing a little unexpectedly, hysterically, as she said it.

J.T. showed signs of waking up, holding him became easier. With his chin still gripped in her hand she used her forearm like a lever against his back. As his legs floated up and he became easier to tow, she began her swim back to shore.

After a few minutes she carefully released his chin and slid her arm across his chest and under his left arm, scissoring her way slowly through the water. The cross-chest carry was the closest they had come to an embrace. She couldn't avoid regretting the reversal of her old lifeguard fantasy. She should be the one drowning, not stuck with a dangerous rescue that she would probably screw up.

Surprised at her own strength and presence of mind, and intrigued by the feel of J.T.'s strong body, she swam steadily toward shore, suppressing a momentary impulse to reach down and stroke his prick, as long as he was mostly unconscious anyway. She'd always wanted to feel one. But she didn't do it. She couldn't. For one thing she would probably drop him and he'd drown. "Yes, officer," she heard herself say to the investigating policeman, "I was towing him in by his penis and drowned him." It was something to think about, especially for a person swimming with as much difficulty as Molly was beginning to have as she grew more and more tired. Could Aunt Louise and the other ladies at the Spa do this, she wondered, or did they just look good?

She stayed calm and swam steadily, holding him in the cross-chest position, stretching out her long legs so that sometimes she could see her pale green feet beneath the water.

Then she saw something else—the deformed fish, more clearly than ever. Fuck you, J.T., she thought in terror, you'll just have to drown. But she didn't let go. The fish seemed to be about three feet long, trailing its long slender body behind as though it were following them. She breathed deeply and swam on.

It was a lamprey, an eel-like fish. She had seen them once before, with her father, when she was a child. Harmless, as far as she knew—she couldn't really remember.

Sometimes it was more clearly visible than other times, but it seemed to be swimming beneath her, or maybe between her and J.T.—or even, at times, between his legs. Don't think about the eel, she thought, just don't think about it. Thank God she had not played with J.T.'s prick. She imagined herself reaching down for a feel and finding instead a three-foot living writhing monster with gills and pectoral fins. I will never go on a blind date again. Not on any kind of date. Ever.

As she swam the eel swam too, always staying in about the same relationship to them. Once it lifted its spineless body into a strange loop so that its back showed for a moment above the surface of the lake like a sea monster, but in the air the lamprey was not so ugly. It was fawn-colored. It did not vary its path or change its position except slightly, sometimes floating closer to the surface, sometimes seeming to have drifted a little to the right or left.

Very tired now, she looked quickly toward the shoreline to be certain she had not confused the time and distance. She had not.

Lampreys can attach themselves to other fish, she thought. Hell, yes! That's what she'd been trying to remember. It's how they eat. Couldn't they do it just as well to J.T.? Her father had shown her a trout with a half dozen or so stuck to its sides, slowly draining the fish's blood, some large, some no more than three inches long, trailing like banners. Parasitic little sons-a-bitches. The sucker mouth draws the blood. She didn't know how long all this would take, probably a long time. It could be hours for all she knew. Days. It had to be. Didn't it? She mustn't worry. Johnny must have seen the fish and stopped swimming, scared half to death probably. It could have attached itself if he were still for a moment or two, she supposed. Oh double shit, how awful. Why did she keep thinking of such things? An even worse thought got through: where it was attached. Could there be any doubt about it? It was on his prick, like an extension hose. The thought was staggering. How could a person stand it? How would J.T.? No, hell no, she thought, it couldn't be there—he had on the swimsuit. Thank God for swim suits. Yet somehow even knowing this, that it was a physical impossibility for the eel to be on his genitals, she didn't feel comforted.

Swimming on, more and more slowly because of her fatigue, she wondered how long they had before there was a danger, before it could actually bore in and start sucking blood. She was almost too tired to care. There was probably more likelihood that they would drown first anyhow. All she could do was swim. If only there were some safe way to shift J.T. to her other arm, but—she didn't try.

The shore was extremely close now. She could see the spot in the woods where they had sat and smoked. Whenever the lamprey touched her leg, her side stroke became frantic and clumsy, though now it touched her and she hardly noticed, growing less and less afraid. She was too exhausted.

When she thought the water might be shallow enough to stand in, she pulled four more hard strokes, her arms burning, and stopped swimming. Her feet sank beneath her into the mud and she held on to J.T., catching her breath, looking for the fish but seeing nothing. J.T. was standing, almost by himself, but leaning heavily against her.

When she had rested she completely astonished herself by reaching into the water, feeling around for the lamprey. As she groped between J.T.'s legs she spoke soothingly to him, as she might to a frightened child. When she had checked his crotch and the fish wasn't there, as she knew it could not have been, she felt better.

She kept searching, running her hand along J.T.'s legs, reaching as deeply into the water as she could. Nothing. What would she do if she found it?

Then, as she drew her hand back toward the surface, it thumped against the lamprey's strange body. Her insides leaped. It was higher up than she had expected. She could see nothing, but the long eel-like creature seemed to float horizontally at about waist level. Reaching down, hopelessly, crazily, she found it again and it moved at her touch. She put her hand around the fish and felt its body, muscular and firm, the skin soft. Though she could not hold it long before it squirmed from her grip, she was able to run her hand along its body, not even frightened any more, until she found the strange head. It was easier to hold than the body and tail.

The sucker-disc mouth was stuck solidly to the smooth skin on J.T.'s right side. For a few seconds she ran her fingers around the spot at which J.T. and the lamprey were connected, feeling the odd lips the size of a quarter, and smoothed her hand along the body until the dorsal fin shivered softly beneath her touch.

J.T. woke up half-crying, stoned and frightened. Molly suddenly felt a little stoned again too. "Snake," he whispered, "snake, snake, snake. . . ." Should she try to release the fish now? The spiny little teeth might already be boring in. She wanted to joke about it but could not.

"It's all right, Johnny," she said; "you're just fine, it's all right." He was confused, distraught. She considered simply jerking the eel away from him if she could, but hesitated.

J.T. was fully awake now, standing by himself but still very weak. His voice was a slow coarse whisper, like a child who is sick. "I've been bit by a snake."

"No, John Thomas, no," she said, "it wasn't a snake. It was an eel—not even a real eel, a lamprey." She started to say, "I'm pretty sure they can't hurt you," but she didn't. He hadn't seemed to hear anyway.

With the lamprey trailing between them they walked a little toward shore into shallower water. Then J.T. stopped. "Molly, I can't go any more."

"Take it easy, John, take it easy. Lampreys are harmless, sort of. As soon as we get out of the water, we can pry it off, maybe. Or—or we can take you to a"—who could help them? A doctor? Her mind was whirling —"to a doctor. . . ."

But she might as well not have spoken. His face became death's head as she watched it, the eyes growing wider and more vacant, the lips curling back in a horrible mirthless grin. He had not known the fish was on him. He ran for the shore, groping vaguely at the whiplike creature which he dragged behind, not crying not even screaming, he vomited sound. Molly chased him clumsily, calling his name. Even in the shallow water the fish hung on and it still hung on when J.T. left the water altogether and ran aimlessly upon the lakebank. Finally his movements were merely a comic and terrible turning and half-turning as he stood in one spot. The lamprey clung to him, swinging first one way then the other, like the untied sash of a little girl's dress.

As Molly caught up, she grabbed it near the head and yanked, popping the mouth away from J.T.'s body with a swack. There was no blood. J.T. sank to the ground with his face between his knees and rolled over, huddled up like a fetus, as Molly carried the lamprey back to the lake's edge. It lay for a moment in the shallows then swam away, not as large as it had first seemed.

She walked slowly back up the bank. A breeze had come up and J.T., who was sitting up now, seemed cold, trembling in the foreground of the ash-colored trees hung with silver moss. The sun was already low—orange and strange and scarcely higher than the trees behind him. She wanted to feel sorry for him but she was too tired. I like you, Johnny, I really do, she thought, but I'm . . . Her swimsuit was binding and uncomfortable; she was tired and sleepy. If J.T. was cold he should do some warm-ups. Hell yes, best thing in the world for him. Sit-ups, knee bends, push-ups. The fucking side-straddle hop. All Molly could think of was a nap. Let Ted Williams and J.T. swing their weighted bats if they needed it, and let Aunt Louise kiss J.T.'s ass, kiss this whacko body freak's fantastically beautiful boring hairless ass if she needed that, but what Molly needed was sleep, an hour. Too tired even to notice that J.T. watched her carefully, Molly stepped lightly from the constrictions of wet polyester and lay in tall grass full of the Gulf breeze.

*Arte Pierce*

## SOMEBODY TO LOVE

We were sitting in the corner in a little restaurant that Vera had made me take her to, a "cafe," sitting on hard white metal chairs, with hard yellow cushions, at a tiny table that would almost fit into a dollhouse. As I expected, we were the only blacks there, out in the sticks, in a shoebox suburb past Fifteen Mile Road. And I was dressed all wrong too; Vera had lied to me; she said it would be casual, that I didn't need to change clothes, probably because she knew I wouldn't have changed anyway, not even for her—I'd told her once, "Anything for you, baby, but I'm not a dress-up guy"; she knew that. Now we were sitting here beside old white ladies in long skirts, though it's funny that Vera was wearing a long skirt too; she hadn't fooled herself with that "casual" talk; I should have known.

She leaned toward me. "Alvin, they've all been watching us ever since we walked in."

I swiveled around in my seat to look.

"Don't stare, dummy," she said, grabbing my wrist. "I'm just pointing it out."

"Oh." I glanced around negatively, and indeed some of the couples had even turned their chairs in our direction. The collar of my denim jacket seemed to be shrinking around my neck and I tugged at it; the room was surprisingly hot; I took Vera's hand in both of mine, though she hardly seemed to notice. "Don't pay it any attention," I said, feeling how tense she must be.

"What?"

"Ignore it. They're old."

She seemed startled. "You think they're old?" she asked.

"Sure. And they're all racists anyway, the old ones worst of all. They don't like to see us out here, but there's not a damn thing they can do. So let them stare. Besides," I added, smiling, "you're looking really good today."

Vera pulled her hand away and began fumbling through her purse for a cigarette.

"I think you're crazy," she said.

"Huh?"

"You're crazy. Paranoid."

I didn't see the connection. "All black people are paranoid," I said. "Try going around for a day thinking that everybody has your best interests at heart and see how long you survive."

She sighed, exasperated. "Alvin, these people are staring at *me,* not us." I choked, trying not to laugh. "It's true. One man even winked at me when we walked in. The one sitting over there under the Eiffel Tower poster."

"And he looks queer to me," I said.

"Alvin! He does not!"

"I'm just kidding, just kidding."

I laughed again but she had really scared me with this talk. I knew she had been dating at least one white guy, maybe more. But did she think they all loved her, even old ones in restaurants? I didn't want to think about it.

A dark-haired waitress wearing too much rouge sat a tiny plate of doll-sized cookies and sandwiches on the table.

"What the hell are these?" I asked Vera after the waitress left.

"Crumpets, pastries, et cetera."

"Pieces of crap," I said.

"It's vulgar to mention crap at the table, Alvin. You shouldn't do that."

I grabbed five of the mini-cookies in my fist and shoved them into my mouth. "And you shouldn't correct my manners either," I said. "To me, *that's* vulgar."

"But remember, you love it, baby," she said, patting my hand. "Take my word for it—you love it." Things had gotten to that point, that kind of love. We couldn't say things to each other we hadn't really thought out, testing them, not caring whether or not they turned out to be true.

"Don't we even get to see a dinner menu?" I asked.

"What dinner? This is all they serve here."

"Cookies? That's all they serve?"

"She's bringing tea now and that's it," Vera answered, lighting another cigarette.

"But I thought we were going out to dinner?"

"We are," she said, laughing at me. "Sucker!"

The other customers were sipping from teacups now, still watching closely, legs crossed at the knee.

Later, in the car, on the way home, the bad times start again. She says it isn't anybody's fault, that she doesn't believe in blame, but that's not true. A lot of it is me, I know. I won't or can't give her many of the things she wants, now or in the future, and I refuse to play along with lies like she is used to from other guys—I'm not promising to change myself for any woman. And so what if I'm in college? She knows it's just barely, because, as she says, I don't step on enough people; I haven't sabotaged anybody's chem experiment to lower the average grade to my advantage. And at that rate I'm never going to be rich, which is what she would like most of all. There are places I don't take her, places she can get to with other guys, especially the white guys, which is fine. And I think she understands all this. Only, understanding isn't enough.

We drive into a gas station, still a few miles outside the city, through a light, night shower of snow. Vera rolls down her window slightly and lights a cigarette.

"You asshole," she mutters, her general assessment.

"But remember, you love me," I tease. "Take my word for it."

The attendant has started the pump and trots back inside the station to get out of the snow. Out of the corner of my eye, I am watching a gang of white teen-agers, maybe six or seven of them, walking past us on the street. They have nearly gone by before they notice us. One of them throws a snowball at the car.

"Roll up your window," I tell Vera calmly, still observing them in the rearview mirror. She hadn't been watching and is slow to understand, but even when she does she decides to defy me.

"What if I don't want to roll up the window?" she taunts, folding her arms and pouting. The snowballs begin pelting the back window rapidly now, savagely. The sounds are muffled, but we can hear them shoving and laughing behind the car, moving closer. I realize that I feel more than simple hatred or fear, though I hate them much more easily, much more completely, than they might think. The image of their jeering blue eyes cut out and mailed to their mothers, still bloody, in small white envelopes the size of thank-you cards, flashes through my head. It makes me smile.

"Roll up the goddamn window," I scream at her. A steady stream of snowballs is pouring in from that side, crashing against the seats and ceiling, covering Vera's face, her hair, eyelashes, with beads of water. She seems in a daze. A freckled blond kid appears in front of the car, half-boy, half-girl, bobbing his head back and forth with laughter, kicking at the headlights. He holds his arms up toward the sky. I reach across Vera's lap and turn the window up myself, getting thoroughly soaked in the process. "Are you all right?" I shout. "Are you?" I pull off my denim jacket and try to cover her.

"What are you going to do about this?" whispers Vera suddenly, sounding strange and determined. The kids have now surrounded the car and are beating it with their fists.

I begin honking the horn but can see through the window that the attendant is afraid to come out. The gas hose is still connected to the car.

"What are you going to do?" she demands again, to the background of fists. "What are you going to do?"

It takes a moment but slowly I begin to laugh. Why not? My car is full of snow, the horn is making me deaf but I'm afraid to stop pushing it, everybody wants something from me—Vera, the little Nazis outside, the attendant who has to be paid. . . .

"Maybe," I suggest, "I can back up just enough to kill one of them. That'll disconnect us without ripping out the gas hose, and I can even throw a credit card out the window before we make our getaway. How about that?"

"Yes, Alvin, do that," she says, clasping my arm tightly, leaning against my shoulder. "Do that for me."

*But I can't do that, Vera, not even in a fantasy. I can't do anything, can't you see?*

We sit in the wet car and wait through a long cold five minutes for the police to drive up, for the kids to scamper away like white rabbits, for strained white apologies, the halfhearted kind, white lies. "It happens," the cop says, and that's true, but why is it true and should it be true? They've learned not to deal with guilt anymore, I think; they're satisfied just to tell the truth, no matter how dirty. Before Vietnam I used to think that they could do anything they wanted, that enough white men together could go anywhere in the world and make it change. But they can't. They're just as weak and worried as everybody else. Like the cop standing outside the car writing down our addresses in his report—his ears and nose and hands are blood-red, sore, cold; his nose is running and he can't even go inside; he's forced to stand here and question me.

"McMillan Street—that's a long way from here," he says. "That's in the city, isn't it?"

"Right."

"Did you—" He looks at Vera who has fallen asleep on my shoulder. "Did you-all have business out this way?"

I sigh and stare up at him with feelings midway between 1968 and exhaustion. Soon he starts writing again, no more questions.

The ride home is numbing, quiet. She doesn't want to talk and I never would force her. I take the slowest route back to town, streets with stop signs on every other corner.

The biggest part of the problem is that Vera insists on having other lovers. It wouldn't matter if we didn't run in to them so often—in the cafeteria, at the movies, out on the streets. It's damn uncomfortable for me, which Vera can't, or won't, understand, to be introduced to Tony and Ira and Paul, to be forced to shake hands with people I feel, by all rights, I should hate. And whenever it happens, a worse part always comes too, a man-to-man side of it, while Vera is running her mouth in the background about the latest phase in her art work, and he and I pretend to listen but really size up each other in our heads: *Does he do it hard? Does he even care if it hurts?*

I believe that I'm mature (aside from this) about what Vera wants and needs, and I wouldn't mind at all if it weren't for the ass-pain of having to deal with these guys. I don't want to know their names or what they do or how they look—it's enough that they exist. She gets into these crazy, bummy, depressed moods sometimes where she begins to chain smoke and stare out the window and make a lot of short phone calls. I can't do anything with her when she's like that—this I learned painfully a long time ago —so when it happens I let loose. It's not a prison, the thing Vera and I have. She disappears for a while when she needs to, and after a few days she turns up at my apartment, usually in the same clothes she was wearing, only dirtier, everything wrinkled. Sometimes we pull her dirty clothes off together, before we've hardly said anything, and I help her into a very hot shower and sit on the sink and we talk, not about where she's been, but other things. I give her credit, too, for having been straight with me about herself from the beginning. She called herself "a born whore," and told me enough stories to make me believe it. I'd only known her for ten or twelve days then, long enough to know that she wasn't what I'd always wanted but somehow came close, with her long straightened black hair that wasn't quite as long as I'd like it, and her strange, hybrid ideas that usually make her disagree with both sides in an argument.

She was faithful to me, so she says and I believe, for the first three months—though I hate that word, the involvement of "faith," but there is no other—maybe because I didn't give her much chance to stray. We met for lunch every day, I followed her around; she always seemed to be a couple of steps ahead, literally walking faster than me, and after a while I realized that maybe I was a nuisance and should stay at home some afternoons. After all, she had worked Downtown for months before she met me and apparently had girlfriends, though I never met any, with whom she liked to eat lunch. My friends say I spoiled Vera by being around so often during those first weeks. I let her see that there was nothing else in my life then, nobody she'd have to compete with.

I hate looking back and realizing that I was so blind and unaware. Everybody gives cues, even I give cues, that show things we really want from other people but can't ask out loud. It's simple: a woman wants a certain kind of man to do things in a given way so that she can be a certain kind of woman. It's obvious to me now that this is what Vera needed, as a woman, and that I just didn't come through. I was talking to her about love or some such shit, frustrating her with commitments she didn't need since love has never been a problem for Vera—it's always been obvious, understood. She says she loved me instantly because she sees love for what it is: a spider's web that binds us together but could be torn away if one of us really wanted: an easy, thin thing, love. She says we shouldn't bow to it, that there are more important things; I know that now; the two of us are falling apart, yet the love is still with us, just as complex as before.

It's amazing, too, the effect that women have on guys. I'm thinking of what Vera did to me versus what I did to her. I'm completely transformed, but Vera's still the same—proud, very proud, like a bird, though I don't mean flighty, not at all. A big, statuesque, coffee-colored bird—a hawk, I think. She took ballet lessons as a child; anyone can tell by the way she paces around the room very slowly and precisely, head up, as if for her even walking is a dance. Vera looks a bit like a bird too, though personally I didn't notice it until other people pointed it out. Her nose is straight and her eyes rather small and round. But she's beautiful, they all admit that I've got a beautiful bird.

Last month, an afternoon, she walked into the plant where I work part-time, a paint factory. The people who work there are grisly-faced old men and a few chem majors like myself from the College. It was perfect, like a movie scene: the foreman, up front, pointing her in my direction, the sudden silence of the others as Vera glided toward me down the center aisle, past rows of machines and gauges, their eyes trailing her. And when, finally, she reached my station, she threw her arms around my neck passionately, like a crazy woman, knowing that they were still watching, that this sort of triumph was the greatest gift she could give me. She gave me a perfect day. She'd never seen me in my uniform before because I always make sure to take a shower and wash the paint out of my hair before she comes over. She was mesmerized by it; she sighed, examining my badges and dirty shirt sleeves with her fingers while we talked. "Don't you dare take this thing off until I come over tonight," she whispered, smiling. She pointed to the thin red textbook jutting from her purse, *Comparative Revolutions*. "I want to fuck a worker tonight," she said.

I was surprised at first that none of the guys commented when she left, since I know that they were listening, envying. After a while their silence made me feel good, though—I understood it. Just as I understand now why several of them insist on introducing me to their frumpy wives and girlfriends who wait outside the gates after work. I have earned their respect because of Vera; they analyze my face when I meet their women, expecting certain signs of approval, the things a man gives to another man. And I don't resist: I pat these guys on the back when they need it and I tell them they're lucky; my smile is easy and convincing, like a clown's; I enjoy pretending that I'm one of them. Because nothing anyone says can convince me that I actually am like them or am one of them. Maybe I'm a bastard to be able to think this way, to be so detached, but that's how I am. I understand it too well— sometimes I think even Vera understands it—this man-to-man thing, the rivalries, the love. I'm bored by it. Yet, I'm sucked into it too, just like all the rest. I could fill a room with girls that I decided to pursue only because some other guy said he thought she was cute or that he had tried with her and struck out. Boring, stupid girls who couldn't understand that all I wanted from them was a victory, the knowledge that they'd given in, that I'd won. That's all. I didn't want to know them personally or add their phone numbers to my list or listen to their plans and ideas, because not a single thing about what we did together was real. And what I enjoyed most of all was later finding the guy who'd put me on to their trail, and telling him in some beautiful, subtle, indirect way, "Buddy, I just did what you couldn't." Once I'd gotten that—it was everything! I could not be defeated.

Vera is in rare form.

"You don't offer me a damn thing," she says over and over, and I agree, which unnerves her even more. I tell her to have her white boyfriends, to have anything she wants that makes her happy. I want her to be happy. For me this is love. But she can't accept this. She starts in on me.

"And you realize that you can't even fuck, Alvin, don't you?" she asks. "Anybody off the street could do a better job?"

"Then why don't you sleep with anybody off the street?"

"I do. I do."

"So why do you come back?"

"Pure kindness. What do you think you'd do without me?"

"You might be surprised." But this is the one attack she knows I can't face. I've always realized that I'm the one who needs, not Vera; but I don't enjoy bringing that fact to the surface.

"I tell Tony about you and we laugh. I tell him about how your feet perspire and you wipe them off before you get in bed, how you try to grip the sides of the mattress when you make love as if you're going to fall off. Tony and I laugh."

"Then go find Tony! Live with Tony!" Only Vera can bring me to the edge like this: I let her do it; she makes me dangle.

"You want to hit me now, don't you?" she says, grinning.

I back down. "I do not want to hit you."

"Yes, you do. You want to hit me, and I want you to, because then it will be over."

"It's already over."

"You're just saying that because you know it isn't true. If you don't do it now there will always be the chance that we'll get it together again. And you're so weak, Alvin, you live for little chances like that, chances to lick my shoes. Just so you can know where I've been walking. Places you'd be afraid to go yourself."

"What an incredible bitch! I hope you make Tony happy."

"Hit me, asshole," says Vera. She grabs my jacket from a chair and swings it above her head like a cape, or wings, dancing. She throws it in my face. "Come on, baby," she coos, stepping close.

I slap her face once, hard, with the back of my hand. "I love you *that* much," I say. "Don't come back."

"Alvin—"

I push her away, but she limps back, like a dog, rubbing against my arm. I push her away again.

She starts impersonating herself, batting her eyelashes coyly like a bird. I don't mention it, it's easier for her this way. "We can still be friends," she says, "can't we, baby?"

As always, I think I mean what I say. But with Vera, how can I know?

"Hell, no," I tell her.

Hell, no. I think.

*Donald Purviance*

## MAGICIANS

I wasn't certain exactly what I expected. Perhaps that an eminent sorcerer would notice me and immediately sense in me some indefinable aptitude for the mysteries. Magicians are very special people, and one should rightfully expect them to fathom potential that is invisible to the rank and file. The sensitive lines of my artist's face, the long, tapering fingers of a conjurer, the grace of my long-limbed gait, the secrets slumbering behind my full lashes. . . .

For hours, I sauntered back and forth through the district that the magicians were rumored to frequent. Any minute, I expected the tap on my shoulder. Even in the late hours, when the foggy dew enveloped me and rumpled my tailored officer's kit, I persisted. . . .

But the famous were elusive. Oh, there were the poseurs, the tedious hopefuls—they were conspicuous, but all were without that special quality that emanates from the truly gifted.

And there were the harlots, creatures who looked especially hideous in the glare of the gas lamps. How they longed to prey upon me. They clutched at me and picked at my medals as I passed by the small shops. Perhaps they only wanted a refuge from the coolness of the night, but how they rebuked me when I refused their advances. One painted crone said to me, "Do you think that you can do it any better with your hands, love?"

In a chophouse, I sought refuge from the disenchantments of my quest. The waitress was appallingly plain, with a pocked and ruddy complexion, fresh from the villages, I supposed. And she was obviously attracted to me; she fawned upon me, to the despair of the other patrons. But she could do nothing about the pitiful state of the fare; her special services and garnishments to my plate could not vitalize the greasy chops and bland cabbage. The proximity of the other diners with the attendant sour aromas and indelicate banter further depressed my appetite.

The lout at the table to my left was particularly ill-mannered. He seemed intent upon my every mouthful. I was extremely annoyed, and so bolted the entire meal—but even considering my haste, my manners bespoke of more restraint than displayed by the regular clientele. They devoured the garbage in great headfuls. I daubed at my mouth with a clean portion of a napkin, and it occurred to me that my expression displayed more than is publicly tasteful. I affected a noncommittal attitude.

"I've been watching you," the man at the adjacent table said. "I've been taking note of your bearing and the way that you handle your implements. Your breeding is apparent."

I cringed, expected next to have some quaint religious pamphlet spread before me. Or a woeful solicitation of funds for some vague emergency. It was my curse to be the constant victim of wayside madmen. So it had been in all of my travels since leaving my own country. I'd passed through terminals and watering places and had attracted the advances of prophets and hungry philosophers.

"You're rather young for the trenches," he said.

"But not for an aviator," I said. "Flying is a young man's avocation."

"Avocation? What is your customary role?"

"I have plans," I said.

"You are an officer," he said. "And you are obviously wearing the colors of a nation other than your own. Are you an idealist?"

"Not at all, but my comrades are idealists. I fly with an élite corps. Our fragile craft bear the sign of the Indian head."

"Ah, the Escadrille. But why do you risk your life without cause?"

"For me, the flying is cause enough," I said. "There is magic in it—the preliminary circling, the flirtatious maneuvers, the joining with one's opponent . . ."

"I suppose that you're on furlough," he said.

"I have been on furlough," I said.

"What plans do you have for a career after military service?"

"I want to be a magician," I said. I was shocked by his familiarity—and by my own candor concerning so private an ambition.

"I knew it," he said. "I knew that you were passing the time in this district because you wanted to be near the haunts of magicians. But one must be careful while in this district. There are many reprehensible types hanging about."

"Indeed," I said. "There is an absolute plague of prostitutes."

He laughed heartily, and then he ordered grogs for us, to stave off the vapors, I supposed. I studied his features. He was an Indian, just as I'd guessed when I'd first heard his high, staccato accent. I would have expected a moderate turban, but he was wearing a beret.

He joined me at my table when the waitress returned with the grogs. She glared at me when she served the drink. I took a sip of it and immediately felt a comforting warmth in my stomach.

"By the way," he said, "I happen to be a magician."

"You're a magician?" asked the lady sitting at the table to my right. I noticed that she was also dining on the cabbage and chops. The dish may well have been her favorite. She was ponderously obese.

"I certainly am a magician," he said.

"Oh, ducks," she said. "I think that your sort is the most interestin' types."

"Thank you, madam," he said, and then he turned to me again, asked where where I'd lived before military service. "What a coincidence," he said, after I'd told him. "I once performed there with a number of famous magicians, possibly a year ago, on the Chautauqua circuit."

I pinched my memory to recall the details of the show. At first, I failed to remember the Indian among the artists. Then I revived the image of a small stage assistant, brown-skinned; they'd vaporized him, cut him in twain, pierced him through with staves. . . . "I remember the show vividly," I said. "Your performance was a high point. . . ."

"Do us a trick, lamb," the lady at the table to my right said. The crowd pressed in, and the Indian performed cliché sleight of hand, astounded the rabble with obvious manipulations of cheap jewelry and worn decks of cards. They were loathe to allow him to terminate the performance, but their interest eventually flagged when he began repeating himself. As we were leaving the chop-house, I noted that he was oddly bowlegged. From squatting so often in the lotus, perhaps.

His rooms were small, overflowing with books and magic props. But the rooms were cozy and warm. I was impressed by the assortment of mementos casually scattered about on low tables. All of them bore inscriptions from the greats of the world of magic. Similarly, the pictures on the wall were all autographed—a wizard here, there a famous satanist, the genious Embalmer, the internationally known escape artist, the greatest illusionist. . . . The greatest illusionist was my idol. I also noted that there were several photographs of young doughboys.

We chatted. The Indian performed a few simple illusions as evidence of his mastery of the craft. I was unimpressed. He expounded on theories underlying the philosophies of the magical disciplines. I was bored, distracted by the pictures on the walls. I interrupted his ramblings and begged at length for anecdotes involving the personalities in the pictures, particularly involving the illusionist. He poured tiny glasses of exotic liqueur for us, then spoke of intimate friendships with the magicians. During a lull in the conversation, he came and sat on my lap.

I recalled conversations in the officers' quarters regarding the proper reaction in such a situation. I was supposed to feel indignation and rage, but I was more uncomfortable than enraged. I trembled, put up an arm to ward off the Indian's clumsy embrace. He immediately got to his feet, and I also stood. I was considerably taller than he, so that I looked down at the top of his head.

"I'm sorry," he said. "I misunderstood. Apparently, you are without experience in such matters. Did I offend you?"

"I suppose not," I said. He was standing near a lamp. He suddenly looked incredibly old and disgusting. There was the stink of the grave about him. His eyes were too viscid-looking within the wrinkled parchment of his face.

"Well, at least I didn't really touch you," he said. "It's just that I thought you wanted to be a magician."

"Are magicians required to indulge in that sort of practice?"

"It helps. Most of us do," he said, and he gestured toward the picture of the illusionist. "Your idol is absolutely notorious."

The little scum blasphemes, I thought. He is desperate and exaggerates. He knows nothing of their private inclinations. I pitied him. I picked up my greatcoat. "I must be getting back to the encampment," I said. "The ship sails tomorrow, and after the crossing, there still remains a long journey to the aerodrome."

"Perhaps you'll stop for a visit when the conflict is over," he said. "If you choose, you're welcome to stay here for a time when you return—until you've established yourself a bit."

He was pathetic. Ridiculous that he should consider himself on a par with the great magicians.

"Thank you," I said. "I'll keep you posted concerning my plans." I started for the door.

"Do some thinking while you're in flight," he said. "About the nature of magicians. You'll have some odd moments for it, in the intervals between the stupefying dives and the shellbursts at your wingtips. Take care of yourself."

I lingered for a moment at the doorway. "When I return"—I said—"when I return, do you suppose that the magicians will find me attractive?"

Judith Stephens

## MONSTER IN THE SEAS

I work in China Basin, which, starting just below the bridge, runs less than a mile to the water on the east side of San Francisco. In the mornings, as I pick my way over cracked sidewalks to my office, the air is heavy with the odor of coffee beans toasted by the ton. The light in China Basin exposes the seams of the buildings; through broken boards I see rotted beams and floors which, in places, merge with mud left by greasy water. Many offices like mine are tucked in with the refineries and warehouses. Business suits are almost as common here as overalls and work cottons. In South Park, where I take my lunch on sunny days, I sit with other secretaries and men who pass bottles in paper bags back and forth, taking long pulls, making halting jokes. Some of them come straight to the park to sit; others have failed that day to be taken on the work-list at some loading dock.

The law office is always undamaged when I arrive. Even in a big earthquake—1906 magnitude—we wouldn't stop working; we would have to keep the office open all night for all the personal injury complaints our clients would invent. The office is always there, always the same, ignorant of holidays, unshaken by any threat of natural disaster. In one of the most perilous cities on earth, it squats over a hamburger joint.

The grim bird paddles into my cubicle without knocking, his fist embracing his last evening's work, a wad of vague instructions in illegible handwriting.

"This is a rush!" he yells in his Brooklyn-transplanted-to-L.A. accent.

The grim bird is a pig, for whom, nonetheless, I maintain a surprising measure of affection. In addition to having the name Joab Gelbhammer, he is funny-looking. His looks are as appropriate to him in his adult state as the dandelions on a lawn. He is a dandelion among men and lawyers, impossibly himself, impossible to defeat; as a child his name and looks must have constituted a real social disability. He is rude, self-centered, and loud. His partner couldn't be more the opposite: handsome, distinguished Walt Madison. Playing Jewish lawyer is killing both men, Joab more obviously. I find myself wishing that it will kill them soon.

"You wanna know why I hire intellectuals? My office is crazy, disorganized. Still I hire intellectuals. Walt, you know what Walt said to me the other day? 'Why don't you hire a career secretary?' 'Because,' I told him, 'they are nothing more than poor white girls. Their class is such that being a secretary is a step up for them. They are dedicated workers, working for a pension, working until they get married. . . .'

"But they bore me, poor white girls do. I need intellectual stimulation around me. So that's why I hire intellectuals."

#### DOWN AND OUT IN BERKELEY AND WALNUT CREEK

"My ironing lady has a Ph.D. What does your ironing lady do?"

"My cleaning lady won the Pulitzer Prize."

"Mabel, you're gettin' a big right arm."

My name is Mabel. Early in my undergraduate career I earned my expenses by ironing the laundry of the more well-to-do than I. Joab is right. Being a secretary is a step up from paid domestic work. It is difficult for a woman graduate to get any kind of job. Thinking ruins you for typing; most office managers won't even consider a slightly fat female, let alone one with a degree. Joab is liberated, and he can also pay me less, since, as he reminds me, I am second-class help.

*Rosalie Fernandez* v. *Dr. Irving Jugular* in the famous case of the infected uterus, and the baby born dead. She was on her third husband and this was her fifth child, a boy, and her husband's first. When there wasn't any son, he reacted by moving back to Mexico where he had been born. He joined the army and went to

Yucatan. Yucatan is where the Mexicans send their black soldiers with the rationale that they can better cope with mucky jungle swamp and bugs and shadowy people skulking behind vine-tumbled pyramids. And so Rosalie wept and sued. But the case advanced slowly as the papers necessary to justice rode back and forth between the counsel on the ponderous tide of the law. She ate compulsively and slapped the children. The lawyers sent her *Interrogatories* and *Supplemental Interrogatories*. The opposing lawyers sent him, there in Yucatan, Interrogatories, written up with "plaintiffs" and "wherefores" and "hereinafters." He wrote back saying, "She, Rosalie, she is wife to me."

Joab is short, with bent shoulders, wide hips, a small-boned face, a large nose, and a very big mouth. He is a victim of the American dream, certainly, and maybe the Protestant ethic as well. He works like work is the only thing which keeps him from dying. He is successful, over and over again. He makes enough money to support the office and a couple of houses each, for his family and Walt's. But he piles on the work like a glutton pouring gravy over mashed potatoes. He never turns a client away even when there isn't a moment left on his calender for another appointment. Somehow he squeezes them in, between hectic and frantic, before dinner.

"Law offices. Hold the line a moment please. Yes, he's on another line would you like to . . . Law offices, hold the line. . . ."

". . . kicking around this office for weeks. You don't know; it's my life's blood! Why should you care? You have no dedication! If I had somebody around here who only cared! Everything leaves your head when you leave here. . . ."

Perhaps I am not really fond of him; maybe I only want to be. For Walt the money seems secondary also. If he were interested in money, as interested as Joab is, he would focus his mind enough to bill his clients, something which he hasn't done in months, or ever, as far as I know. He is a television lawyer; he has crisp, curly gray hair, sparkling blue eyes, firm chin. He is impeccable in the court scenes, perfect with the clients, always amiable. His conscience is written across his teeth. As I do not know his original family name, I have never seen the man behind the actor. Walt was the person who began the firm, taking Joab in as a partner. He does not respond to Joab or react to his antics. Does a man criticize the other side of himself?

"And do you know why I like to ski?"

Contacts. I bet he's the devil himself in a ski suit. Big, black, padded executive chair, ski poles, down the slope forty miles an hour, no turn signals.

"And we'll call this a . . . *comes now* the defendant and for a . . . says . . ."

*Jesus.*

My dream: a tall, square plastic trash can is central in my vision, half filled with orange blood, steaming. In it is a wadded carbon paper and a used-up piece of eraser tape. Down, way down below my eyes to the right, he's lying, the victim, with his black plastic frame glasses and his plump cheeks and diplomat suit. "My God. This time you've done it. This is Henry Kissinger. You can't use him this way. He has *talent.*"

I am tired, but I will survive this morning. I just need a transfusion for Henry.

"Are you going out for lunch? If you're going out for lunch . . ."

I'm starving, really starving, and I'm going to have a beer and a piece of pie and burp in the park and read and look at the birds crapping from off the olive tree. . . .

"Will you get the money from petty cash and get me a . . . let's see, tuna sandwich from the health juice bar if it's open and if it's not, will you . . ."

Get you a bird-poop sandwich from the health juice bar.

*Ann Thompson.* Annie Thompson. Will the heirs of Annie Thompson please step forward and for a cause of action plead.

"Law offices."

"Is Walt there? This Miz Thompson . . . Annie's brain wave . . . it flattened out. . . . Walt, the hospital just call and . . . they want to know can they . . . unplug the machines. . . ."

The machine is plugged into my ears. The voice blares and now drops to an after-lunch mumble. When it is plugged into me, my will is bypassed. A huge bird is sitting on my shoulders with his legs wrapped around my neck, and he's controlling my hands to make them type a letter to Santa Monica. The dictaphone wears on just one part of a brain, the part with words. It uses it all day, without bothering any of the rest of the mass—better to keep that asleep—so that at the end of a dictaphone day, all of the words are worn out. Any that remain are wasted ghosts in my head. Anything else in the jelly, anything at all that would normally have agitated it, is locked in or blocked out. I feel nothing with the dictaphone replacing my senses—no fear, no hate. My concentration is taken up with fuzzy spoken words, implied meanings, phrases clogging the back of my brain. My job is to pull the phrases out, making sure my fingers tap each letter of each word of each phrase in the correct order, so that he can grunt satisfaction at his hard day's work when I present him with the clean formal gold I have spun from the moldy straw he has given me. And all the time that I spin, Joab and Walt blare, mumble into their machines, dictating more. Or Joab yells and yells it's his life's blood. Not his. Not.

"What do you do? That woman just told me her daughter's brain wave flattened out. And should she tell them to turn off the machines? And should she tell the kids their mama is dead? What can I do? The Supreme Court . . . legal death. She's gone of course. But I had to tell her to leave them on, the machines . . . legally better. . . ."

QUESTION: And do you claim to have suffered injuries in the above incident? If you did, list each symptom, its duration, frequency, and treatment.
ANSWER: Yes. Severe headaches, lasting eight to nine hours, and an inability to push or pull or dance. Pains in my back, resulting from . . .

"Mabel! Come in here! This is a rush job!"

"Everything is a rush around here, Walt."

"Now goddam it, you come in here and sit down when I tell you to! When I say it's a rush, it's a rush! And I don't want any back talk out of you. Look at this letter. The bottom line is crooked where I put on the P.S., and you misspelled *pro duces tecum*. Now doesn't that look like bird poop?"

. . . pains in my back resulting from permanently tensed muscles. I was sitting in my bathtub, listening to the radio and playing with bubbles. A car crashed through the wall, tipping over the bathtub and causing me . . .

*Judith Stephens*

"My God, *why doesn't anything ever get done around here!*"
. . . over the bathtub and causing me to career awash headfirst through . . .

"Law offices. Yes, Mr. Gelbhammer is in. Who can I tell him is calling? Law offices, would you hold a moment, please? He's on another line. Law offices, may I help you?"
. . . career awash headfirst through the bathroom door, causing severe splintering.

QUESTION: Describe when you first saw defendant's automobile and how fast it was going when it struck.

ANSWER: I first saw the car as I was dangling nakedly wedged through the door. . . .

"Mabel! Type this letter right now! My God, I dictated this . . ."

"Law offices. Yes, he's right here, Mr. Mason."

". . . tape *four days ago! I could get disbarred!* Hello? How are you, Perry?"
. . . wedged through the door. It seemed to me that defendant's car began to bark, but I was dazed and could not be sure. I do not know how fast defendant's car was going or whether the brakes were on.

QUESTION: Describe whether defendant's car or your vehicle moved on impact, or after impact, and how far. Describe what part of defendant's vehicle came into contact with your vehicle. Describe how it was that you went through the door headfirst.

ANSWER: My vehicle, my bathtub, moved northwest . . .

"Mabel! Who's on the phone?"

"It's for Joab, Walt."

"Oh."
. . . my bathtub, moved northwest about four feet and tipped over. Front of defendant's car hit right rear side of tub, knocking off claw . . .

"Oh my God. This is terrible. *Why didn't these interrogatories get filed last week?* If I had somebody with dedication, she would stay until the work is done, no matter what. Just a little loyalty, that's all I ask."
. . . rear side of tub, knocking off . . .

"Law offices. No, he's gone to court. Would you like to speak to . . . We expect him back about four-thirty. I'll give him the message sir."

. . . claw foot.

"Mabel. Could you make some more coffee?"

. . . I was sitting in my bathtub on my feet. . . .

My chair has become agonizing to sit on. It is tiny, with rollers. The seat is padded, but the edge cuts into the back of my upper leg, shutting off circulation. My legs hurt. I can't rest my back; the chair is designed to keep me in optimum working posture, not for resting my back. I can't type while I'm resting my back. So I sit on my feet on the chair with my knees up beside my elbows. I propel myself around the office this way, from desk to desk, squealing and grunting, the rollers on the chair digging ruts in the rug. Most of the ruts run to the coffee maker. . . . knocking off claw foot. I was sitting in my bathtub on my feet, with my knees around my elbows, playing, I said, with bubbles. When defendant's car came into contact with my tub, it sent me sailing headfirst. I later hid behind the artichoke plant in the garden.

"You now, you're mature. You don't let your domestic problems screw up the office. What's that?"

"I'm putting an ad in the *Bay Guardian* for my ex-husband."

"He's still your child. He's still your child."

"He lives in a mobile home in Mendocino County. I don't mind doing him a favor."

"You're not telling me the truth. You still treat him like your child."

Lawyering bores Walt. He can't seem to keep his mind on it. He dictates incomprehensible letters:

"Take a letter to mumble Swinerton in . . . ah . . . lemme see . . . ah . . . and say 'Dear mumber' . . . commer . . . Wait. Look in the file. There should be a listing of three deeds ah lemme see . . . ah . . . And say Dear mumba . . ." He believes that he hires secretaries to do all the tiresome stuff. If only I could figure out which tiresome stuff, which case, and whether Mumba Swinerton is a client, lawyer, or simply a friend he is giving free advice to.

Walt does have his fun-loving side.

"There were these two old Jewish grandmas in New York and one of them runs up to the other and says, 'Mabel, didya hear the good news? The pope decided the Jews didn't kill Christ.' And the other says, 'The Jews didn't kill Christ? I wonder who did?' The first one pauses and says, 'I don't know. Maybe it was the Puerto Ricans.' The Puerto Ricans!" His blue eyes twinkle devilishly.

I feel exposed. San Francisco is a fragile city; it has perched its ponderously weighted ass on a trembling sandbar. The bridge dangles in the path of inland winds funneling down the river valleys leading to the bay. It jerks at its moorings as ocean storms blast it from the west. It may be any morning as I drive to work that the bridge will begin to jump and buckle wildly under me. I will just keep driving over the sickening, heaving pavement, trusting to some mysterious rule of physics that my car can ride and not fall. I will keep on driving until I reach the chasm and the water, or I will descend through fallen freeways to broken streets and a city flaming from its gasline veins.

I know how delicate my skin is. The heights are waiting to fall on me. I can see them, avalanches of granite and concrete and glass. The people scream through the streets, crash their cars into each other, into sudden fissures. A cable car breaks its tether, rushing down and down and sailing and falling on splintered humans already downed by the glass. The glass. I cry: How will I ever get home?

"Hey, Mabel. Didya hear the one about the Transylvanian grandmother?"

"Yes, you . . ."

"There was this Transylvanian grandmother, see. And she was telling her cute little grandchild how to fend off vampires—by holding up a cross, because everybody knows vampires can't stand crosses, right? So the little kid is in bed and wakes up with somebody coming in through the window and over to his bed and he sees that it's a vampire. So he holds up the cross in front of him and the vampire says, 'Oy, pupila, have you ever got the wrong vampire!'"

I can't finish my work. I am locked like an invalid to my chair, typing frantically, answering the phone, writing letters, transcribing, making files, hundreds of new files. I go out for sandwiches. My trashcan spills over with . . . Don't look. My pile of work recedes, surges up like a wave threatening to crush me, drown me. My spine is a tower in the wind, my muscles cables, pulling. I must finish this work now. I must finish it all today so that I will be able to get Henry his transfusion. He is dying. He generates only enough to barely breathe asleep, day after day while I finish all my little chores. He must have a transfusion soon; something is siphoning all his blood into my wastebasket.

Wrap me as a mummy lies, with tattered linen coming unstuck from my face. I am alone in here. I know my words are faint. I am alone and need someone to see that I am alive inside these bandages. Things are dank at first in tombs, but they get very dusty as the dead dry out. Can anyone hear me?

"Law offices. May I help you?"

The Transylvanian grandmother has crept up behind me. "How's your work load, Mabel? Are you pretty well caught up?"

I hold up my cross and his blue eyes twinkle and he smiles with his bottom teeth.

Out to sea, its contour obscured by the fog bank, something as yet unlit is moving. So far out is it that even its darkness is muted, its hugeness not to be believed.


To Whom It May Concern: I, Robert Jugular, M.D. hereby make my report. When I first saw the patient, she was comatose, and also in very poor condition. There is a slit in her gall bladder, neatly healing. Since her heart tends to stop every time we turn around, we have attached an electrical pacemaker so that the blood pumps around like it should. Or else the patient would die. Everything is in its proper place, but her lungs have ceased to function alone and she no longer seems to feel anything when we stick her with pins. When we noticed that she had no brain wave, we were tempted to turn off the machines. Instead we put plugs in her ears to keep the mush in.

"Take a letter to ah lemme see, I think it's Ed Sewell. And say: Dear Ed commer and say . . ."

"Speak louder, I can hardly hear you. This tape is worn out."

"I'm trying to tell you, listen. The bandages, my voice is weak, and the bandages."

"You know why I like to ski? It's nonverbal. You know, when I used to go out for lunch, I would take an hour and just walk around, sit in that little park, ride the bus to Union Square, just sit. It cleared my mind out you know? Like skiing.

"Well, the reason we eat lunch at our desks, see, is about a year or two ago, Joab discovered that if you eat lunch at your desk we can deduct the cost of the food from our Transylvanian grandmother as a business expense. So that's why I don't clear out my head anymore. Except on weekends."

"Law offices." Hold it just a minute, mister. That is not an island you see out there. That is the top of a head. And that is big black ape hair. Soon you will see the glowing orbs, greedily eyeing this whole city, ready, ready to start its demolition.

"Yeah, hello, this is Joab. Deposition? My client isn't here. You mean she isn't there? Oh my God. I was waiting for her. No, cancel it. We'll pay the reporter's fee. No, well, you see our main problem around here is secretarial. . . .

"Oh my God. I forgot all about that deposition. Those guys in that big office really must think . . . Hello, Rosalie? Listen, where are you? I've been waiting. I didn't call before because I thought you'd be here any minute. This deposition is very important. (That's why I forgot. If she'd have been here, I'd have remembered.) OK, dear, well, I don't know. They'll set up another one. I'll let you know. Gee, it's a shame you forgot. Bye, dear.

"Oh my God. *I could get disbarred. Clients* have no respon*sibility.* Look at this place, will you? What a crummy mess. You know what? Walt and *I donate* our services around here. You know that secretarial *help* takes up the major part of our office expenses? And office expenses take up 60 per cent of what we make? Why do I work? You just come in here and collect money. You don't worry about it when you leave. *You don't care.* And the clients! I take poor people, people who would have no access to good legal help if I didn't take them. And what thanks.

*"My God,* I don't know what to do. *I'm trapped.* I built this office up and I take it with me when I leave. All I want to do is lie on the beach, but I can't dump this office. My main problem is *secretaries.* I can't get a secretary to care!"


On the line of the ocean's horizon in the west, two eyes blink thoughtfully, taking in the city. One might almost think they were two suns setting in the red haze of the Pacific. They are the eyes of an ape, an ape at least a thousand feet tall. He is not standing as I first thought, with his monstrous feet in the ooze beyond the continental shelf, walking in. No, I think he will not just stroll in, stamping as he nears the land, shaking and smashing the anthill city as if he were stubbing his great toe. I think he will not plant his big black ape foot in the middle of the bay—a puddle in his path—swamping the docks and marinas that ring it, ripping out the fragile bridge gates from his chosen course. That ape is sitting, much closer than I imagined, watching, with his knees up around his elbows. He waits.

Joab is lounging in his chair, snuggled into its vinyl-covered billows.

"I can see you're suffering. I can see it on your face. This work gets to you, doesn't it? You walk in here and the look on your face is awful. But I need you. I need intellectuals around me for the stimulation. You understand, don't you? So don't suffer in my office. I don't want to see you suffer. Don't you realize that as a legal worker, you have the power to *destroy me?*"

Yes, yes I do.

At the bottom of the stairs, the air is stale with the breath of the last cigar to leave last night. Feel very good. Carpet nubble gritty, grit on knuckles. Shoulders bang each on walls going up. Fire door. Push with head, door open. Hall clear. Feel good. Squeal. Air is good in chest, big chest. I am strong. Open door. Air smells bad in here. My hair is black in hall. Kick damn door shut. This place is mine.

Old desk is better to sit on than chair. Typewriter hungry? Have banana, I will peel. Here. Roll into mouth. Nice, eh? Hum and burp. Leave rest on spinning ball. IBM Selectric ball, banana-cock angle. Dictaphone want juice. Plug in wall. Too much juice; ear-piece puddle. Who needs coffee? Adding machine. Add faster. More coffee.

"Who? Who? who who who who?" Feel good. Beat on chest. Big air, big booming. Good to dance. Dance on desk. Telephone is squealing. Kick it.

"Madison and Gelbhammer. This is the answering service. May I help you?"

Squeal.

"Answer, please. Who's there? May I help you?"

Squeal. Grunt loud in phone. Squeal and squeal.

"Who's there? Who? Who? Answer, please."

Files. Big files. Litter files. Jump. Files snag hands, stick between toes. Taste bad, dry. Rip files. Throw them. Words come off sheets, slide on carpet. Sticky words, "offer to compromise," "guardian ad litem," "attorney of record." These words come off. Sticky black mess. Letters float in air, and words. "And each of them" "defendant" "plaintiff" float and stick to others and come apart. Sneeze. Sneeze. Nose does not like.

Tiptoe on big toes. Quiet. Copy machine is here all alone. Careful, no hair on rug. No one will know I visit here. Copy machine. Pee in toner bottle, no drips. Yellow copies. Tiptoe out.

Typewriter is sick. Type banana. Make words on wall. White out. Taste is thick. Spit. Stays on lips, on chin. Nasty. Pour into telephone.

Rest. Office of Joab. I will have music from radio, sit in big soft chair. Eyes are tired. What's this? Dictaphone recorder. Noisy. Hurts. Make it quiet.

Walt's big padded chair. How to muffle two dictaphones? Put in chair. Still noisy. Mummbly-blat. Squat. Ahhh. Big pile. Eat many bananas. Yellow pile. No one will hear them again. Dead. Buried. Quiet.

Someone comes to door. Scamper to little cage. Sit on silly chair.

"Who's here? Oh my God. Who? *Who?*"

Roll chair on mat, back and forth. Chair squeak. Eyes burn. Air is red. Sun sets in my eyes. Here he comes! Hop down. Walk proud. I am strong and big. Hair is stiff on head. Hands itch. Knuckle walk, stiff arms. Very strong.

"Who?" Scream. "Who? Who?"

Grin big at this Joab, he who loves thinking workers. Not lover of big yellow fangs. I speak big. . . .

My name is Mabel. I work in China Basin. I destroy the city every time I cross the bay.

# II  MONOLOGUE AND INTERVIEW

*Talent is extremely common. What is extremely rare is the willingness to endure the life of a writer. The problems are physiological, among other things. Sitting still is something the body was never meant to do for any length of time. Enduring solitude is something the human mind was never intended to put up with for very long. Writers have no one to talk shop to. The work itself is exceedingly tedious. It is like making wallpaper by hand for the Sistine Chapel.*

from "An Authors' Symposium for Congress,"
KURT VONNEGUT

*George Garrett and Stephen Kendrick*

## *HOW IT IS; HOW IT WAS; HOW IT WILL BE*

1.

Let's begin with two quotations, epigraphs and texts. Some notions expressed by other writers earlier in this century. Ideas which have sometimes been very helpful to me and, I hope, may possibly be helpful to other writers. Call them texts for a writer's wall calendar or for posters. Sometimes I think if I had room enough, skin enough, I would have these tattooed on me, fore and aft, so as never to be able to forget to remember them.

One comes from William Faulkner, written for an introduction to an edition of *The Sound and the Fury,* an introduction which was never used. He mentioned the relative and deceptive ease with which his first two novels—*Soldier's Pay* and *Mosquitoes*—had been published. Followed by the seriously disappointing difficulties he faced in finding any publisher willing to publish his third novel, the first of the great Yoknapatawpha series, which was finally published in truncated form as *Sartoris,* and, not long ago and posthumously, published more or less, as he wrote and wanted it to be, as *Flags in the Dust.* Faced with crippling frustration, he found a way from there to freedom. "One day," he wrote, "I seemed to shut a door between myself and all publishers' addresses and book lists. I said to myself, 'Now I can write.'" The first thing he wrote was *The Sound and the Fury,* beginning one of the most remarkable explosions of creative power in this century, resulting, in a very short time, in the writing and publication of *As I Lay Dying, Sanctuary, These 13,* and *Light in August.*

The other statement comes from Joyce Cary, in the Preface to the Carfax edition of *The Horse's Mouth.* He is describing some of the qualities of Gulley Jimson which serve him well as an artist: "He is a creator, and has lived in creation all his life, and so he understands and continually reminds himself that in a world of everlasting creation there is no justice. The original artist who *counts* on understanding and reward is a fool."

### 2.

What a Successful Agent tried to teach me: "Listen! You gotta understand. This is a *business!* Art is for kids."

### 3.

A couple of years ago I gave The Talk for the first time. More or less by accident. I had to fill in, on short notice, for somebody else at a writers' conference and give a talk on the general and assigned topic of "The Writer and the Publishing Scene." A blank check, really, and fair enough. About which, frankly and obviously, I didn't (still don't) know much. Of course, I've been writing all my life, and my first book, a collection of poems, was published twenty years ago. I've been writing and also editing books ever since then—fourteen of my own so far and editor or coeditor of sixteen others. Not counting paperbacks and foreign editions, this has involved my dealing with eighteen different publishers. On the other side, I've worked as editor or coeditor for four literary magazines. I was poetry editor for the (now defunct) Contemporary Poetry Series of the University of North Carolina Press. And, off and on, I've been a judge, reader, part-time editor, advisor, consultant, etc., for a dozen or so university presses and a couple of commercial houses. Nothing special or unusual in all that. I can think of any number of writers of roughly my own age who have been much more actively engaged in many aspects of publishing.

All this is common enough. Promises no expertise or special knowledge. Of course, I have observed the scene—from a distance and safe in the certainties of relative ignorance. I have read what I could, have talked to a good many people who are professionally involved in publishing, and have listened to some of the professionals in public, speaking alone or on panels, discuss modern publishing. Also I might as well confess that my wife once worked in publishing and was good at her job. She knows about the business, but she honestly doesn't think it is a very interesting subject. "Publishers are not very interesting people," she says.

In that original and accidental Talk, I called upon my own fairly typical experience and limited knowledge, which had allowed me to form some opinions and come to some tentative conclusions, and I succeeded in depressing everyone who was present. Which was exactly the opposite of my intention. I had hoped that a brief and unblinking look at what the translators of the Geneva Bible (1560) called "hard places" would, insofar as it was true, work toward the goal of freedom. Freedom of the spirit seemed an obviously desirable goal for any artist. I hoped that shedding some cheap veils of illusion and dispensing with certain common misconceptions would serve to help young and beginning writers—in fact any serious writers, for one distinct characteristic of the contemporary literary situation is that, with the noted exception of a very few celebrated stars, we are all of us always only beginners with each and every new work—to concentrate more completely on whatever work is at hand without dissipating precious time, energy, faith, hope, and sacrifice on the altars of false gods. My audience didn't get that message. I seemed to lose them somewhere among rocks and hard places. The happy ending, out of the wilderness and into the garden, couldn't displace the prevailing mood of depression.

Well, I thought, that's that. Never again.

But ever since then I have been asked to give what amounts to the same Talk in a variety of versions and situations and places. Sometimes in the company of editors, who, to my surprise, seemed to settle into the same state of depression as everyone else. I expected to be challenged and maybe to be corrected by these professionals. Instead the usual reaction was a long sigh, followed by the wish that I had talked about something more cheerful and uplifting. Followed, finally, by an invitation to impose the same experience on some other unsuspecting group. People nowadays seem to want to be depressed. They are willing to come together in modest crowds to cultivate their feelings of communal gloom. And that depresses me. I would much rather be cheerful and

uplifting. So, in order to exorcise these drab demons and to re-
duce The Talk to the plain neutrality of printed words on a page
(in the strong hope that thereby I may never be asked again to
deliver the sad news) I've decided to put it in writing; not The
Talk itself or even an imitation of the tone and style of it, but anyway the notions and arguments, unadorned, without camouflage
or concealment, in a brisk and fragmentary form.

Because, like the late William Faulkner, I want to shut the door
and write. But first I want to show how reasonable it was and is
and will be to do just that.

4.

Later, the trade came more and more into the
hands of an inferior class, until the great
majority of those who dealt in books were
tradesmen pure and simple, regarding their
business solely from the point of view of
immediate returns.

—R. B. McKerrow in *Shakespeare's England*

I lost by your last book, and you know there
is many a one that pays me largely for the
printing of their inventions, but for all of
this you shall have 40 shillings and an odde
pottle of wine.

—*The Returne from Parnassas*

In one sense the agent was right. Publishing in the United States
(which is the only kind that matters much for American writers)
is a business. Just that. Just another business. It is not, by any
standards at all, a very good business or a very important one;
but, anyway, it runs along and is run more or less like any other
contemporary American corporate enterprise. Another piece of
the same pie. Publishing has pretty much the same virtues and
vices as all the others except that it is generally a little less
efficiently and thoughtfully managed.

Publishing reflects with accuracy most of the changes which

have taken place in American business and society in this century. Originally small and oriented toward the goals of a modest, cumulative profit and depending on the slow, almost organic growth of a reputation for responsibility, reliability, and integrity, it is now part and parcel of the universal, conglomerate system of consumer business aiming for quick, large, profitable returns . . . or none at all. Feast or famine. Publishing has become, by and large and despite backlists, etc., a brief, seasonal, short-term affair. Today the average life of a commercially published book is about sixteen weeks from the date of its publication. After which it is most likely to be remaindered. Most likely these days it will be pulped. The paper is the most valuable part of the book.

What has all this got to do with me? you ask. Wait, I say, wait and see. But I will say one thing here and now. The writer is part of this system, like it or not. Whenever you submit anything for possible publication, you are tacitly supporting that system.

One of the things this shortened life span for most books means is that most contemporary writers, like their publishers and unlike either the writers or the publishers of a generation or two ago, cannot enjoy the luxury of a *reputation*. Very little is cumulative anymore. Each work, each season is a beginning from scratch. Which also means that, allowing for a very few exceptions, all our writers, young or old, experienced or beginners, are equal.

There are about 40,000 titles published in America a year. The place of the serious writer of poetry, fiction, and even non-fiction is a very small one. A tiny and, in terms of measurement by numbers and percentages, an almost negligible part of the picture. Here is Kurt Vonnegut ("An Authors' Symposium for Congress," June 18, 1975) saluting, with hearty optimism it seems to me, first novelists: "There are 2,700 colleges in this country, and out of them will come 150 first novels this year. Here's lots of luck to would-be writers! Of the 150 first novels published, all will be commercial flops, virtually." Put on your thinking caps. Out of 40,000 titles published about 150 will be first novels. How important are first novels in the publishing business? My handy-dandy Texas Instruments calculator informs me that first novels represent .375 per cent of the business.

Of course, in all fairness and justice, publishing in America, the whole thing, is a tiny, almost negligible part of the economy. Some recent figures show that the annual gross business of all American publishing is $3.2 billion. A billion of anything, soybeans or paper clips, is a lot. But in the big picture $3.2 billion is not all that grand or extraordinary. Retail shoplifting in America, what they call "shrinkage," is estimated to be a matter of $6.7 billion a year. A smart aleck might infer that publishing is (in dollars and cents) about half as important as retail shoplifting.

The U. S. Chamber of Commerce estimates, conservatively, that white collar crime (fraud, embezzlement, tax evasion, etc., including, of course, some white collar crime in the publishing business) amounts to $40 billion a year, a little over ten times the impact of publishing. It is, as they often say, all a matter of priorities.

Take some other numbers for the sake of argument and perspective. One of the major and most profitable parts of American publishing is the publication and sales of textbooks. It is a $500 million a year business and offers some opportunities for real profit to publishers. Interestingly enough, this figure is almost exactly equivalent to the estimated annual cost of vandalism in our public schools. And the vandalism is growing faster; will soon surpass textbooks as an expense in public education.

Nobody I know of seems to be able to come up with any accurate estimate of the net, the profit of American publishing. However, it is safe to say that it is piddling in any serious comparative sense. It is safe to say that if all the publishers got together and pooled and invested their $3.2 billion in ordinary savings accounts, they would all earn much more money than they do now.

The earnings and salaries of the top management of the most successful publishing houses are considerably below those of the second-string level of corporate executives. Editors, even the most senior, get very modest salaries (in a relative sense), sometimes beefed up by fringe benefits and expense-account perquisites.

What all this adds up to is that there is no big money in publishing. Not for anybody. Least of all for the lumpen proletariat—the writers. Their part of the action is inconsequential. Except for (again) a very, very few, most of the writers make a good deal less from their endeavors than, say, part-time help in any given publisher's mailroom.

It is a fact that no serious writer of fiction or poetry has or will have even the ghost of a percentage of a chance of earning a living by and from writing alone. (Most of the pop writers don't either.) Maybe John Updike is an exception of a kind, but the only serious writer in this century to create and leave a real estate, worthy, say, of a doctor or a lawyer or a reasonably successful corporate executive, was John O'Hara. That sort of capitalistic accumulation would not be possible now. And even among those already noted, the very, very few, none could be defined as really wealthy, in terms of earnings derived from the exercise of their craft or art, except in comparison with other writers. Last year, for example, Kurt Vonnegut, Phillip Roth, and Joseph Heller were teaching part-time. Just like the rest of us. One is at least entitled to doubt that any of them were doing this just to pass the time or for the fun of it or because they prefer the company of the young or because they love the academic life.

All of which means that any sane and reasonable writer must be able to disregard almost completely the economic aspects of the craft. These not only can, but also should, be ignored.

In his entertaining blast against the publishing business, *The End of Intelligent Writing,* Richard Kostelanetz defines the relationship of the writer to the publisher as being closely modeled on the relationship of sharecropper to landowner. But there is a happy difference. In fact the writer need not be helplessly beholden and humble in the presence of any ole Massa in the publishing business. If the writer works for a living (in any other enterprise than publishing), chances are he or she will be making as good a living as anybody with whom he or she will ever have to deal. Wallace Stevens, poet and insurance executive, probably earned more than anyone in American publishing.

Economics is boring to most writers. But it is worth thinking about if only briefly. Especially in America where, for the first time in our history, we have a considerable and growing number of young writers who are not even modestly well-to-do and who come from families which are not well off. This is one of the great sources of strength and energy in our present literature. But for survival and, equally important, freedom as writers, these young writers must not delude themselves that writing itself offers a way to wealth or even much "upward mobility." They must either find the ways and means to earn a living in other ways, or the writing of fiction and poetry in America will soon be left exclusively (like a country club or a hunting preserve) to the lucky, the well-born, or the well-to-do who can afford to cultivate the habit.

Conclusions:

Publishing is a business. In general business terms it is a trivial and unimportant business. By the same general business terms (only), the people engaged in the publishing business are trivial and unimportant people.

The art and craft of writing is not trivial. It is not a business at all and has not been so for most of this century.

The American economy could get along just fine, probably even thrive and prosper, in the absence of any publishing whatsoever. If all the publishing houses vanished and all the people working for them went on welfare tomorrow, it would make no appreciable waves.

Serious writing, the absence of which would be a national disaster and a national shame, is outside of the network of the economy.

By definition, then, serious writing is not a matter of dollars and cents.

Forget about dollars and cents.

5.

Bureaucracy does not rest upon honor; it rests upon ambition—a stronger force.

—Tom Braden in *The Washington Post,* November 29, 1975

A word about the people, about the personal relationship of writers and publishers.

First the writer. Above and beyond a passionate love affair with words, which passion identifies the writer, writers are also supposed to be devoted celebrants of the active imagination. Which is why the writer must continually labor and strive to push his/her imaginative capabilities to the limits of consciousness. One characteristic of an active, engaged imagination is the ability (from time to time) to conceive of other creatures—animal and vegetable and even mineral—as something more than, if not other than, objects. The active and honest imagination recognizes, among other things, that there is a mystery at the center of every other human being which in some way corresponds to the mystery at the center of the imagining self. Which mystery cannot be fully known or named or defined, but can be felt and acknowledged in awe and with wonder.

Two of the greatest dangers to the purity of the imagination are, first, the common delusion that the wounds and joys of others may somehow be possessed (sentimentality) and, second, the notion that one's own deepest feelings may be willfully imposed upon others (rhetoric).

The power of an active and honest imagination (an original impulse which must constantly and consciously be tested and disciplined and trained) is urgently important in the context of the corporate, institutional social world in which we have to live. Institutions do not have any imagination. The imaginations of institutional people are strictly limited. To the extent that people think and act institutionally they are forced to deny the imaginative impulse.

In their dealings with publishers, writers should be able to recognize that they are dealing with institutions through institutional people. There is not much chance or occasion for a genuinely imaginative encounter.

It has to be assumed that the desires, both practical and personal, of people in publishing are in large part bound up with the institutions which they serve. Which is to say that beyond the level of civilized amenity and the most perfunctory and rudimentary lip service, they cannot be seriously concerned with art in general or you in particular. Motivated, as they must be, by simple self-interest, by the hope for survival within the institution or a similar institution, and by the desire for such power, privilege, and rewards as the institution may be able to confer upon them, they have, paradoxically, already surrendered at least part of the freedom which is necessary to achieve these ends and to enjoy them. The surrender may make them comfortable; for freedom is often extremely uncomfortable. But, because they cannot wholly stifle the imaginative impulse, it cannot make them happy with their work or themselves.

Thus the potential for freedom enjoyed by the writer is, inevitably, offensive to the institution and to the institutional servant.

Which is why the relationship between the writer and the publisher, no matter how friendly and polite, is always an adversary relationship.

As to the nature of the institutional people one must encounter, the best assumption is that one will meet with just as many (or as few) knaves and fools in publishing as there are in any other contemporary institution. To the extent that our society is corrupted and corruptible, so are they.

The edge that the publisher has is institutional. The writer, as writer lacking an institutional armor, must depend upon imagination. Which can at least offer some solace and counteract the gnawings of self-pity when he loses. Which can also check the excesses of pride and vanity if and when he wins.

6.

Fame is but the breath of people and
that often unwholesome.

—An Elizabethan proverb

—Never mind all that, some voices say. If not for fortune, then for fame.

And how shall we define fame? Fanny Foxe, Johnny Carson, Linda Lovelace, Squeaky Fromme, and John Dean, for example, are better known to more people than any American writer living or dead.

—Oh, that is only notoriety, celebrity.

I agree, but question, in passing, whether there is or can be or will be anything which can be called fame, other than some form of notoriety or celebrity. I question whether fame is a worthy possibility in our time. We have public figures. There are a very large number of people who can be called public figures. Very few of them, at any given time, are writers.

—What about Norman Mailer and James Dickey and Erica Jong?

What about Joseph Hergesheimer and Floyd Dell and Lizette Woodworth Reese?

Seriously, there is nothing inherently wrong with being a public figure. And nothing wrong with giving appropriate attention to at least some writers who have produced significant and influential works. Since we are part of the American scene, we, too, must have our own stars, celebrities, and public figures. There is a question, however, aside from social habits and models, whether or not a literary star system bears any relationship not only to the facts—small public, small marketplace—but also to the reality of contemporary American letters. There may well be some small value for publishers and, as well, to readers. Celebrity is an important factor in marketing books. Publishers are trying, more or less, to sell books. It is a little easier to sell the books of stars. Not a whole lot easier. For instance, in poetry we are talking about the difference of a few hundred copies between the sales of a James Dickey and those of an unknown. In both cases there is a huge gap, several thousand copies in fact, between either Dickey and the unknown poet and the magical and mysterious Break Even Point where the book may be said to have paid for itself and can therefore be considered as something other than a kind of advertising or conspicuous consumption on the part of the publisher. The difference in sales between the poems of Mr. or Ms. Unknown and James Dickey (or anybody else alive except, say, Rod McKuen) is not very much. They are much closer to each other than to any point of breaking even.

Not many people or institutions purchase books of poetry in the United States. A rough estimate of the average sale of a book of poems by a commercial publisher in the United States (university presses do a little better because they are able to keep their books in print for a while) is about 600 to 800 copies in hardcover, 1,000 to 1,200 in paperback. There are more published poets than that. See *A Directory of American Poets,* which lists more than 1,400 poets and is far from complete.

I often wonder how many of these poets actually buy books of poems. Not many, it is clear. If all the people who write poems and submit them for publication purchased, say, four books of poetry a year, the whole situation would be greatly changed.

How is this relevant to the subject of fame, or, anyway, that more modern term—recognition?

Well, I have suggested that there is, in fact, a community of poets. If you include serious writers of fiction and so forth, it is a very large community indeed; unique, in its size, range, and variety, in all literary history, as far as I can tell. The only analogy I can think of is the situation in England in the closing years of the sixteenth century. Our great masters of the earlier part of this century, even though most were not recognized as masters until our own time, lived and worked in a very different world. One might conclude that fame of some sort was a rational goal for them. I suggest that it is not a sane wish for a writer in our time.

Looking objectively at the scene, most people would agree that the kind of recognition which passes for fame today is largely arbitrary and accidental. It is more Calvinistic than Catholic. Some are elected and some are damned. Good works have very little to do with it. It is a matter of faith and out of the writer's hands.

There are others, with their own (sometimes honorable) vested interests, for whom there is at least some rationale in preserving a star system.

Critics and reviewers, for example, being primarily concerned with their own fame and fortune as critics and reviewers, are not often free to be pioneers. Discovery and rediscovery, creating or resisting fashions and trends, are not their strong suits. It is about enough to expect them to keep up with such trends and fashions as there are. They are essentially conservative because they have to be.

Teachers are interested in literary works which can be taught in fifty-minute periods during a sequence of fifteen-week semesters and twelve-week quarters. And they are mainly concerned (or anyway, ought to be) with works which are teachable and from which young students can learn something. In a more practical way they are also limited by the availability of works in relatively inexpensive editions. It is easier, in those terms, to teach a book by John Updike or Kurt Vonnegut, whose works are in print in paperback editions, than it is to teach works by, say, Wright Morris or Joyce Cary, most of whose works are not. Of course, sustained exposure in the classroom may not be entirely beneficial to any writer's reputation. But the absence of available choices, and, for beginning writers, of the fullest possible range of normative models, does not seem likely to lead toward new directions, or, for that matter, toward the legitimate academic goal of seeking to preserve the best of the past.

Then there are the editors, overwhelmed by the tidal waves of manuscripts coming to them from the huge, growing community of writers. Aside from the paramount practical matters, the editors, one assumes, are interested in quality. Because of the nature of things, and the pressures of time, quality must be easily recognized. Even that which is to be called experimental or avant garde must be quickly identifiable as such. What this means is that even the most adventurous editors have to be profoundly conservative. They can only recognize qualities which they have seen before.

Thus none of the professionals can help the writer much. Elected or damned or simply ignored, you are all by your lonesome, all alone. Recognition can be given or denied, but neither the gift nor the denial can add one cubit to your stature.

I sometimes think that the most celebrated writers I know of are really worse off than all the others. In the bright moments of success, they must be sorely tempted to believe there is some rational system at work, that virtue is rewarded and vice is punished. The comfort of that illusion renders them singularly vulnerable to misfortune. The Elizabethans called people in that position the slaves of Fortune. And they pitied them.

I also have the impression that the appetite for recognition, like the hunger for love and approval, is never satisfied. There isn't enough recognition in the world to satisfy even one cultivated appetite.

Conclusions:

Forget about dollars and cents except as a means to survive and to follow the hard road of your chosen craft.

Forget about recognition except to toughen and train yourself to bear the equally dangerous times when it may be given or withheld.

The only sane and reasonable thing for the writer to do is to concentrate, as much and as deeply as possible, on the art and craft of writing. That devotion is the source of the writer's freedom. Though the writer works freely and alone, there are nevertheless certain obligations which are not isolated, but communal. Dedication to the art and craft of writing brings to the writer the knowledge, a joyous knowledge, that he or she is part of a real community of artists, living and dead, known and unknown. Whether the writer succeeds or fails, he or she is nevertheless a full member of that ghostly community and has an obligation to it.

Secondly the writer has an obligation to the reader. An imaginary reader. Not an audience or a public; for no matter how many people may freely choose to read or ignore the writer's work, that work is addressed to one reader. The deepest obligation is to the one imaginary reader. An obligation to use all the resources of the liar's craft not to cheat, not to deceive or delude the reader. And not merely to depend upon technical competence or even virtuosity. Rather to employ all craft in order to engage the active imagination of that reader so that there may be a meeting of sense and mind and spirit, an awareness of the center of mystery from which imagination draws its human energy.

What this means is that the writer's work, in whatever shape and form, must be worthy of the attention of the imaginary reader. Who deserves more than most of us are able to give. Who should not be challenged by any less than all that we can offer.

—George Garrett

TO PRESERVE THE CHILD: A TAPED INTERVIEW WITH GEORGE GARRETT BY STEPHEN KENDRICK

SK: Let's talk about some things young writers like myself need to know and yet seem to be ignorant of. You've taught at several schools over the years—have you noticed a real separation between your students' expectations and the reality that you sense after twenty-five years in the fray?

GG: I think that the separation between expectation and the hard facts is basic to education in anything. Maybe I'm just getting old, but I think that expectations and illusions seem to be a part of youth and built into being young. We make choices about as whimsically as in "The Road Not Taken." In a way, that's kind of too bad because that means that frequently the information—if not the wisdom—of one generation cannot be passed on.

SK: You mean the new generation just won't listen?

GG: It seems to be beyond the capacity of human imagination. They can listen and absorb notions intellectually, but it's like Freud saying that the one thing people can't imagine is their own death. Well, I think there are a lot of things that people can't imagine until they have to.

SK: You mean like literary death?

GG: Yes. . . . The problem here is that there's such a divide between my generation and the previous generation of writers in America. It's very, very different than it was in the time of Faulkner, Fitzgerald, Steinbeck. This being so, most of the lessons that we would have learned and perhaps may have learned are today inapplicable except in a general way. This is how the use of the past works in a strange way. You can see how things that have come to pass were beginning then, but only retroactively. They didn't see these things happening. They simply assumed the future would be an extension of the past. Therefore, some of the tin drums that I am banging on, saying "You've gotta recognize the facts of life; it's gonna help you"— some of these things may not be true at all in a very short time. It may be possible that beyond our imagining there may be ways, methods of publication that no one has really conceived of yet, that may change everything quite drastically. But it doesn't look like it's going to (laughter).

SK: Then how can a student plan ahead? How can he find a niche to survive within? What are some of the favorite niches of the writer?

GG: Well, of course the prime niche right now is in Academe. One of the thrusts of the monologue was to point out that every young writer should find a way to earn his living.

SK: It seems to me that writing is a wildly impractical business.

GG: That's right.

SK: Then why can't students go about it in a businesslike way? It seems to be the only way that they can survive.

GG: I can't really answer that. The only thing I can figure is that the notions, a) the idea of practicality in thinking ahead that far, and b) the imaginative notion that one will ever get old both seem to be beyond most people, including writers. In a sense, writers are deceiving themselves. The only things they ever read about writing are news stories and these all deal with great success. There are enough of those to deceive those who have no concept of the whole picture. Thus, they don't have enough accurate information to base their decisions on. And beyond that, it seems that it is harder than ever for young people to plan ahead, whether or not they are writers. Unlike writers of a generation ago, young writers, if they want to reach their goal, will have to make certain preliminary psychological adjustments because these goals have now become statistically unlikely. What is odd to me is that young college writers— and about 99.9 per cent of all writers these days are college educated—are quite able to deal with deans of students, bursars, and registrars, but become extremely naive and ignorant when dealing with publishers. This is one reason, I think, why even publishers get depressed when I give The Talk. They realize that there is some obvious truth to it, even if they do not want to admit it. It's like someone going around the streets saying: "Listen—you're gonna die!" It's okay to do it in a cheerful form, like commercials, when they tell you that you only go "round once in life; live it with gusto." Everyone knows this, but they don't want to admit it. They would prefer not to believe it.

SK: Then why can't writers institutionalize themselves to deal more effectively with the institutions of publishing?

GG: There are writer's organizations. But the problem here is that you have to have some product that a lot of people want. The day may come when serious fiction and poetry are not only desirable, but necessary, to a large number of people. But right now, for example, the audience of serious contemporary poetry in the United States is less than a thousand people. A lot of them are probably poets. If all the poets writing were part of the readership, it would double the audience. And we know that the audience for serious fiction numbers from about three thousand to about twenty thousand.

SK: These are the people who actually go out and buy a hardback book?

GG: Yes. But we don't know if they read it or not. . . .

SK: You can't count people who rely on libraries or who are students and can't afford to buy hardcovers?

GG: Even libraries are having to cut back on the numbers of books they can buy. Here we have a product with no real clout, so there isn't any point in unionization. You might have a club—on the theory that misery loves company.

SK: Why is it that the market for short stories has just about dried up? Isn't it ironic that the market that young writers are most suited for and most need is completely closed to them?

GG: That's the thing they do best in fiction. Because they either don't have the time or the material to concentrate on a novel, which is, after all, a hard thing to do. The market *has* dried up, outside of the literary magazines, of course. Some critics say that people's needs for fiction have been transferred to television and movies, where they see lots of narrative, cop shows, cowboy shows, and domestic soap operas. Alfred Hitchcock says that the closest literary form to the movie is the short story, not the novel.

SK: Let's talk about first novels. What is the most realistic thing that someone can expect in terms of the twin "f's" that you were talking about: fame and fortune? What can a first novelist really expect to get?

GG: I don't know whether they can really *expect* to get anything. What they can realistically hope for is an advance against royalties somewhere between $1,500 and $3,000, which, it would also be realistic to expect, is all the writer would ever see, because the advance would not be made back by sales. There are exceptions—*Jaws,* of course. . . .

SK: That's about it. . . .

GG: . . . And there are some first novels lately that people have gotten advances of, oh, say $7,500 for. Again, the chances of making back the advance are slim, barring something like a major paperback sale of some kind. So, you spend a year on a novel. Some people spend a good deal more. And that's the most they can expect on it. And they cannot expect that it will be widely reviewed, significantly reviewed, anywhere. Only a handful of the first novels are touched on at all by any reviewers. The home town paper might review it. That's a satisfaction. . . .

SK: It might get in the hometown library. . . .

GG: Right . . . or even statewide. And strangely enough, there are still some areas in the country where enough people have a sort of local allegiance. I've been told, for example, that in North Carolina there are enough people who buy books by North Carolina writers that they do at least as well locally as they would nationally. But, for the most part, expectations should be severely limited. The main thing that will happen is the fact that it appears in hardcover with a jacket. At least it's been published.

SK: What advice do you have for the first novelist? Say a person has completed a manuscript, but doesn't know anything, doesn't know who to send it to. He goes out and buys *Writers Market,* and it says "have a literary agent" or whatever. What should he do? What advice should he ignore and what advice should he take?

GG: Practical advice would be that, at the present, it is extremely difficult to get an agent. It would be helpful, perhaps, to have an agent to do the sending around for you. However, it is extremely difficult these days for a beginning writer to get an agent. The number of agents has declined considerably over the last ten years, and furthermore, they don't really have the time or energy or incentive to spend their efforts on first novels. I was recently on a panel with five writers, all of whom were, in my view, pretty successful, more successful than I. And none of them had an agent when the question came up from the audience. They said that it was just too much trouble. I was the least successful writer there and the only one with an agent. But, coming back to it, I think that the most *practical* thing to do is to determine who are the fiction editors of the major publishing houses where one would like to see one's book published. There are a number of ways of doing this . . . through *The Literary Marketplace,* through simply calling or asking the publisher "Who are your fiction editors?" Anyway, try writing first. Just sending the unsolicited manuscript is bad news, because there are thousands of them, and it just gets lost. For the most part, publishers don't pay any attention to them. But if you should write a letter: a) introduce yourself, b) describe the book briefly, and c) ask them if they want to see it. That's half the battle. Those who say yes should get a copy of it. Those who say yes will read it promptly. Whether or not it is accepted may not have anything to do with quality, but with their finances, their booklist, other things out of your control. But it is a way, in effect, of getting your own manuscript solicited by a publisher. I imagine that beyond a certain level of literacy and competency, most books today are published or not published on the basis of their subject . . . and the treatment. And if your letter indicates what the subject is, and gives some indication of how it is treated—it's almost like writing a blurb for yourself, but it can't show—at least they have two of the major criteria for rejecting it disposed of. And if they still want to see it—and read it—then it would seem that you've got a foot in the door and a chance.

SK: Would you advise sending along maybe a portion of the manuscript, too?

GG: No, I would think—I'm not sure this has always worked, but it has worked for some who were students of mine—that a brief letter, not more than a page, page and a half, would do these three things. The letter establishes, among other things, that you are sane. Publishers get thousands of crank letters; therefore, that should be in the back of your mind, that "the narrator of this letter is sane, comma, cool, and collected." The hardest part is the second part: reducing your novel to subject and treatment in a very few words and with some accuracy. I mean, not being too modest or too extravagant—not saying, for example, "and then with wonderful agility and adroit symbolism, the author . . ." But, if you say, "I have written a novel about a cross-eyed trumpet player from Louisiana . . . told in the first person from the point of view of the trumpet . . . ," this will give them a fair idea of whether they want to look at it or not. Some people, no doubt, would look at that novel.

SK: What pitfalls should a young writer be wary of?

GG: Are you still talking about the first novel?

SK: Yes.

GG: One of the things we had in *Intro 6* was a very interesting symposium about the first novel, and in there, James Landis, who is an editor at William Morrow and who has published a lot of first novels, pointed out something that might have slipped by some people: that almost no first novels were, in fact, first novels. Some people had written five or six before the first one got published; and while discouraged, they got better all the time and finally did publish. They were then able, among other things, perhaps, to publish the earlier work, out of sequence. The thing that the young writer can realize is that you have that extra strength: you should certainly fight very hard, with great patience and fortitude, to try to get the work published in the sequence of its composition, but you have another out —"I'll come back to you later." You have that possibility, and that's your ace-in-the-hole. I think it may have been Arnold Bennett, referring to William Faulkner, who said that the mark of the good novelist—it could be any literary artist—is the conservation of literary material; that is, nothing is wasted, the feeling that sooner or later things that didn't work out will take another form, another shape. That confidence or knowledge, I think, is like the knowledge of a gambler in a long evening of poker playing. I remember a professional gambler saying the great danger —and we know most professional gamblers cheat—was to try to wrap it up too quickly. You've got to learn to play all night long and make your windfall at the end look like a natural accident. Well, in a sense, that's the position of the professional writer. The distinction between the professional and the amateur is that the professional does have the longer view. A great number of the younger writers give up a little bit quickly. I've been told, on pretty good authority, that some sixty—in excess of sixty—publishers turned down *Catch 22* before it finally caught hold, and that took a long time. Once it did, it was a rarely successful first novel.

SK: Well, what do you say to people who say to themselves: 150 first novels do come out every year, that's not asking too much—I have 150 chances a year. Isn't this statistic encouraging?

GG: Statistically, it's very clear that it isn't, because they have 150 chances out of maybe 20,000 . . . maybe more. Thousands of novels get submitted. The odds are always there. Luck plays a part in it. Also, I think, in a statistical bind like that, with the odds that much against you, it is pointless to waste time on anything except something you care about a great deal. That's the difference. It would be foolish to try to beat the system logically if it were something you didn't really care about very much. You don't get many times at bat, therefore you must put your absolute best effort, nothing less than that, into it.

SK: The attitude of a lot of people, I think, is to bemoan the fact that 150 first novels are published a year. Can America absorb any more than that?

GG: Let's look at that; 150 first novels are published a year; they can't all be good: there aren't that many good books published in a year. They may be competent. I'm sure that the first thing that one should realize is that competence is not enough. That's a good lesson for a writer. Even a certain virtuosity, the right use of techniques or tools, the kind of thing for which you get a pat on the back at school, are taken for granted. This is moving up into the big leagues, and the ability to catch the ball is presumed. Writers should be well aware that talent, intelligence, and competence are not enough; there have to be other dimensions. Vonnegut, whom we quoted at the beginning of the monologue, and John D. MacDonald have emphasized the sheer physical durability, that it's very hard on you. You should be training yourself for the terrific burden you are going to put on your body by sitting at a desk too many hours. There are extra dimensions and I suppose the difference between an amateur and a professional in this day and age, since it cannot be measured by financial returns, is not really a matter of talent, either. There may be amateurs who are more talented, more naturally gifted than professionals. But the real difference lies in persistence, toughness, the capacity to perform productively. William Faulkner said that a professional writer is somebody who can produce a book about every two years. That eliminates a lot of great writers, but that's about the way Faulkner's career worked out. This again involves character more than it does talent. It averages out—Sometimes you have bursts, several things come at once, and then you might go through several dry years.

SK: David Slavitt said that his real audience, besides himself, of course, was his wife, and eleven friends.

GG: I think he is an optimist.

SK: How much does a writer sense an audience beyond that, out there in the real world?

GG: I think it depends. Writers I know who work in nonfiction tell me they get lots of letters and lots of response—John McPhee and Annie Dillard regularly get a great many letters from readers. I'm not sure that writers of fiction, except in so far as they touch upon highly topical subjects, get much sense of audience or response. And I'm not sure that would be a good thing. After all, nonfiction writers finally, no matter how you cut it, no matter how fine they are as writers, are talking about topical things of immediate interest, and the novelist is not—*should* not be. A novelist is not of a season. Books are *merchandized* by the season, spring and fall, but not necessarily for that particular season. I suppose finally the relationship with the reader is with some kind of ideal, imaginary reader.

SK: Can the creative writing teacher, in all honesty, ever advise a student to go ahead and try and make a career out of writing? And what if the student asks him directly? What are some of the moral things involved?

GG: I don't think it is the business of the creative writing teacher to discourage people (this is not necessarily the same thing as encouraging them), or try to dampen their desire or ardor to write. The creative writing teacher can recognize and encourage talent and is able to say at a certain point in dealing with a writer that there appears to be a natural talent or a learned talent there. That should be encouraging to the writer if he or she wishes to proceed. You can be encouraging, but you must be realistic. They should understand as much as possible about what's involved in a career of writing. That leads to a discussion of goals, expectations; beyond establishing some sort of ground rules and reality, it is not your place to discourage. Although I can quite honestly discourage somebody who hands me a manuscript—which I feel is not good—and says "I plan to submit this to publishers and make a fortune and be celebrated as a major American novelist," I can easily enough say "Good luck to you, but it's not going to happen." Then he'll probably go back and rewrite it and prove I'm wrong.

SK: Have you ever been proved wrong like that?

GG: Oh, sure. I have been surprised, very often. But that makes it all the more complex. Looking back over the years, I can say this: Some of the most talented of the students have not produced, have drifted into other things, or maybe will produce later. Some who had less initial evidence of gifts or talent have grown up and changed, simply done the hard work and been persistent, and have produced very well indeed. Again, it's a matter of character: how much the writer wants to produce or publish, how much there is a need, and then a lot of luck. . . .

SK: If luck plays such a part in things, then that implies that weaker writers sometimes come up on top. Isn't that perversely some sort of encouragement for all of us? I mean, we all doubt how good we are.

GG: That's a good point. You can look at it either way. Luck is out of your hands, except for whatever rituals of knocking wood, sharpening pencils, short prayers to the Muses, etc., that you have. You can do your ritual propitiations to luck, if you like, but beyond that, there is nothing you can do, good or bad, except to try to survive. The writer must be a gambler. There certainly are more gamblers in America—by far—than there are readers, or even writers. It's a gamble, but it's always a possibility, and that can be a very positive thought. Tomorrow my luck may change.

SK: I understand you used to have your students go back and read old newspapers, reviews, etc., from the twenties, the thirties, and check out the literary situation at the time. What did they find and why did you have them do that?

GG: What we would do is assign each student a different year, and for a couple of weeks they researched from the original sources, not with present histories, but going back and reading all the New York *Times* and—in those days—the *Herald Tribune,* reading all the book reviews. They discovered many of our most famous writers were certainly not very well known at that time and that a great many people who were well known, widely discussed, are now almost totally unknown. This was salutary, as long as they did not fall into the trap of thinking that people in 1925 were characterized by an invincible ignorance that would not be present today. The quickest way is simply to get an almanac out and look down the printed list of Pulitzer prize winners over the years.

SK: It's surprising how few you even recognize.

GG: Few names would you even recognize. . . . It is always the belief of every generation that they will not repeat the same kinds of mistakes that earlier generations made. But literary history indicates that each generation makes pretty much the same mistakes. Ours is struggling manfully not to. Which is a peculiar thing, and is part of our peculiar self-consciousness. We attempt constantly to control history. This has its effect on literary history, too. However, one thing I can assure all critics and scholars who have valiantly over the last ten years tried to lock in an acceptable establishment view of the modern scene: History is finally written by historians. And they are people that come along later. And one thing they don't like is people who try to do their job for them. So, if anything, the portents and omens are that our period will be more heavily rewritten in the future and revised than any other, precisely because our self-conscious critics and scholars, etc., tried to write the history before it happened.

SK: It always makes me a bit uneasy when I see on the front page of the New York *Times Book Review* that here is finally the Book of the Decade.

GG: The point is that we see this about once every two months. And you try to remember "What was that last Book of the Decade?" I suppose the only way to keep track of it would be to paper your room with the front page reviews of the New York *Times Book Review* and then you could re-member about half of them.

SK: James Michener's book has just come out in paperback, and it's described as "The Book of the Century"—this is what it reads on all the little paperback stands—that's such a strange feeling.

GG: That puts it above Proust, Joyce, Mann . . .

SK: *Ulysses* fades into insignificance.

GG: . . . All of Faulkner . . . All of Hemingway . . . Well, that's a superb example of the very thing we've been talk-ing about: the marketplace mentality. It isn't a horse race, but any good gambler realizes there are whole series of races which can make or break you, and tomorrow the track will be open again. I think that it has reached the point of silliness. . . . That's interesting, though . . . "The Novel of the Century."

SK: If art is for kids, then what is there for grown-ups?

GG: One has to be very grown-up to preserve the child within— the good child within you. We've exaggerated the virtues of children a great deal: I'm inclined to agree with W. C. Fields both about Philadelphia and children; but never-theless, it takes every bit of grown-up savvy and toughness and sanity to preserve the child within. From an agent's point of view, that's true: Art is for kids, and he's not in-terested in that. From the writer's point of view, he's des-perately anxious in every way he can to preserve the child. Unless you want to be totally dependent, like Blanche, in

*Streetcar Named Desire,* upon the kindness of strangers (you might end up like she did, carried away by guys in white suits), unless you want that, you're going to have to preserve your own child, and I think that can be done.

SK: The subtitle of this volume, *The Liar's Craft,* is very interesting to me because it points out the two different usages of the word "craft": in the sense of being sly and crafty and then the sense of the writer's craft itself. What does the liar's craft mean to you?

GG: Well, of course it is the title of one of the better stories in this *Intro.* The *liar* is the part that interests me more than the double sense of the word craft. From the earliest times, from classical times and through the Middle Ages, etc., poets and fiction writers were described as liars. They were like the Thebans who cannot tell the truth. They were described as people able to tell lies which could contain great truths and which couldn't be told in any other fashion. That's really what it's all about. I guess that's why it is an appropriate title for this book. These are fictions, therefore, in a sense, lies. But through craft those lies contain a truth that ideally could not otherwise be expressed or shared.

SK: You said something in an earlier published interview that I really liked, and that was that a writer must face the fact, as he looks back on his career, that maybe he's worked forty years and he's produced nothing. And what I liked about the way you said it was that this was a very necessary risk, that there's no other way to look at being a writer.

GG: This is the first risk that a writer has to take. This was mentioned by Vonnegut about Joseph Heller. He said— I'm not quoting him directly—Joseph Heller worked for fourteen years on *Catch 22* with the full knowledge that it could have been a piece of garbage. It might well have been.

SK: A lot of publishing companies thought it was.

GG: Yes, a lot of people thought it was a piece of garbage. Even at the beginning—that risk was required before it had a chance to be a successful work on its own terms, and he had to be willing to take that risk. Another superb example of this idea is in the title story of the Iowa Short Fiction winner by Barry Targan, called "Harry Belten and the Mendelssohn Violin Concerto," which uses as its epigraph —"Anything worth doing is worth doing badly." That's really the starting point for the kind of sacrifice that is involved, that is necessary to do any good writing. And that may be a good thing. We've come around full circle. That is, in the past there were some rational, reasonable rewards. Therefore, their approach was a little bit different. They didn't have to take the Joseph Heller risk or the Robert Frost risk. They had a shot at something definite. They either achieved those goals or they didn't. Now we have a shot at something definitely. . . .

SK: Indefinite?

GG: Yes, and it should make—who can say?—it should make for more commitment and, in many ways, better work, from the survivors.

SK: We're running out of tape now, so we need a bit of inspiration. Is this really the last time you're going to give The Talk?

GG: I don't want to ever give The Talk again. Some people like to hear it for some reason, though.

SK: Perverse enjoyment?

GG: It goes in one ear and out the other.

SK: Well, now that we have it in permanent form, thank you.

# III  POETRY

*So this is the beginning,*
*standing naked on the stairs.*

from *"Nu Descendant Un Escalier,"*
by PATRICIA SHEPPARD

## THE TRUTH IS:
## ASSASSINS KEEP DIARIES

Except for winter, the trees,
though not the trees themselves, are

a kind of threat—as if I'll pass under
the click of something caliber. This

is the age: we have our thoughts & load
ourselves with knots. In rooms, warm

& laden with heavy china, I am polite.
In kitchens or parking lots, overcome

with craving, with a silent afterburner,
I might seek a specific attention. It's

not that I don't date. I do. Women
have been smooth & complimentary. Nights

go by when I lug flowers & listen to tropical
orchestras. At home, I move things away

from the edge of things. I know the dust
is not deliberately cruel & the closets,

the place where women have hung their slim
uniforms, are sparse. I hide nothing. If

I have a pattern, perhaps it is this: when
it rains, you'll find me personal; in the dark

of a street's alcove, I am circumspect. You
would expect that. At a party, this party,

I'm the first to drink your farewell toast.

—HOWARD AARON

## ROBINSON'S LAST PROM
—for Weldon Kees and Tiajuana

Robinson on his haunches in his attic taking counsel
From spiders. Baldfaced, a single lightbulb contributes its
Jaundiced view of mementos and family albums. Pressed cor-
    sages,
Brittle ticket stubs, and programs hold hands with tuxedo snap-
    shots.

This one: Robinson an amateur wild man with rhythm. Living
    proof
The hully gully and twist don't damage the spine. It's too dark
To tell if that's Robinson nailing "Roll Over Beethoven"
To the music department upright.

Or this one: Basketball nets ballooning with crepe paper, star fish,
Paper mache clams, and, barely seen but nonetheless noticed,
Robinson's missing jock strap. The theme
A Night in Neptune's Kingdom.

Or: Robinson in the backseat grappling organdy
While her breasts jut with the tide. The desire to kiss
Black stones beneath the bridge
Débuted that night.

Outside, the Robinson baby boom bells the cat
With firecrackers, but it should be Robinson whooping it up
in Yucatan. Second wife Robinson downstairs watches
Joe DiMaggio pop out in The World Series.

Under his cobweb sombrero, listening to Django Reinhardt
Plunking in the rafters, Robinson surveys the state of his union
Suspecting that here, as on the Golden Gate Bridge,
It's the top of the night.

—VerKuilen Ager

## RACOON

The animal strains
when the stars align;

gaping, artless.

Entering the racoon's eye,
I take her breath,
I follow in her legs,
I forget the moon and her uneaten clams,
the locust growing in his shell,
becoming old, bending his legs.

The sky is turning;
we are lost to the wood,
fallen in the clutch of weeds
the fur parts, our haunches tremble,
the blood comes,
one by one the creatures burst;
low murmurs
and the stars break to pieces over our body,
we lick them, they learn to breathe,
they settle in our skin.

—CATHY ANDERSON


# WINTER BEACH


The icy gulls, high flakes of white,
at daybreak cry and whirl and flare,
and sharp on shallow skies and bright
as crystal kites, they drive to where
the sullen sun, a wet hole, wears
into the waiting air. Light brings
the winter sea gulls, snow with wings.

—MICHAEL ANDERSON

## OLD MEN

The day has gone to rain.

Birds turn grey and quibble
with the old men who gather chestnuts
in Central Park.

Later on Fifth or Wall
they flock around smoking stands,
picking shells in the gutters.

The old men, necks deep in shabby coats,
carefully finger my offered coins.
Grey stubble on their faces
feathered with frost,
their eyes are their weather,
following me as I take the extended bag
and leave without the change,
afraid the claws of the outthrust hand
might close around my wrist.

My father is dragging
the broken wings of his body
across the East River,
his clothes flapping and cawing around him.

Below the river pulls at the mist.

—ADELAIDE BLOMFIELD

# THE HARD GHAZALS

I

The hard ghazals rise blind,
out of themselves, feeling for you.

Empty, blue, unveined, unthinking,
my hands unfold in your shadow.

Night air tells lies in high branches.
Behind your hair, somewhere, you listen.

Underneath feet, underneath kneeling,
underneath wet palms, arched bones: a dark river.

In a white room you slowly undress.
Across the city I bring sour milk to my lips.

II

Light from a black moon poisons your face.
Deep frogs bloat the stillness.

Everywhere, in clouds heavy with summer,
in thin grasses, in my wrists, the insomnia of you.

Lying here beside my shadow,
I whisper your secrets, and he believes me.

In a mirror anything can happen.
On the other side I crave your absence.

Dogs scold a nervous breeze.
My lungs remember your breath.

III

Rain splays my bones in every dream.
Thinking of you, it's hard to keep my eyes open.

Winged insects have their burdens of haloes,
but the darkness draws back in your path.

When blood goes far he forgets your name.
I turn blue to hear him pounding it out again.

Pieces of black snow, cracked circles, broken words:
the wreckage we leave at dawn.

Dust in its throat, the room asleep.
I wrap myself with arms like huge roots
in your pale smoke.

—DAVID BREWSTER

## OTHER LOVERS

There were others that winter.
All the girls in Boston were clutching
their fiancés, their eyes blazing
with diamonds.
I clutched your arm on the ice
and laughed. At night
I sang to you, while the stars
washed their discs in the woods.
That spring your best friend married
and I vowed I never would,
a woman of imagination.

Yet if I sleep with your smell
for years, I still can't imagine you;
You, who know how my breath snaps
during nightmares, with your mouth
on mine pulling me ashore;
if I live with you forever
this way, entering the dark
nightly, each time knowing
I have just begun.

—DEBRA BRUCE

## THE PREGNANT NUN

Under a hobo star,
        she wanders
through sparse city copse,
        gown dappled
with wolfish faces,
        wafer-thin and
        mooncast.
Near a streaming ditch
of sewer
        she contemplates
her grief-filled belly
and years of longing.
        Grown uncertain
of Mary's
        lamb-fed boy,

she turns to what's left
      of her derelict lover
      and prays for
a useless, vagrant look
in those beautiful
      bastard eyes—
a look no wildman
      fisherman
      or harlot
would want to follow
      anywhere.

—EDWARD BURCH

## MIRE
### (*Reflections after being propositioned by a prostitute at the City Market*)

1

Root and pith, leaf and bud
Love the fertile dirt, their home.
Deft fingers probe into the mud
And rock and loam
As root provides for bud and leaf.

Till the sap has wasted in the stem
They suck life from what they love.

## 2

The wanton boar roots in the mire,
The wanton sow mires in the mud.
They grovel, matching leer with leer,
And mingle blood.
King and Queen of their earthy realm,

They labor in desire for lard
And love their sausage, loin, and ham.

## 3

After sufficient greens and ham,
Man and woman cling and cleave,
Evolve and elevate, at home,
And never rove
From domestic bed and cozy hearth.

They whisper of their souls' true love:
Their souls, buried, wail through the earth.

—BRAD BURKHOLDER

## THE HOUSE

Flocks of migratory birds
fly into the Midwestern sunset:

A woman in an old white shawl
passes

eating an apple,
her husband holding

their child
into a white painted cupola house.

THE RAIN
All the new green leaves on the trees
are still.
The wind drives out the children.
White petals swirl an alien blizzard snow.

Three mud darkened men
carry a young girl away
deep into the city park.
The white petals are plastered
all over
the stables and the tomb
of the unknown soldier.

A man takes a picture
and walks on.

—JIM BUSHEY

## WHERE IT ALL BEGAN

This is the place
where it all began

where young children dance
to the tunes of an old country

where chairs outlast their owners

and the yellowed letters
of elderly women
are kept in a tin box

in a trunk
that is never opened

with trinkets
once worn by an unknown saint

—EDWARD BYRNE

# AFTER THE PERFORMANCE OF THE NATIONAL THEATRE OF THE DEAF

How great the distance
between the feel of the wind
and the rustle of leaves?
To be silent amid silence
no ear perceives.

Had I met you alone
and tilting your head you said
"Tell me of love in a sound,"
I would never have thought
of silence or a touch,
when any word I might have found
would have been too little
or too much.

—CHARLIE CHARETTE

# *VACANT*

Mukilteo had been a ghost town,
a classical setting
where the young
grew younger and the old
grew neither way;
a legend of cattails straighter
than the wicked rays
of sun that yellowed the parched
FOR SALE
signs that rose
from the earth more quickly
than each blade
of deadened grass,
and they looked like wordy
tombstones
as they stood,
some slanting
toward the ground
almost waiting
for that last nudge to knock them
flat
like rows of dominoes
or the Great Wall of China;
and beyond that too
were the lives
of those shy deserters
more gifted than potential itself
that had been cast
adrift somewhere
between this body and that
like featherweight fuzz
on a wilted dandelion,
too late to be picked again
by still another stranger
but not by
me.

—Victoria Coen

# THE HOUSE ON THE BANK

The house on the bank had a garden
Just over the hill.
I remember cucumbers and sweet potatoes.
There were scrub pines
And a field where dewberries grew
In behind the deep gullies,
Each side of the road.

One foot on tar,
The other in the ditch,
I checked the mailbox daily
In all seasons.
Once, I found a note to the mailman
From my old maid aunt: There is no one
Who lives here by the name of Occupant.

There was a black walnut, plum trees
And a covered well under a large oak;
A shed of some kind where we played
"I'll show you mine, if you'll, me yours."
The girls in the village loved that game.
It meant the future held some hope.

There was no grass in the yard.
Jaydene and I had to sweep it clean
With brushbrooms every Saturday.

Then, soldiers came and put bayonets
Through flags made by my sisters.
Hurrah for the bonny blue flag.
The flag of the simple blue star.
They sang. No reason not.
Their cloth was pierced and sagging,
But n'er the spirit of it's original toil.
My sisters knew what time it was
When their watches had stopped.

Sister Lorna hid the food under a rock
Behind the outhouse.
When the tough-guy soldiers left,
Their jeeps kicking up dust
On my father's gnarled and loved trees,
We always sat down to a hot meal,
House still intact,
Spirits ringing in the wooden, pegged rafters.

Snails and slugs did more annual harm
To my mother's flowers
Than all the little Hitlers
With their big heeled boots.

I guess if you keep the music clean,
All varieties of pest
Can only lose in the long run.

—BRAD DINSMORE, JR.


## CENTAUR


She trotted all summer
on beer cans clamped to her sneakers,
a rope between her teeth
and one tied to her belt loop.
She held the ends of the first one
in either hand,
clucking and spurring herself,
both rider and horse.
Once the dog yanked her bridle,
pulled two of her teeth.

216

More than once she skidded into the gravel—
tail wound up in her spokes.
Tenderer than horsehide
she bled and scabbed, bruised
until she called herself a pinto.
She suffered to be a horse!
Years later, stylishly maned,
a psych major told her
"All girls fall in love with horses
because of their dongs,
which are huge and purple erect,
barbed and heavy like the maces
knights carry to battle."
"I've never seen one," she said,
"that's not why I loved them."
"Well, then, you sensed them,"
he nickered, pawing the ground.

—CAT DOTY


## GENEALOGY


Cut
from this skein
of yarn
somewhere in the
center     or
maybe toward the end

I cannot see
where it was spun
where it was joined
and wound
and braided      what fingers
twirled, bleeding
                the eyes
grown ragged watching
                the numb foot
tapping with the rhythm of
the wheel.

There is no history
here
no memory of pipes
and drums or
sweaty pubs
the clannish plaid
fading
through Ellis Island
turnstiles into sackcloth
of Virginia foothills
and Ohio's patchwork
valleys.

I do not know you
but sometimes
combing through my
light and wavy hair      I
catch a tangled
knot and hear a
distant spinner
scream.

                —JUDITH DUNAWAY

218

# HALF TRUTH

My body only contains me
It does not sing a sweet shuddering poem
I feel cold in my bones
Bed like a grave
Sheets like a shroud
Covering the smiling lie.

—P. R. FARROW

# THE ART OF LEATHERCRAFT

1.
To pound blindly at this flesh
is madness. To cut
deeply into the sheath of last night's steak
is little more than the drinking
of unclean water.
The water must be boiled,
thickened with the blood of cattle,
or this carved leather is worthless.
Just as the snake who watches,
this must be danced on.

2.
Hand and mallet
wrestle in the dirty sheets of sweat,
pots under the table rattle with each impact.
The tea kettle behind me screams,
but I keep on working,
cutting and pounding, faster
and faster with an urgency worthy of the craft.
My cigarette, ash phallic and withered,
has long since gone out.

Outside, toads call for their mates.
The neighborhood kids have run inside
for fear of death under
the moon's jagged jaw.
A hammer cracks
on the inner walls of the skull,
and already, skin begins
to tighten and crawl.

—Vernon Fowlkes, Jr.


## AMONG PROGRESS IN MINNEAPOLIS


It is hard to remember my home town.
At dusk, young black mothers
across the street scream
their children home.
Their jewels & sequined gowns
glitter dimly in a sun less often known;
slender limousines, made waiting
among their own fumes. Things here

you kind of expect to happen happen:
Super America hold-up men
leave a liquor store cop face down;
narcotics drift; crouched in the shadow
of a porch, vicious with rabies, a squirrel shakes,
ready to attack anything

that moves. And everything moves. Anymore
my home town is no longer:
while fired-up bulldozers & caterpillars
sit dimming the sky with fumes,
a wealthy man named Skogman
closes a deal for land. In the greasy name
of progress, he builds houses that all look the same.

Minneapolis; Cedar Rapids—
even their names vaguely rhyme.
And at dawn in either city, now ragged & forlorn,
those younger mothers, black or white,
return to empty homes. In the night their children
have crept away toward crime,
sick of screaming, mad with spite,
forgetting their ways back home.

—DAVID GRIFFITH

## GAMBLING WOMAN

No one fondles
my dice. I roll
independently.

Snake eyes suit me:
Black drills
boring little soloists.

—JILL GROSSMAN


# LETTER TO WILLIAM STAFFORD
## from PILOT ROCK, OREGON


i

Yellow hills melt us
Like butter in the sun
We assume the shape of our land
Fields like corn loaves
Keep a brown road running
Off to announce a ranch

Mountains think of covered wagons
Dust remarks how clouds begin
Smoke signals on the ridge
Pronouncing old fires
Stars and time are motionless
We are the ones who move

ii

A man said: Corn silage is good for wintering cows
If you have a strong rope
Blows them up like balloons he said
It's good for cleaning the barn
During the snows

I feed them once a week with silage—they float
A foot off the floor
And I spread new straw
But keep a short rope

One morning Rinso spooked at standing in mid-air
She liked to kick the roof
Right off before I got her down
Out of the rafters

iii

Some cows never touch the ground
They just rove on their noses
From grass row to grass row
Hanging on with their rolling mouths

—LAURA GROVER

# A HORSESHOE MATING AT CHATHAM BAY AFTER VICTORY IN VIETNAM

It is late spring and leaptide.
Again the ocean has curved up
in the fertilizing pull of the moon.
Cod-boats sleep closer to the constellations,
their nets a dark litter of fish.

Along Nauset spit the crabs have formed up
like a necklace of German helmets.
They grind their souls at water's edge
and leave everything else at peace.

But we who have come to do the same
stand unsexed in the strong moonlight
as these thin-blooded things big as shields
drill another generation
into the high-water stain.

—JEFFREY HAGEDORN


## LIVING ALONE


There's the same woman on the bridge;
Perhaps today she'll go a little farther
Toward the other side,
Though it looks now as if she's motioning
From up there to something
She just saw move. A friend
Of hers. He's been waiting a long time.
But it doesn't matter, he won't come any nearer.
He wants to, but he can't.
Now a scarf of fog
Begins to close around the bridge
And the figure there. She will disappear.
It's frightening, the way she slides
So easily from view, turning less gray,
Less gray and more white;
Then it doesn't matter if she was there or not.
I know tomorrow at this time
She'll re-appear. I know how gently
The fog comes in here.

—BRENDA HILLMAN

## POEM

During a needle-sharp moment
   the stranger within you steps out
He straightens your tie
   dries your forehead with his sleeve
     and counts the number of lines in your palm
Then leaves

You follow from a distance
   fitting your step exactly into each footprint
     he has left behind

For a moment you know your arms around his chest
   as you say,
"The river is dying.   Time
has frozen to concrete as heavy as a human breath."

He folds like a paper map
   and he fits snug in the darkness of your breast pocket

—TIM HJELMELAND

## THE RABBITS

The hound nosed open
the unlocked hatch,
shook the white clumps,
and left them.

225

The children cried.
The dog was hit on the nose
with a newspaper.
The sun went down.

Miranda, staring at a square
of linoleum, said:
"Since they're already dead
why don't we eat them?"

Her mother, finding no reason
not to, skinned them,
stewed them in onions and thick
white gravy.

Only the father sat apart,
straining on the skinny legs
of the kitchen chair, his hands
curled in his lap like a rose.

—SANDRA HOBEN

## SARABANDE

dream like quality of Sarabande
sense of fatalism—the way the jagged dissonances
turn into the Sarabande

—MARTHA GRAHAM, *Notebooks*

We lie

on the back porch,

his chest a burlap mat,
my braid a diamond-backed snake
coiling for the strike.

My teeth burn sunspots into his neck.

He rolls over, his hair
rippling like the priest's cloak.
I dig ruts with my fingers,
the same fingers
that scrape the dirt for the new road to town.

He does not notice these invasions.

Dissipated, we sleep,
his hand pressed
into my back.
I dream of wedged
Waves, and sandy saffron rice.

My lace bruised,
The moon silently curls into orbit.

—MARIA KATZENBACH

# RECITAL OF WATER OVER STONE
## (for Robert Creeley)

We wait to see you nail down
your voice to the floor.
You stand near the rear door
talking clothes off pale dreams.
The groupie in the front row
wears lavender stockings—
knows Blue Nun and Panama Red,
stares at the glass ceiling,
flutters like many crimson birds,
as if poets hide among rafters.
You step up to the podium,
drag on a cigarette, and touch
the halfdead microphone—
songs leap into your mouth.
You've slept in a hollowed log,
lived dogdays, hardtimes.
You lead us through Osage orange
groves, exposing white bones,
drums buried under dirt.

—YUSEF KOMUNYAKAA

## PARTS OF SPEECH OF ABRAHAM LINCOLN'S BIRTHDAY 1975
(*for T. S. Cushman*)

No ADVERBS this morning

Though I've
not yet
come back from Carolina

there's to be an
Opening of the Nikonos
this day

PRONOUNS and your sexual apocalypse

Who
or
whom
is
the
object?

What
and
how
could
that be?

VERB AS ADJECTIVE

The
Lust*
List
starts
with
L.

A
girl
named
L.                * Not love that list but lust
                      (though slightly scorched)
admissable along the spectrum—somewhere—of our sex


EXCLAMATIONS (S)

But which one fits
when everybody's
everybody's
teacher sloshes
thermos coffee
into her English lap?


My sister the ARTICLE sung of
Elliott
(Not Schwartz who synthesizes
with the Portland Symphony) but he
who loved to fill
his belliott
with green gum

who traveled miles too many
much too fast
miles too many
much too fast
too fast

PREPOSITION

The madman gave up
long ago
on punning—
too glib—and easy as
alliteration
—demoted to the slogan
in the '70's—
the clack of IBM's
—electric—from the
muse next door

—D. B. KREITZBERG

## THE LAUREATE'S HANGOVER

All the sun waking, dawn halts my sleep
(Ernest Dowson and Mallarmé)
i lordly bid the sun to hell,
and to hell with Shropshire reveille

as rough strife rolls through my senses
and remembrances dawn within my head—
things pass, but to no use: i can't
remember how i got to bed.

My brain feels mashed, my breath smells sour,
and overturned upon the floor
an empty bottle rests that held
Jim Beam erect the night before.

I've Joyce's vision—literally—
(Dylan Thomas and Oscar Wilde)
my head has somewhat settled on
my neck, and i feel reconciled

to a morning dripped from coffee cups
and carrioncomfortinscape stressed,
but the comfort of *Beamus Erectus* will ease
such woes before the day has passed.

Be always drunk, said Baudelaire,
and i, by eternal radiance stained
(but better acquainted with night), agree:
Be always drunk, or at least be stoned—

and though *la fleur* could be drunk with passion
(John Berryman and Christopher Smart)
he was best versed in the gnomic blurb:
"Truly drunk is drunk with Art":

Swinburne liftingly lilted a glass,
ethereally wafting with wine went Crane,
when Poe's ravenous thirst went dry
Rimbaud flew off with Paul Verlaine:

inebriates of art they were,
and art the finer for what they did;
i'd swill all hell's mixed metaphors
to toast their company when i'm dead.

Thus i, musing on their dreams
(with up so floating many shots down)
look around me in the morning light
for more to drink, if only to drown.

—CARL LAUNIUS

232

# APAXNE
## LOXOSCELES RECLUSEA

A silver sliver board long fallen
From the winding stack with weeds
Pushing the edges. And after I
Pulled afar this false sky there
It stood in the flood of light,
In a fear stare. Eight swollen
Banded knees above hairy hanging eyes.
Fat fangs below the eyes. Then a
Furryscurry into the drying.

Riding home on the bus
I rehearse the poem

> Past the passive willows,
> The low flooded fields, wheat grown
> Too tall to mow, seedpods rattling
> On black locust in final revival

In my head.
A vexing poem;

> Cones of lavender and white lilacs.
> Deep blue streams wandering from
>     the hills
> Slowly being drown by thru streets
> Then sewered past my house.

Never finished,
Never improving.

> My desk is shingled with paper
> Spotted blue and green paraffin,
>     pencil,
> Ink, eraser shavings, with a few
> Marked lines to start again.

I have sightsinging
And Soc. to study.

> I light the overflowing
> Candle; straighten the lexicon,

Almanac, and the poems. Hold
   them upright
With the railroad spike.

I have new poems
To work on.

The Tonkinese jumps up, sits
On my paper. Slowly squints. Purring
Hopeful I will pet her. Outside
The clouds are orange and blue
   heather.

Besides, I hate
My typewriter.

Heather filled the mountainsides.
We took the mountain's beautiful
   time
(With a break for bush hunting)
To scramble up from the bugbog.

The "C" and "p"
Stick at the ribbon.

Sweat filling my eyebrows and
   sleeving
My arms. Sweat transferring the dye
From the backbands onto my shirt.
Deerflies bite off steaks of skin.

It jumps spaces
The line never rings.

A droning hummingbird inspects
The huge red flower on my back.
The streams do green lightning
Backwards on the valley walls.

It forces me
To have titles and endings.

Tahoma is far off and all white.
Peaks of permasnow become clouds
Where the earth ends.
The world is only mountains
   forever.

—RICHARD LE COMPTE

# JOURNEY INTO CORNFLAKES

with these two boxtops (and thirty-five cents)
you can get a piece of land far off the map
you colored in fifth-grade geography, or a full-
size map of jesse james and the lone
ranger. this is a one-shot deal.
like deciding to go west for gold or rob
trains. which? the future is wearing
a mask and firing silver bullets.
do not send stamps or coins.
like waiting everyday for twenty-five
years, just for a two-week delivery.
another spoonful, another bullet
to bite. dear kellogg's cereal: i have read
the box fourteen times and i would like
to discover the west, but there are
very few physical areas left to explore.

—KENT ROBERT MAHAN

# CAST PARTY

Zippers shoot up sequin costumes
Rubber dolls in glass slippers do the Alley Cat
kicking up ruffled petticoats
like lettuce leaves sprung from the ground

On the terrace
he savors her
like a papaya

It rains

she plucks velvet spiders
from his whispers

They awaken later that night
in a puddle
of silver quarters

—ADRIENNE MAHER

## BOB DYLAN VISITS CARL SANDBURG
### (and finds him home)

In an old Ford
Up from here
In New England

The story was told
On one frosty morning
While touring

He knocked at the poet's door
Introduced his intention
And was invited inside

To talk their poetry
He, of course, admired the poet
Who had not yet heard the records

—Michael  Malinowitz

## *LEARNING  CHINESE*

Lao-Tzu comes to my place
twice a week

I am a slow learner
I mix up words

*Shan* says Lao-Tzu
Say *Shan*

*Shan* I say

No no that means *grave*
Say *Shan,* say *mountain*

*Shan* I say
Lao-Tzu shakes his head
Try *Shiang, mutual*

As it is written:
The tree and the eye
They look at each other
Mutual

*Shiang* I say

No no that means *think* says Old Lao
Think is the same
tree, yes, the same eye
but underneath it all
is heart

Now say *Shiang*

And so it goes
Each day with its confusion

Like today
I couldn't say *Yea*
which means artistic, and elegant

I kept saying
*Yea*
hoarse, dumb

—DAWN MCGUIRE


## *THE FLIGHT*


He said that he would do it and he did.

It was so hard to fathom the subtleties
of air current in and around Bethany.
Strange, sibilant sound seemed to sneak and tickle
                              from secret.

The mission got a green light despite the elements.

Boy, he flew by the seat of his pants;
doing barrel rolls and loop the loops,
talking and blessing.
He punched a thumbs up at us
                              at liftoff.

The noise of the crowd was deafening.

"He's moving!" "He's getting up there!"
"Go you sumbitch!" "Look at him go!"
I yelled so hard I've been hoarse
                              for centuries.

Looked like he had enough power,

To make the heaven of heavens
without even an attitude change.
There was a general excitement,
                              a joyful cry.

A commemorative coin is to be minted.

On the one side it will say: "Bon voyage."
The reverse: A field of stars, a human face,
and a simple, straightforward plea:
                    R.S.V.P.

                              —Jim McGuire

## PORT CALL
### (*An Aubade for Sue*)


Daybreak.
A muffled bay.
Bell buoys sound the channel
As the bobbing bow slices through the swells.

I see you lying among windless sails
And shout across wrinkles of silk:
Ahoy, Ahoy.
And when you answer through a fog,

We rise from battered sloops
And roll together
In the wake of dawn.

—DAVID R. MEMMOTT


## WEARING FINE


I
Crystals of ginger
poppy seeds
whole cloves—
small obsidian flowers
dissemble
in my wooden mortar
their pungent dust
drifts out of the bowl
around the pounding
pestle

## II

Once the sky was thick
the earth has whirled
it thin so
transparent now
the moon is an egg
rocking on glass
when the air breaks
the world will spin around
the rim of space still
clotted with fragrant stars

## III

My friend whose mother
was an archaeologist
brought out the old
basalt mortar
we ground pollen
and grass seeds
swaying, the yellow powder
bitter in our mouths
the knob of the pestle
had milled the hollow
smooth

## IV

Now I am worn fine
out of the bowl
of bone curving
between my hips
the bruised scent
of vanilla rises
into all my nights

—MELINDA MUELLER

# CARPENTRY

Work that lasts and is strongest must be done
by hand, the family men believe. Quality oak
will stand through hard rain, grief,
inconstancy, if fastenings are tight,
if lines are plumb. Good handiwork will never change.
They made my grandmother's casket and did not clean up
the shavings, splinters, sawdust underneath the boards.
Terrible labor leaves its grit.
At her confinements and lyings-in,
her strains and cries and wrenching spine
were secretive, and sheets were burned
to mute the rupture stains. Later the hammers
and files resounded until they closed her in.
Veins and darkenings and knots
were sanded to one consistent grain.

All the men have been carpenters,
fixing planes, notching ends, filing and putting things
flat. My husband works on cabinets all day, and frames,
and windowboxes soundly braced. Jealous of edges,
he adjusts and bevels adjoining faces
with exacting tools. I smile to approve the craft
I could not do: the snug design, weight secured,
the walnut grain sealed and smoothed. In raw material
he can see and measure dimensions that fit a plan.
My father, too, would go out mornings,
trap young trees and find them good
for splitting. They cracked like backbone
frames as he peeled them open
to make them wood.

—LINDA MIZEJEWSKI

# CANADA: BELOW THE ARCTIC CIRCLE

Ten of us went:
Seventy miles along the west side
Of Mistassini Lake;
Portaged three miles through spruce
To Cold Water River;
Up Cold Water fifteen miles
To Cold Water Lake;
There three days rested.
Portaged one mile through mud
To Mistassini River;
Down Mistassini one hundred eighty miles
To Chicoutimi.

Charlot, the guide, was drunk the first night out.
He crept back to the reservation drunk—
The nine of us, asleep, didn't hear him go—
And we found him drunk in bed at ten
The next morning. Bob threw the bottle out.

You wake at dawn. The mist clings damply to your face.
Your stiff and swollen fingers zip the sleep
From the down bag, rub it from half-shut eyes.
At breakfast you are beat;
You sit and shiver, staring at the fire,
Eating oatmeal. You give the dog a bowl to lick,
And hunch nearer the coals.

You make an eddy-turn above a run
Of white water. The other three canoes
Slip in beside. There's low and hurried talk
As the river rushes past, under the thin
Bent bones of the canoe on which your knees
Are jammed. You pull for shore, beach,
And haul up the wet canoe by the middle thwart.
You dump water from your boots, and eat dried beef,
While rain falls from a greying sky.

At night the four canoes are overturned.
You make curried rice, and Charlot's shot
A pair of geese. His pipe is lit
To drive the goddamn bugs away. You watch
As Jim smears iodine on his gashed knee.
Later, you lean back from the fire, flushed,
And stare at spruce outlined against a still black sky.
The rain drips slowly in your eyes.

At Cold Water Lake, I lay
On the hard bottom ribs of an aimless canoe,
Circling slowly in the looking-glass lake,
Empty except for my naked body.
I saw a thin cloud shredded
Against a blank blue sky.
Another formed, and hung motionless
Ten thousand feet above my body.
The canoe stopped.
Unmoving in soundless air,
I lay naked.
Then I felt that cloud on my cheek:
Ten thousand feet above water,
I hung motionless,
Touching cloud,
Ten thousand feet above water,
Suspended.

Then my heart beat once,
And I heard the water lapping gently
On the canoe's side.
I slept.

*Returning is the motion of the Tao.*
*Yielding is the way of the Tao.*
*The ten thousand things are born of being.*
*Being is born of not being.*

—Nicholas Morgan

## RUSHING
### (*to J. F.*)


Sunning out from under the road,
a clear corridor of sound
charmed my mind like the children's
behind bushes I heard pretend
with bright-colored blocks
and little trucks that surrounded them.

Leaning over the railing,
I stared at swirling sky,
the leaves twice green
and round rocks below.
At the fountain I came
upon surprised, shopping,
two children walked the rim—
round and round that circle
never falling, laughing eyes connected.
For them there was only the fountain.

For me, the stream holds a minute.
(Then, I made dams til dinner
in rolled-up pants wet to the knees
in rushing      caught salamanders.)
I hurry to think about your comment
"In Kubla Khan the flow was sexual."
Smiling, you said, "Creative."
You are one of the particles
I dam, make muddy and slow.
The fountain must be simple.
Rocks will rise to road
if I go slower,
listen to the stream longer
before I go.

—ANGELA PECKENPAUGH

245

## LETTER COMPOSED IN RM. 310
## CALHOUN HOTEL, SEATTLE 9/14/75
### (Addendum to a note)


I missed you back east again.
Your landlord thought you'd gone south
for the weekend, some new gig
with the symphony, left
only an hour ago, he said.
He called you Susan.
I listened at your door so long
I swore I heard you sigh, and E string's
lament, and silence.
'Got yr address from yr sister
in Seattle,' I wrote, 'Will write,
                              Love.'


I write this now, knowing that note
remains folded under your door,
knowledgeable too of all it doesn't say.
Dumbly it withholds what might pass
unspoken between us, had I
arrived one hour sooner.
The flight back was too fast; I still
address you in this town, wondering
where summer went, when we met again
as for the first time, a new tide
and we stood shivering at the ferry's rail,
facing west.


Now, in off the Pacific, a slight breeze,
the hand of some sad salt history
brushing my cheek, trailing its perfumed
glove through these same streets. Finally
registered for the same sleazy room
you and I had that last time,

with the same window and 3 a.m., the
purring city and lights like smiling
fish eyes, when we made terrific love
with dark and whispers trailing off
tender til sleep and lunar memory
that breathes-in its tides.

But this time I got the room for only
5 bucks. A hard young man with no
luggage but a memory, they figured,
not much dirt. I bought a paper and
upstairs and undressed searched for you
in bylines marked *Cincinnati*. Nothing.
And then the want-ads for work—nothing.
Nothing but gray pictures on the last page,
nothing but the long night sea lanes
northward and cold, held to by
tug-scows bound for Prudhoe, but now
just specks blinking through the fog . . .

And the silent night men out there.
The reporter then goes on to describe
how a seaman's daughter cried in transmission
over the tug's only radio. That she
hadn't seen her father in so long
and that it was mom's birthday
and that she loved him. And then
the wife came on and said she
loved him and he answered yes
that he loved her too. And the entire
crew—from watch to engine room
could hear, and they listened. . . .

Beyond shame they listened to the woman's
calling, the voice distorted, yet
there in the dark, at sea, so sudden
so intimate as a breath upon the ear.
And dreaming the men said nothing,
but guessed where the moon would be
had there been. Nothing. So I watch

the twirling light of the elevator
scale the Space Needle from deep
inside a darkness and 2 thousand miles,
where you ride your highway home, and a note
unfolds on the floor a virgin's thighs.

—GEOFF PETERSON

## WHILE I AM WRITING THIS

I am shooting a slingshot
at a shiny pie pan
hung from a rafter in the loft of my barn.
I stretch back the bands.
Between my forefinger and thumb
I squeeze the small square of leather
around a .22 shot.
Now the pan is framed in the slingshot's prongs
like a face peering through a window.
I am shooting myself.

—JAMES PINSON

# ECLIPSE

Cover that
eclipse
with a blinding stare
of your own,
throw a glass stone or two
past the center,
imagine life on
Mars, or your
erotic dreams coming in
herds
to trample you.

Your fingers dig into
my wrist,
holding.

—GARY PULEO

# VISIT FROM FRED CHAPPELL

He hesitates on my stairway like a stutter;
a four a.m. stare
falls upon his drooping cigarette.

Unlikely, the Poet.

At home in a strange chair
he bows
humbly—
squats intent as a Sumo
about to butt heads with the world.
Drawls swears into soft prayers
and pauses
stooped,
a casualty.

My wife takes his picture.

He looks asleep.

—JAMES REED

## POEM

al is burrowing deep to
make it.
waiting for good thick snow
heavy ice cover
over old wood and
air drafts.
a place found early in
summer
to hole up the winter.
it's flat.
no heat
no light
no gas

no tax
no rent
sleeping wall to wall
with a spring across the
railroad tracks and
down,
he passed the months.
boats float down the sun
glazed river knowing;
    "goddamn winter's coming on;
the sun goes out.
i can almost hear it.
click.
it's gas around the moon and
cold.
god, it gets
cold."

once, with a buddy,
a whole winter wrapped in
shipping blankets in a
cardboard refrigerator box
on a flat garage roof.
huddling up at night
the cold never bothered
at all. funneling warm soup and
sharing the last straw;
it isn't love.
yes, it is.

        —BILL REHAHN

# I WANTED TO SAY
## (for carolyn)


the tuxedo of consolation worn
on my tongue
i offered you monuments
to fashion your sorrow after
great statues of grief

i propped your chin
with the crutch of passing time

i wanted to say crowds
pressed their hearts toward you
eyes   like dresses of water
danced dust into rain
the silence
on your son's tongue was
the fall
of petals
in the wind

—FRANK ROSSINI


# AUGUST: PAPER MILL VILLAGE


I
Say there were brown feathers graying,
an olive belly, a neck of ringed reflections:
you would be wrong, it would be spring.
It is not. The doves become mute, on the verge
of October.

252

## II

A breast of horse dung on the path between two places
marks the disappearance of one striped tent, two fools,
three sequined leotards. That tremendous flock of mist
over the ridge means nothing.

## III

A man walks. All day, one step after another.
A burst of shrapnel bursts in front of him
all year, one day after another. He is a particular
man in a peculiar place. He has taken off his hat,
that the people might have something to notice.

## IV

A salt edge rings the lake, the children are bathing
in brown water: there, by the coal shed, fleas drink
at the pool of a black dog's eye.

## V

Plenty of food this new moon: green grapes,
a cluster of clairvoyant eyes, rot in the mouth
of a doll.

## VI

When the small change begins to disappear look
for it here, covered with cloth and sewn on our
shirts, where the buttons fell loose.

## VII

The sound of a slow whistle in July.
This month, the year we so carefully
placed is spread flat on the rail.

## VIII

A town knows its need to ignore
for a time the talk of its people,
but for the doublecrossed man with a tool
in his hand boring holes in the wood:
a place for the ear is important.

IX

Now is the coming of going, the factories
move closer together: only the odd ask for
their sight restored; no voice of ours begs
for the visible birch. All words evaporate
in that direction.

X

Knees amputated by grass: a run of animals
down the same drunken path they will beat
again in snow, the swerve of last August
in a frozen glance: see always behind you
this life, the heartbeat of lizards in a coma.

—MARY RUEFLE

## ON NOT REMEMBERING MY DREAMS

Waking in the night,
I look at my hands
                    & wonder
where they have been.
Over whose dead head
they might have drifted
on their way to the harem
                        where
they acted like such fools.

Hands,
why did you keep me in such darkness,
while high above, little people
jumped with their parachutes on fire?

254

I do not ask for truth,
which you disguise as a horse, or a nurse,
or a room filled with water.
I ask only to tag along
to the arena, & the picnics
where lovers throw their bones at the moon.

—GARY RUST


## MOUNTED PATROL
### (detroit police department no. 26)

red lights and
stop signs.
cowboys can't
compete with
two ton
chevrolets
on woodward.
no more
cattle drives
or saloons
or chuck
wagons.
but the smell
of horseshit
on cass,
always,
reminds me
of your
presence.

—KEN SAVICH

# NU DESCENDANT UN ESCALIER

It is the inside of the year.
snow is on the river.

I find myself
on the staircase
holding only color
in my wake.
I move when I stand still.

Was I going upstairs,
tired, to bed?
Or, did I sleep well,
and with whom, and
start down for bread and cheese?
I now face
what I believe to be east.

So this is the beginning,
standing naked on the stairs.

—PATRICIA SHEPPARD


## MARE'S-NEST

Against my mouth your teeth are thin & white
as eggshell.

The sun stiffens the day migraine bright.

Vulnerable as the skin under a Jesuit's collar,
I curl up inside your pocket watch.

You toss horseshoes, stacking them around my leg.

Your belt buckle, a carved brass eagle, rides your stomach,
above an imagined phoenix.

Sun burns my air-conditioning pallor fresh orange like a carrot,
I handwash my mantilla of Queen-Anne's lace.

My nose feels like the knot of a Chinese-silk cravat.

—ALEDA SHIRLEY

## ALONG THE FLYWAY

In the blue haze of morning
river bluffs rise from bottomland
like the humped backs of bison.
A frozen lake is spotted with beaver houses.
Patches of snow lie in dark furrows.
With harsh, muted calls
black-winged geese settle on the fields
to search for fallen grain.
Their shadows pass across the ground
as their formations fill the sky,
driving the winter toward Canada.

—SALLY SMITH

# PLATO'S SKY

is here
in this warm clarity
after the heat of a merciless day

a gentle spirit
in the olive trees
off the highway's appetite

an abundance of silver
mixed with the darkness
magnificent trees in the wind
foaming torch songs of rivers

this river
is a mouth
full of stars

—LARRY SPARKS

# POEM

all the maleness i knew
hung in sawblades, proper ones
        proper times
    the mystery of childhood
    "when is it proper"

who tells you
what hammer to use
    standing in the garage
    wood-oil smells

ball-peen hammer, tack hammer,
    mallet
    how do i know which

    you were never there
    i squatted in the garden
staring through the cyclone fence
california humming
shorts and t-shirt

with no one close
    Rosemary, mother, terrible crazy
            lady
    cut up   dying
so i hide
in the geraniums      tin sword
                      clutched
    grandma bought for me,
    China-town
where the man was
stabbed                i think stabbed
    too much blood on the night floor

for just an accident,

    i flew so quickly,
    Pow's arms lifting me
            away
            to sit here

hidden
deep green      red pungent
corduroy shorts    small sandals
        pretty soon my uncle
        is coming
        but now i wonder

about airplanes
    saws
and the proper time.

—JEFF STONE

## *REPULSION*

the things beneath
our feet
are slow moving,
viscous.
we trust them
to be slow moving
until our deaths.

we cannot
stand to see
the floors
sink beneath
our feet,
or the imprint
of our faces
in the walls,
in the walls

that crack
beneath the strain
of a hundred moving
things,
the weight of all
the stars.

beyond
in spaces,
movements,
is our fear,

no words.

—THEODORA TODD


## LOCKJAW


He said the victims never screamed
for help. They whined through the nose,
their eyes gone white, and their spines
warped backward till they broke.
Death came from nails, from punctures,
from tetanus—death any child could catch
by accident. So sleep, he said.
Sleep, and you'll wake up safe.
I was ten, had begged for terror.
He was the safe man, the father, the swindler.

—CHASE TWICHELL

# COMPLAINT

How bitter this gold
makes green berries taste
when nothing ripens.

Not corn, nor
wheat, nor her
young breasts.

Take them—
they close the moon
in her blouse.

She will not unfasten
even if I die
and drift starless

or women lift me
from doorsills, turning
husks from my pockets.

—LEE WALMSLEY

# THE LIFE OF A NAVAJO
# MEDICINE MAN

Buffalo hide rattles
filled with rough dreams
chase away diseased spirits

from the hung breast of a weathered man.
Seated in a hogan baked by the Arizona sun,
at eighty-five, again Long Salt is assured
as simply as the strings of frustration
are cut from his sooted body.

And I,
I buckle the belt tightly
around my perma-pressed waist
bought by my grandmother with doe skins
and beads,
then leave the strange bathroom in Juarez.
Back to the den filled with talk that races smoke
to the beamed ceiling.
With each glass of wine
I offer more of myself
to the students surrounding me,
with each emptied glass
I know I have less to give,
till the bottle lies on its side drained.

Yet, Long Salt smiles.
He believes in life because there is nothing more.
He keeps it in neat bundles of hollow reeds
and eagle feathers.

And I,
I unlock my trunk at the American border
to prove its emptiness
so I can return to El Paso.

—DOROTHY WARD

# APPLES
## (for my father)


I was the clumsy child
who stole apples
from your favorite tree
to toss them into the lake.

I have no excuse, but
those apples were never lost.
Each night, while you slept,
as apples bobbed in moonlight,

I waited in shallow water
until the apples washed ashore.
Each time I gave you an apple.
Sometimes I remember that desire

to take whatever belongs to you
so I can return it.
Now there are windless nights,
when the lake lies still,

when I have another dream:
I gather you in my arms,
after death, and ease you
like a basketful of apples

into the moonlit water,
and we float home,
with an awkward grace,
to a continent dark with apples.

—MICHAEL WATERS

# LEARNING A FOREIGN LANGUAGE

It was during the war, in France, captured,
during the sleepless interrogation

that the questions became unanswerable.
Left speechless by insistent German logic

even name, rank, and serial number
were an unknown tongue to him, and left

the unpalatable taste of blood in his mouth.
The pain in his fingers, snapped off

like wax beans, went limp. He remembers
like a scar how they persisted. *Talk,*

they whispered, cutting out his tongue,
tell us what we want to know. *Talk.*

It was not enough to swallow the silence,
to cluck and sputter with eloquence.

—RICHARD WEAVER

## LIBRA'S CHILD

```
                              God
           I balance      how I hate it          I'll blow
        my checkbook           s               fifty dollars
       weigh decisions         o              for fun tell my
    budget time am always      m            boss to go to hell
    prompt and dependable      e           not show up for work
  a stabilizing influence . . .  d       spend all day making wave
                               a
                               y
                           I'll tilt
```

—MARY LEE WE▶

## A SPOOKY, BUT POETIC, VIGNETTE

Upon her bare, tanned leg
a roach crawls, pauses.
His antenna quiver obscenely in the darkness.
And she turns
smiles
shows her teeth
and whispers:
"Not here."

—JOHN WOOLEY

# CHILDBIRTH

Bare trees flow upward into the sky
from a yard where two cows patiently
stand into slanting ice, parts
of a difficult wooden puzzle
in which heaped-up rubble
and three split log sheds repeat
the monotonous shades of ground and sky.

A chink of light beckons
from the front room where a child
stands in brightness. She parts the lace
curtains, watching for a man who carries
a baby, blue with its cold sleep,
within his leather bag.

Sleet lowers the heads of the animals
and of the doctor; the beasts
dream of powdery snow stamped
with human footprints.

In the back room a forest
of ice grows heavy inside the mother.
Her mind fills slowly with the winter
as she recedes into fields
of stark, piled-up sheets.

—Marlene Youmans

# BIOGRAPHICAL NOTES

*Fiction*

JAMES L. BOND was born and grew up in Ione, Washington, did a trick and a number as a computer programmer in the big city (Kansas City), and now studies creative writing with John Keeble at Eastern Washington State College.

VAUGHN D. BROWN lives in Tucson and studies at the University of Arizona. Born in Malden, Missouri, he has lived in small towns in Georgia, Tennessee, Missouri, and Arkansas.

JOHN GREGORY BRYAN, a graduate student at the University of Denver, also studied at Notre Dame, Southern Mississippi, and the School of Irish Studies in Dublin. His work has appeared in *Mississippi Review* and *Cimarron Review*.

JANE BUTLER did a lot of different things including "factory work, grooming horses, modeling for artists, and every imaginable kind of waitressing" before settling down to study at Miami University, where she edits and designs the literary magazine.

RAYMOND COTHERN, a native of Louisiana, studied under Warren Eyster and Walker Percy at LSU. He has been an actor and owned a bookstore and is now writing a novel.

TAMA JANOWITZ, who has studied at Goldsmith's College of the University of London, attends Barnard. She has published both poetry and fiction in little magazines.

JAMES KNUDSEN grew up in Glen Ellyn, Illinois, and attended the University of Missouri and the University of Iowa. He is in the M.F.A. program at the University of Massachusetts.

TOM KRIKSCIUN has lived in Europe for four years and made two extended journeys to the Far East. Most recently he has been studying at Hollins with R. H. W. Dillard and Allen Wier.

KAREN LOEB comes from Chicago and lives in Bowling Green, Ohio. Her short stories have been published in various magazines including *Aeon, North American Review,* and *Wisconsin Review.*

SARA MCAULAY was a student at California State University at Hayward when she wrote "The Liar's Craft." She had a first novel published by Knopf in 1975 and has been represented in Whit Burnett's *Story* anthology.

LEE MCCARTHY grew up in Arkansas, and studied at Tennessee and San Francisco State. She was a Stegner Fellow at Stanford during 1974–75, and writes both poetry and fiction.

LEWIS NORDAN lives in Fayetteville, Arkansas, with his wife and two sons. He studied at Auburn University and has published poems and stories in a variety of journals.

ARTE PIERCE comes from Detroit and graduated from Michigan in 1975. He is a three-time winner of the Avery Hopwood Award for Fiction. He is now in medical school at the University of Michigan.

DONALD PURVIANCE resigned from the Internal Revenue Service in 1975 to study at the Iowa Writers Workshop. He is writing a comic novel about the IRS and a series of stories on the theme of magic.

JUDITH STEPHENS was born in Washington, D.C., but has lived most of her life in the west. She studied anthropology at Berkeley and is now working for an M.A. at San Francisco State. She has held all kinds of jobs—from legal secretary to model to bone expert in a museum.

*Poetry*

HOWARD AARON, whose poetry appeared in *Intro 7,* has published in many magazines and quarterlies. He is a student in the Writers Workshop at the University of Iowa.

VERKUILEN AGER, whose work was represented in *Intro 7,* spent seven years in Vietnam in the U. S. Navy. He has recently graduated from Roger Williams College in Bristol, Rhode Island.

CATHY ANDERSON was born in Detroit and was brought up there and in Kansas City. She studied philosophy at the University of Missouri and poetry under Larry Levis there.

MICHAEL ANDERSON studied with James P. White at the University of Texas of the Permian Basin. He is editor of *The Pawn Review,* and his poems and articles have appeared in many little magazines and anthologies.

ADELAIDE BLOMFIELD lives in Anchorage, Alaska, and studies at the University of Alaska.

DAVID BREWSTER was born and raised in Portland, Oregon, graduated from Reed College, and is presently studying at the University of Washington. His work has appeared in a number of magazines, including *Poetry Northwest* and *Northwest Review.*

DEBRA BRUCE has just received her M.A. from Brown University. Her work has been published in the *Iowa Review, Seneca Review, Southern Poetry Review,* and *Poetry Now*.

EDWARD BURCH is a native of Louisville, Kentucky, and is working for an M.A. at the University of Louisville.

BRAD BURKHOLDER was born in Roanoke and grew up in the Blue Ridge Mountains. A graduate of Madison College, he is working toward an M.F.A. degree at the University of North Carolina at Greensboro.

JAMES BUSHEY has studied writing with Samuel Moon at Knox College in Galesburg, Illinois. He edited *Catch,* the literary magazine there, and hopes to go into publishing.

EDWARD BYRNE was born in 1951 and studied with John Ashbery in the Brooklyn College Program in Creative Writing. His poetry has been published in many journals.

CHARLIE CHARETTE was born (1953) in Scranton, Pennsylvania, and studied at Keystone Junior College and Lock Haven State College. She is working on a novel.

VICTORIA COEN is a native of the Pacific Northwest and has just graduated from Western Washington State College where she majored in psychology.

BRAD DINSMORE, JR., is a young jazz pianist and singer well-known in Paris and Amsterdam. A graduate of Virginia, he has finished a first novel called *The Jazz God Giggles*.

CAT DOTY, who works as a cartoonist, is a graduate of Upsala College in New Jersey and has just received her M.F.A. at the Iowa Writers Workshop. She won an Academy of American Poets Award in 1975.

JUDITH DUNAWAY has been studying at Bowling Green State University with Phil O'Connor and Howard McCord.

P. R. FARROW worked for Revlon before studying architecture and urban planning at Princeton. She writes both fiction and poetry.

VERNON FOWLKES, JR., is an undergraduate in the LSU-Baton Rouge Creative Writing Program. He has published in *The Southern Review* and *Manchac*.

DAVID GRIFFITH graduated from Iowa in 1973. Subsequently he has lived in Minneapolis and Missoula, Montana, and plans to join the Iowa Writers Workshop during 1976–77.

JILL GROSSMAN, who comes from Washington, D.C., attends Columbia College in Chicago. She has had her poems published in the *Paris Review* and the *American Review*.

LAURA GROVER, a graduate student at the University of Washington (Seattle), has been published in *Kansas Quarterly, Hawaii Review,* the *Pacific,* and other little magazines. She is writing a novel and a book of poems.

JEFFREY HAGEDORN comes originally from New Britain, Connecticut. He graduated from Hobart College and is presently enrolled in the Writing Workshop at Arkansas.

BRENDA HILLMAN studied at the Iowa Writers Workshop. She lives and works in Kensington, California.

TIM HJELMELAND graduated from St. Cloud State University and is presently a teacher of high school English and drama in Minnesota.

SANDRA HOBEN has a B.A. from St. John's in Annapolis, an M.A. from California State College at Fresno, where she studied with

Phil Levine and Peter Everwine, and is currently working for a Ph.D. at the University of Utah.

MARIA KATZENBACH has published poems in *The Denver Quarterly*. An excerpt from her novel, *The Grab,* appeared in *Intro 7.*

YUSEF KOMUNYAKAA appears in *Intro* for the second time. He is a student and lives in Colorado Springs.

D. B. KREITZBERG studied poetry and writing at the New School for Social Research.

CARL LAUNIUS received a B.A. from the University of Illinois and is presently in the Creative Writing Program at Arkansas. He was also published in *Intro 7.*

RICHARD LE COMPTE was born, raised, and educated in Spokane, Washington. When he is not bicycling, backpacking, or mountain climbing, he attends Eastern Washington State College.

KENT ROBERT MAHAN holds a B.A. from the University of Redlands, California. Having studied at both Cambridge and Oxford, he is now a graduate student at Bowling Green. Armchair Press published his chapbook *cornflakes.*

ADRIENNE MAHER comes from a family of classical musicians and is, herself, a pianist, guitarist, singer, and beginning violinist. She attended Roger Williams College and has done all kinds of work to support her habit of writing poetry.

MICHAEL MALINOWITZ is a graduate of Brooklyn College's M.F.A. program, where he studied with John Ashbery. He reports he never met either Carl Sandburg or Bob Dylan.

DAWN MCGUIRE is an outstanding young photographer whose work has been widely exhibited. She lives, takes her pictures, and writes her poems in Princeton, New Jersey.

JAMES MCGUIRE has been working in Bellingham, Washington, with Annie Dillard and Robert Huff. He has published poetry in several magazines including *Jeopardy* and *St. Andrews Review.*

DAVID R. MEMMOTT attended Clatsop Community College in Astoria, Oregon, served in the U. S. Air Force, and now studies with George Venn at Eastern Oregon State College in La Grande.

LINDA MIZEJEWSKI lives in Richmond and teaches at Virginia Commonwealth University. She attended Wheeling College and the University of Cincinnati. She plans to enter the Writing Workshop at the University of Arkansas.

NICHOLAS MORGAN is a graduate student in English at the University of Virginia. He is presently working on a long poem about George Reeves/Superman.

MELINDA MUELLER is a student of botany at the University of Washington (Seattle). Her work has been published by a number of little magazines, and she has served as an editor for the Washington student literary magazine.

ANGELA PECKENPAUGH is currently enrolled in the M.F.A. program at the University of Massachusetts. She has published widely in little magazines and quarterlies, and some of her work will appear in forthcoming issues of the *Virginia Quarterly Review* and *Southern Poetry Review*.

GEOFF PETERSON has studied with James McAuley, John Keeble, and others at Eastern Washington State in Cheney, Washington.

JAMES PINSON is a student at the University of Missouri in Columbia. He comes from Independence and lived three blocks away from Harry Truman.

GARY PULEO lives in Norristown, Pennsylvania, and is a student at West Chester State College.

JIM REED studies with Jim Whitehead and Miller Williams at Arkansas. He was an undergraduate at William Jewell College and worked for a while as an accountant.

BILL REHAHN, who says he has "lived pretty much in Dee-troit, Boston, and the Woods," attended Oakland University and Wayne State. He's been an editor for *art-beat magazine* and is "editor publisher printer distributor" of *the great mohasky press*.

FRANK ROSSINI is working in migrant education and studying at the University of Oregon. He has had work published in a number of the little magazines and quarterlies.

MARY RUEFLE studied at Hollins College but this is all she wanted in her biographical note: "Mary Ruefle is a waitress in North Bennington, Vermont."

GARY RUST studied with Phillip Dacey and Stephen Dunn in Minnesota. He is presently a teaching assistant at Wichita State University.

KEN SAVICH was born in 1954 in Detroit and has lived there ever since. He attends Wayne State University.

PATRICIA SHEPPARD comes from Pensacola, Florida, graduated from Yale in 1974, and is currently studying at the Iowa Writers Workshop.

ALEDA SHIRLEY, who comes from Myrtle Beach, South Carolina, is twenty and a student at the University of Louisville. She has published in a number of magazines, including the *Kansas Quarterly*.

SALLY SMITH, who has studied with Hillary Masters and others at Drake University in Des Moines, won the Iowa Poetry Association Contest for 1975.

LARRY SPARKS attended San Francisco State University, studying in the writing program directed by William Dickey.

JEFF STONE comes from Moscow, Idaho, is a bookseller in the winter, and in the summer works on a Lookout Tower in the Boise National Forest. He studied T.V. and film at the University of Idaho.

THEODORA TODD, who is twenty-one, studies at Wichita State University and edits *Gazebo,* the poetry journal there. She has published poems in several little magazines.

CHASE TWICHELL is, in Real Life, a printer and bookbinder in New England. She has also recently earned an M.F.A. degree at the Iowa Writers Workshop.

AMELIE WALMSLEY grew up in New Orleans, attended Princeton University, and reports that she "is currently studying to be a caretaker."

DOROTHY WARD was born in Heidelberg, Germany, and is a student of creative writing at the University of Texas at El Paso.

MICHAEL WATERS is in the Ph.D. program at Ohio University. In 1974–75 he was Poet-in-Residence for the South Carolina Arts Commission. His work (poems and criticism) has appeared in *American Poetry Review, Iowa Review, Ohio Review,* and other magazines.

RICHARD WEAVER lives in Tuscaloosa and studies with Thomas Rabbit at the University of Alabama.

MARY LEE WEBB is presently a student at Oklahoma Central State University.

JOHN WOOLEY attended Oklahoma State University and served two years on the helicopter carrier *New Orleans* before enrolling as a graduate student at Central State University. His first professional publication was a comic book script he sold to *Eerie* magazine. He is currently writing what he describes as "possibly the world's first 'hard-boiled' fantasy novel."

MARLENE YOUMANS, who comes from Cullowhee, North Carolina, studied at Hollins College and Brown. She has published poems and translations in many magazines, chapbooks, and anthologies.